THE SILVER SCREEN

JEREMIAH BASS

Library of Congress Cataloguing-in-Publication Data
ISBN: 979-8-9904474-9-3
Names: Bass, Jeremiah
Title: The Silver Screen | by Jeremiah Bass
Description: First Edition | Macabrest Press [2025] | Wisconsin, USA

Subjects: Fiction | Fantasy – Contemporary | Romance – Supernatural

10 9 8 7 6 5 4 3 2 1

Thanks

While many believe writing is a solo sport, it's clear to me that writing takes a team. While the early drafts are something we may do alone, to improve we must have others point out the things we're blind to. On a project this large, it's often hard to see the forest for the trees. So, thanks to my writing group: Andy, Dan, and Kevin who always help me see what I'm missing. Thanks to early readers, Jade and Chris, who've helped identify obvious flaws in characters. Without the feedback of this team of dedicated readers this story wouldn't have come to fruition. Infinite thanks to my editor, Daniel, who has spent countless hours tightening my sloppy punctuation. Most of all, thanks to Casie, who constantly inspires me to do better, be better.

THE SILVER SCREEN

Chapter 1

Wyatt

I was staring at the crooked ceiling tile, twenty feet above me, when my wind-up alarm clock started clattering on the five-gallon bucket I used as a nightstand. I didn't have to look to know that the short hand rested over the dimly glowing five, while the long hand stood at full attention. I rolled over and pushed in the little plastic knob that stopped the alarm clock's clatter then rolled back over, unwilling to drag my old joints out of bed. It wasn't fear of arthritic pain that kept me hunkered under my blankets. My joints were as fresh and supple as they had been when I was thirty-five. The rest of my body was too.

No, the courage I needed wasn't about overcoming old bones. The courage I had to muster was about facing another day. Another day in a body that refused to obey the laws of nature. Another visit with my dying brother. Another day that I'd have to eat and drink alone.

I didn't want to get out of bed but eventually, like every other day, I mustered the courage to throw my feet over the edge of my king-sized onto cold concrete. I worked my way through a hundred pushups like I had most every morning for the last sixty-five years—ever since my brother and I first saw Jack LaLanne's fitness show. On my back, I squeezed out two hundred crunches. With my body warmed up enough to hit the road, I put on a pair of rotting sweatpants, worn-out running shoes and a "wife-beater" tank top.

At eighty-eight years old, and completely alone, I was living in an old, poorly remodeled theater. It still had its big, rusting, red and white marquee above the entrance and the huge silver screen in the main hall. I added a small section I called the bedroom. It had a king-size mattress lying on a tarp on the floor, and a five-gallon bucket turned upside-down for a nightstand—post-depression, newlywed chic. Beside it, I had a worn-out couch that I never sat on. The kitchen, on the other side of the theater, was complete with stove and fridge sitting on either side of a plywood bar with a sink in it. I also had some second-hand cabinets, repainted, and mounted to the cinderblock wall. A small Formica table sat a few feet from the stove, serving as both countertop and dining area.

The theater itself had been built about eighty years before, on Main Street in a small Minnesota town called Ely. The town rests on the edge of Shagawa Lake and is home to just under four thousand people. My wife and I moved there shortly after our son died. My wife died a little over a decade later.

In my lifetime, I buried my wife, June; only son, Wyatt Jr.; only nephew, Jeffery, and sister-in-law, Hilda in St. Louis. My folks were buried there, too. Only Russell, my twin brother, still lived in that shithole city.

When our son died, June and I had to get out. After seven decades in that city, memories assaulted us at every crumbling corner; they drove us from our home like the cold winter wind drives Ely inhabitants from snow-covered streets. Every inhabitant but me, that is. Over time, I got comfortable with the cold. I even started to like the icy morning air against my bare skin. I liked the frost crunching under my feet.

Dressed and as warm as my body ever got, I walked through the glass doors of my movie theater into a blustery spring morning. Wind shot through the holes in my worn-out sweats, up my legs, shriveling my manly bits. That cold wind always took my breath away; stung my bare skin. But after that initial sting, the cold faded. It was almost like I knew it should be cold, knew the bitterness of that cold air, but my body didn't react to the cold anymore. Maybe as I'd aged, I really had lost some of my senses…

I started my morning jog—a ten-mile jaunt to the edge of the lake, down the side of the frozen shore, and back. A few blocks from my theater, the bank's flashing thermometer read 24°. "Brisk," I mumbled, my voice matching that of a gunslinger from a 1960s spaghetti western. Since The Big One, World War Two, when I was imprisoned and tortured until I screamed my throat bloody, I spoke with that gruff, ragged, raspy twang. In twelve torturous hours, my voice turned from silk to sandpaper; a constant reminder of the cutting, burning, and slicing I endured in the Stalag.

I jogged north, into the wind, toward the lake, and by the time I reached the shores of Lake Shagawa, I had a good rhythm going. During my first winter in Ely, my morning jogs were the talk of the town. Few other residents liked to get out and move before the sun. Those that did spread rumors of a "crazy guy jogging in summer garb." The rumors stretched from one side of town to the other like wildfire in a dry Montana summer. It wasn't long before I became something of a town legend.

One of the beauties of small towns is their ability to assign abnormal stories to normal people. Sometimes those stories are based on a single odd behavior; other times they're legitimate. When I was a kid and our neighborhood in St. Louis still had a small-town feel, we'd taken notice of a man with two dozen cats and no friends, family, or spouse. This was during the Depression, when feeding stray animals wasn't something people did. Neighborhood kids talked about the old man's cats more than we talked about him. Kids said that his clowder of cats was always changing. They said the cats were raised, butchered, and sold to the Chinese people who lived down the street. They said that he ate them and that he used them to lure little girls into his house.

Kids can be cruel.

In Ely, people started telling stories about my tolerance of the cold. They speculated that I was a Russian ex-pat who missed my special forces training so badly that I kept myself on the same torturous exercise routine. Others said I was training for the Iditarod but wasn't planning on using dogs.

"Small towns equal small minds," my friend Hersh used to say.

The simple truth was I liked that running took my mind off almost everything else. Almost.

A few months before June died, we permanently closed our theater. We'd spent ten years showing classics in that theater, and both of us had fallen back in love with film. When June asked if we could close the theater to take a long vacation, I knew it was time. I didn't know it was *her* time, but I was ready to close the theater, too. To be free of late-night showings, of mopping sticky soda off the tile floors. Of sweeping piles of popcorn from between the seats. I didn't realize that when we closed the theater for a long vacation, it was going to be permanent.

After she died, the theater and my dying brother were all I had left. I sold the house in Ely and moved into the theater full-time. The rumor-mongering townspeople would say I became a shut-in—an old recluse. I didn't shop in the local grocery, I didn't drive, I didn't go to the shops that surrounded my theater in Ely's "Historic District." I didn't go to festivals or the county fair. I never went to church. In fact, other than my morning runs, it appeared to the Ely-ites that I didn't leave the comforts of my home at all.

Rounding the last mile of my jog, I passed a pair of drunken men staggering down the alleyway behind the local, all-night

"Bingo-N-Booze." They were dressed, like most others, in layers of heavy clothes. Their sock hats stood mostly upright on their heads, with only the pom-poms drooping over to one side or the other.

I glared at them as I ran past; my tolerance for sloppy drunks and drug addicts had died in Vietnam. But I didn't say a word. I just put on my grimmest face and hoped my body language would speak for me. And I wouldn't have said anything if they'd kept their Goddamn mouths shut.

"Did you feel that?" Drunk One, a punk kid with a Timberwolves sock cap, spat as I slipped by.

"What?" Drunk Two, a fat boy with a Vikings coat and scraggly beard, asked.

"It was like, like cold wind and mist," Timberwolves said.

"'Wind and mist?' Every rooftop nearby has a foot of snow on top of it. It's Minnesota, of course there's cold wind," Vikings mocked. "Unless…unless you're afraid of those rumors about the old theater."

"Fuck off! Let's just get out of here," Timberwolves mumbled.

The idea that anyone would be afraid of my theater had me curious. I slowed my pace and slipped into a doorway behind "Crazy Daisy's Discount Shop," waiting to hear the rest.

"You honestly think that Old Man Gaumond is out here? Creeping around?" Vikings asked, laughter lacing his voice.

"Come on, let's go!"

"What do you think he's going to do? Come out here with his Kalashnikov and start spraying the alley? That old bastard hasn't been seen in years. If he is in that theater, he's rotting away. He and his *bitch* wife. You know one time when I came to the theater with my parents, she wouldn't let me use the toilet because she 'already cleaned it for the night'?" Vikings said, with emphasized air quotes. He staggered to one side and bumped into a dumpster, then looked at the dumpster like it was its fault for being there. He went on, "I was a kid; I almost pissed myself before I got home."

I stopped myself from shouting at him, but that didn't mean I was going to let it go without any repercussions. He'd crossed a line I couldn't let him cross. No one insulted my wife right in front of me. Especially a drunken, pencil-dick, fat-boy with a Goddamn pompom on his hat.

I hadn't been in a good fight in years, and maybe I was looking for one. I know I still had a bit of that old blood rage in me from all the shit I'd been through. I fought for two years in The Big One, did a six-month tour in Korea, two and a half years in Nam, did some underground work in Lebanon, and finished my career covering George H. W. Bush's *Gulf War*. After The Big One, aside from some individual paid "favors" for my longtime friend Hersh, I wasn't military. I was a photojournalist willing to do almost anything for the right shots and story. You know those full-page glossies in *National Geographic, Time,* and *Life?* A lot of those were my work. My brother and business partner thought we were close to the Pulitzer a few times. But we were always overlooked; we couldn't get the right balance published. We always ended up with either a great photo and a so-so article or a great article and a so-so photo.

Looking back on it, I'm sickened that I was paid to glorify war. After the things I saw, I can assure you, there's nothing glorious about it. It was demoralizing for me, the troops, and it should have been for the American people, but they were almost completely unaware of what happened in war. That's why I spent my life trying to show the world what was really going on—even if the world didn't want to see it. Of it all, Nam was by far the worst. No one wanted us there, and no one wanted to be there. Our guys fought shadows in forests they weren't equipped to walk through. They fought high, drunk, and angry. They fought among themselves, and they fought against themselves. They hated what they were doing but saw no escape short of death or dismemberment—and some willingly took that second route rather than step foot in the jungle again.

When I was there, I personally saw a kid taken from her mother's arms and killed by American soldiers. The young staff sergeant who did it was trying to get information about "Charlie." His interrogation tactics were absurd; the woman didn't even speak English. When the staff sergeant shot the child as a method of coercion, his troops turned on him. They shot him in the back…then they shot the screaming mother. It was madness. True madness. *Apocalypse Now* is the scariest movie I've ever seen, because it's probably the most accurate war movie that ever graced the silver screen—it was hyperbolic, yes, but terrifying, nonetheless. Men lost their minds in that war. If the jungle didn't break them, the violence or the drugs did.

I got a roll of photos of that incident, but the soldiers who'd just shot their commanding officer took my camera, opened the back, and tossed the film into a rice paddy. They told me that if I ever spoke out, they'd kill me. After what I saw, I had every reason to believe it.

A soldier I met in a bar a few months later told me a similar story. He saw a mother carrying a naked little girl across a muddy street get shot through the head. The soldier thought a Viet Kong sniper did it. Who was I to tell him it was just as likely that an American sniper was the culprit. "The little girl," the soldier told me, "lay in the street covered with her mother's ichor"—that was the word he used, "ichor." Though he knew it was wrong, he and his platoon left, unwilling to step in front of sniper fire for a crying "gook" child. His eyes teared up as he told me the story, and his hand reached automatically for the tarnished silver cross hanging from his neck. I talked to that soldier all night. I cried with him because, like mine, his life as he knew it was over. He didn't calm down until he was halfway through his seventh *33 Export*—a cheap Vietnamese beer.

A full-page candid of that soldier, tears running down his face, beer bottle about to make contact with his lips, once made the cover of *Time*. Under it, only three of my words had been printed: "The American Soldier." *Time* refused to print the rest of the story. While the combat violence was horrid—unspeakable as *Time* proved—those of us who witnessed the war also saw soldiers kill themselves with drugs. Heroin was as available as aspirin. Vials of liquid opium were sold at stands like bags of oranges, on the sides of busy Floridian streets. Drugs, booze, murder, chaos…no wonder nobody wanted us there.

Most soldiers who did come back were never the same. That war made men aggressive, or addicted, or lazy, or turned their minds to mush. PTSD wasn't a term back then; they just called it "Post-Vietnam Syndrome." I had some of that post-war syndrome from The Big One, but they called it "shell shock" back then. I handled it: I drank a little too much and distanced myself from my family. I went back to the trenches because it seemed I could tolerate the flashbacks if they were caused by a fight, a gunshot, or a bombing rather than some domestic event. For the most part, when my blood was up, the fear stayed at bay; it gave me an edge, made me hard. If a car backfired in front of my house in St. Louis and I ducked for cover, it made me feel soft, weak. If my wife hit a pothole while driving and my mind got tossed back into a war zone, it was too much to explain to her; it was just another reason to stay away. I *handled* it; the soldiers in Nam couldn't handle it.

As the years in Nam passed, a lot changed. I still wanted to show the world the fight our guys were going through, and I often did. I got the good shots; I got full-page glossies; I got half-burned men and bombing victims. I got body parts scattered mid-explosion. I got kids crying. I got soldiers screaming in bloodlust.

But when my nephew, Jeffery, the son of my twin brother, Russell, died in Nam, suddenly every photo I took was someone's family member. A son here, a grandson there; a father, a boyfriend, a husband. They weren't faceless bodies anymore; they were all Jeffery. They were all that young soldier who cried into his beer as he told me about the little girl covered in her mother's ichor.

They were all me.

Back in the alley behind my theater, as the two drunks who'd never seen the horrors I'd seen mocked me and called my wife a bitch, I saw red.

I'd lived through hell. I was scarred both physically and emotionally. I was alone and angry. But I wasn't afraid.

I stepped out of the doorway behind "Crazy Daisy's," turned to the boys that were so blatantly disrespecting me and my June and screamed, "One more word and I'll cut your peckers off and shove 'em down your Goddamn throats!"

The boys, who'd been tussling and laughing, froze. They spun around so fast and wobbly I thought they'd fall over. The one who'd called June a bitch turned pale and looked like he'd just shit himself, and for a second, just a split second, I was sure he was my dead nephew, Jeffrey. He looked almost the same—and the fear in his eyes, fear I'd caused, stung worse than the cold Minnesota air. They turned and ran like children who knew a whipping was coming.

I wasn't going to chase them; scaring them was enough. I turned and walked back onto Main Street, back to the front entrance of my theater. By the time I made it to the huge, rusting red and white marquee above the entrance, my heart had slowed, and my temper was cool. Cool enough, anyway.

* * *

Emma

I opened my eyes in total darkness. My palms were sweating and heart racing. I was terrified of…I didn't know just yet. I was engulfed in cool, damp, mildewy shadows. The only hint of light was a tiny sliver filtering through a crack in the doorway on the other side of the room. I searched my coat's pockets, hoping for a flashlight, lighter, or book of matches; anything to push away the absolute blackness. In one pocket, I found a small metal flashlight with just enough juice to emit a faint orange glow.

The green military coat I wore was stained black around the cuffs. Patches added by a once-proud Army man lined the arms and the chest. The nametag was torn, but there was a "Gau," and a curved line that could have been an "r" an "n" or an "m", but the rest was gone. Aside from the dirty military coat, all I had to keep myself warm was a worn-out old mattress and ragged blanket.

The stench in that tiny room was enough to rouse me. "Room," being an overstatement, it wasn't tall enough to sit up in without bumping my head. It was hardly long enough to lie down in without my feet touching one end and my head touching the other.

I had no idea where I was or how I'd gotten there; I just wanted out. I felt like I'd been asleep in there for years. Though awake now, my body was still exhausted, weak, like I was sick.

I took a deep breath; the stale air burned my lungs. When I released it, a breathy fog filled the tiny chamber with the stench of death. I felt sick, but the stench that came from my mouth was a dead giveaway. I was beyond sick; I was dying. I could tell that from the smell alone.

Despite not knowing how I got there, I knew the cubby was an open space under an abandoned movie theater's stage. I knew I lived in a place called The Valley. I wasn't sure if The Valley was a town, city, street, neighborhood, suburb, or a nickname, but the name gave me a small rush of adrenaline. It sounded beautiful, peaceful; but at the same time, it didn't feel like home. Just a distant memory of a long-forgotten past.

The nostalgic feeling of home didn't stop my body from shivering under the heavy canvas coat and ragged blanket, though. It didn't stop the nausea from welling up in my throat—that excess of saliva just before you… Aches thrummed through my body with every beat of my weak heart. Despite everything telling me I should just close my eyes, give up, and die, I forced myself to move. There was a nagging sense of purpose driving me on.

Shivering and exhausted, I used the stiff side of the mattress as a type of handle and pulled until my feet rolled off the edge. The mattress didn't sit high enough off the ground for the weight of my legs to help pull me into a sitting position, but I gathered strength, some hidden will to continue on, and pulled my body up. Sitting fully upright, I had to slouch so the top of my head wouldn't touch the ceiling. I caught my balance as my body started to lean too far to one side and, with my shivering hand, found a half-empty pill bottle.

The dying flashlight was just bright enough for me to see the name on the bottle, Emma, and the prescription—Vicodin. The rest of the label had been worn away, leaving me with no indicator of my doctor's name, contact info, or my own last name. I felt around and also found two other pill bottles—Chlorambucil and Meprobamate—neither of which had complete labels to help fill the blanks in my missing memory. I didn't have a clue what either of those pills did, but I put one of each in my mouth, along with a Vicodin, just to cover all my bases. Then I thought better of it and took a second of each.

I looked around for water to wash the pills down, but all I found was an old paper cup with forty-two cents in it. Forty-two cents, the clothes on my back, the mattress, a flashlight, some pills, a blanket I wouldn't usually let a dog sleep on, and a filthy paper cup was all I had. I assumed my name was Emma, the name from the torn labels on the pill bottles. But given the state of things in that tiny cubby under the stage, it was just as likely that I'd robbed some old woman's medicine cabinet.

With shaky, frail legs and weak arms, I unlatched an oddly placed hasp that kept the cubby locked from the inside and slithered out from under the stage. I felt like a creature sliding my way out of the black lagoon. On the outside of the cubby, as I closed the black doors, a chill unrelated to the near-freezing temperature ran up my back.

There was less mildew and death scent on this side of the doors, but the air was even colder in the main part of the theater. Stale, humid air laid a sloppy, wet kiss on every bit of my exposed skin, making me shiver.

Fever. I knew what that felt like, and I was coursing with it. But what else?

What year is it? What day? How old am I? Why do I live under a stage in a rundown old theater? There were so many unanswerable questions running through my head. Most importantly: *Where the fuck can I get some food?* It wasn't hunger; I had no appetite; it was a need. My body was weak, and if I didn't eat soon…

With the hope that breakfast and a glass of water would make the pills I'd just dry swallowed settle in my stomach, I moved toward the only light source in the building—a faint glow under the main doors that led to the theater's glass fronted lobby.

I paused at the glass panels, taking in my appearance. My clothes were mismatched and tattered, my shoes were holey, pink house slippers, my auburn hair was tangled, and my face was thin, beyond thin…skeletal. I may have been pretty once, but I needed to gain forty pounds before anyone would be able to tell that. I was young, too. Maybe not in my teens, but not far out of them, either.

I looked past myself, through the floor to ceiling glass panels at the cars parked on the street. They looked "modern," but that didn't tell me anything. I didn't know if they were modern for 1945 or 1995.

My appearance, this theater, my lack of memory, even the world around me…none of it made any sense.

I walked through the front doors with no specific destination. I walked down poorly paved sidewalks, wandering. Several blocks later, I crossed a deserted street and headed into a Piggly Wiggly.

"All we have left in this neighborhood is the Piggly Wiggly. And that's where I'll be working, Emma," a cigarette-damaged, but still nurturing voice grumbled somewhere in the back of my head.

An elderly greeter stood on the other side of the Piggly Wiggly's double glass doors, but I didn't get a greeting. Her job was handing out coupons and getting carts for shoppers, but she didn't even look up when I walked in. It was as if I didn't exist. I looked down at my filthy, worn-out "Gau" coat and understood why. It was obvious; I was homeless. One of those invisible members of our society that the world wished would just go away.

I saw the greeter though, and I recognized her. She was the first thing I'd recognized since I woke up. She had one of those old lady cotton ball haircuts that grandmas with thinning hair always have. Her face was pruning, especially around the lips, where she'd spent most of her life sucking on "cancer sticks". But I also knew her snickerdoodle smell and her pearly white dentures. I knew her heavy blue eyeshadow and her polyester pants.

"Morning, Grandma," I said, my voice shaky and weak. My grandmother turned to me with a tormented look on her face. She looked at me like I *was* the creature from the Black Lagoon, and I'd just slinked into her store. I was as disgusted with myself as she appeared to be, so I didn't hold her revulsion against her. But I moved closer. I kept walking toward her, putting one exhausted foot in front of the other. I needed more than just a face I recognized. I needed someone who knew me. Someone who could tell me who I was, where I was, fuck…when I was. I needed the soothing, heartfelt voice of my grandma.

In a hushed voice she said, "Your face is flushed, Emma. You're sick again; I can see it in your eyes. But…you're not supposed to be here." Then, even more aggressively, she growled, "You're *not supposed to be here!* Why did you come back?"

"Grandma, I just need breakfast. Can you loan me some—"

"Child, go back where you came from. Go back, go back…" she said as she backpedaled away from me, a terrified look on her face.

My eyes filled with tears as the rejection sank in. I dropped my shoulders, took a step back from the old woman, and said, "Thanks anyway, Grandma." I turned and started to walk away, but something…an urge I couldn't quite explain made me turn back and add: "You know, you always did right by me. I never blamed you for anything. You were the one person that made me feel good when I was a kid." It was like my voice was on autopilot. I didn't understand the words coming out of my mouth, and I didn't know why I was saying them. But I couldn't hold them back, either. They'd spilled out of me like oil from a floundering tanker.

I left my grandmother standing by the grocery store's front door, handing out coupons to people who'd come in behind me. I didn't know what she meant by the things she'd said. I didn't know what I'd meant by the things I'd said. I didn't know how Grandma had "done right by me." But the words came out of my mouth as if they'd been pre-programmed. It was like I'd been waiting to say those words for years, decades, and when they came out, I felt relief of an odd sort. Relief that I'd gotten to tell her how much she'd meant to me.

My body and mind, it seemed, were acting on instinct; so I let my instincts have free rein. I moved toward the produce aisle, where I set a bunch of bananas on a nearby scale, weighed out as close to a pound as I could, pulled an extra banana off the bunch, then roamed, looking for something else I thought I could tolerate. A display of the first spring strawberries caught my eye. Pulling one of the green cardboard containers to my nose, I sniffed.

Oh, the smell of early spring strawberries! Sweet and rich and full of hope.

I remembered that smell. I remembered Topes Strawberry Farm just outside of The Valley; a long, narrow field of green, with speckles of red berries lining trimmed, grassy paths. I remembered when I was a kid, and Grandma would take me to pick strawberries. We'd pick a peck, and she'd cut them up, add sugar, and pour the mixture over sweet, buttered biscuits.

Strawberry Shortcake. It was the first thing I'd truly remembered since I'd woken up.

I turned back to Grandma to ask if I could come by, but she wasn't there. She'd disappeared like fog after the morning sun rises over the horizon.

Before I knew what had happened, before I knew how it happened, I was outside the Piggly Wiggly—an odd sense of accomplishment filling me. I didn't remember going through the checkout aisle. I didn't remember paying. But there I was outside, a bundle of bananas in one hand, a cardboard basket of strawberries in the other. Under one arm, a plastic bottle of water.

I scanned the store one last time for Grandma's puffy white hair. But she was gone.

And again, I felt utterly alone, scared, and confused.

Chapter 2

Wyatt

My brother, and only living relative, Russell, still resided in St. Louis—a city that, over my eighty-eight years, I watched wax and wane. I watched the country tear itself apart during the Civil Rights movement—my city included. I saw gang violence spread like a plague during the crack epidemic. I saw a city eating itself alive. When St. Louis became one of the nation's most dangerous cities, June and I had seen enough. We headed north.

Russell was the only thing that kept me tethered to that city so long. When June and I moved, he remained in St. Louis. The stubborn bastard said, "I'm not leaving my family," even though they were all dead. The sad truth was, he wouldn't have handled a new town well. He was already starting to slip when June and I left St. Louis, and just a few short years after we moved, the police started calling me about my brother. "Have someone pick him up," they'd say. Or they'd call and say, "We had to take him home again. We're not going to keep doing this. He can't live on his own much longer."

He'd get lost, forget his keys, forget his name, he'd go to my old house instead of his; he got into multiple driving accidents. The police were right; it couldn't go on like that. I made the hard

16

choice and convinced Russell to move to a "home" that dealt specifically with dementia and Alzheimer's patients.

Dementia was the only thing in this world that scared the hell out of me. I saw my father live through it, and watching Russell live in a type of purgatory before purgatory—a land of the dying where no one knew how to get out or how they got there—only terrified me more. Every man in Russell's home was a young man at heart and an aging, confused man on the outside. They were angry, scared, and left there to rot.

Because of my aversion to nursing homes in general, I chose the nicest home I could find, the home my father died in: Paradise Garden. Not only did I know the place firsthand, albeit many years before, but their pamphlets mentioned things like, "Nice staff," "No nursing home odor!" and "Good food," all things Russell deserved. He was my twin, for God's sake, and I'd want the same for me. I paid the outrageous monthly fees, and I visited often.

The commute from Ely, Minnesota, to St. Louis, Missouri, was roughly 800 miles. Nearly twelve hours by car. Airplanes can make the trip in just under four. I could really rack up the frequent flyer miles, but I had other means of travel. That morning, after my run and my shower, I shoved fifty dollars in my back pocket—emergency money—and walked across the main room in my theater. The hundreds of original Art Deco seats had been removed and sold or given away years before June and I bought the place. Some jackass had plans of making the theater into a gymnastics academy. A gymnastics academy in Ely, Minnesota…go figure.

When his money fell through, we bought the place for a song. Before we reopened it to show classic films that reminded us of better days, we bought a hundred leather recliners and bolted them to the floor. If we sold out—which we often did—we'd set up folding chairs in the back of the theater, sell those tickets for half price, and give the patrons stuck in folding chairs free popcorn. We never once got complaints. Some people even started bringing their own folding chairs, hoping to get the half-price tickets.

In addition to my "living spaces" when I moved in, I had to add a real bathroom, not just a stool. And with the ancient plumbing, the bathroom was the least user-friendly part of my limited renovations. I'm handy, don't get me wrong, but the old building had been set up for three toilets, a urinal, and two sinks: no shower, tub, or washing machine. My temporary solution was a shower that drained directly into one of the old toilet drains. I had to keep it capped during the day because the drain was trapless. Without capping, it would let in the most God-awful smells you could imagine.

The entryway/concession now served as the garage—where I kept the new woodworking tools I bought myself after June died. Russell and I kept ourselves busy with woodworking when we were freshly retired, but these tools, I'd never once used. The still-packaged tools sat in the garage, a reminder of how the ambitions I'd once had melted away like piles of snow during the spring thaw.

Ironically, the theater was furnished much like my first apartment. The big differences were the garage, the five thousand square feet filled with recliners, the stage, the screen, the projection room filled with old movie reels and little treasures I'd collected throughout my life, and the stack of boxes that sat beside the couch I never used. In the corner of the "living room," those boxes stared ominously, begging to be opened so the memories within could finish crushing my aching heart. I often considered moving them to the projector room with the rest of my wife's and son's things—out of sight, out of mind—but never found the energy to take on that task.

There was a pang of loss that struck me every time I saw those boxes, but sometimes it was nice to see them, too. A lifetime of memories stacked up nice and neat. Seeing the boxes was like looking at the worn cover of your favorite book; you know what's inside, and you can hit the highlights without even opening it. So, they stood there. And, though some days it stung to see them, on others it was almost cathartic.

When we bought the place, the theater came with a few dozen hand-me-downs, too. Most of which, including a squatter's old mattress and nasty old blanket, I tossed; I did keep a few things, though. In the projector room, there was an old box, much like those in my living room, but emblazoned with a big red stripe down the middle. Unlike the boxes in my living room, it made me feel so uncomfortable to look at that I buried it under a stack of reels for an obscure Japanese horror film we used to show at our Halloween double-feature, called *Portrait of Hell*. In the years I've owned, worked in, and lived in my theater, I never opened that box. It just sits up there like the monster in the closet, the gremlin under the bed. I hate that Goddamn box but don't dare throw it away.

I don't even want to touch it.

I don't want to think about it.

Emergency fifty dollars in my pocket, I headed through the sea of recliners. My leather-bottomed shoes echoed off the empty theater's bare black walls as I neared the massive silver screen. Small tears were beginning to form at the bottom of the silken-silver screen, so I had to be careful with it. I jumped onto the stage—despite my real age, my un-aged body was still nimble enough to do such things. In front of the screen, I stopped, took a deep breath, felt the energy of life surrounding me, pulled that energy through my shoes, through the stage, through the concrete, through the earth, through the air, and into me. My body filled with the numbing hum of lifeforce—that's what I called it because

I didn't know what else to call it. When I had gathered enough, I placed my hand gently on the deteriorating screen and forced that energy into it.

For a second, the screen felt solid, soft, flexible, and I had to be careful not to push my hand through its decaying surface. But, when I transferred enough stored-up energy into the screen, my hand pushed through. Not a tear. A cool, wet; like an ocean wave frozen in time; water that stood upright, disobeying all laws of gravity. A dense cloud; a haze of uncertainty.

When the screen was "charged" enough for me to step through, that cloudy, watery appearance changed to a shimmering light so bright I could hardly stand to look at it. I didn't know if I needed to or not, but I always took a deep breath before I walked through the shining white liquid.

On the other side of that white light, a hallway with thousands of doors—maybe hundreds of thousands—stretched out as far as you could see in both directions. Behind me, the screen I'd just walked through shrank from a vast openness into another door—a door that slammed abruptly. The hallway of doors stretched out as far as I could see. The one that had just slammed shut was green; the word "Home" inscribed across it in black marker. The other doors were painted red—I didn't know why; that's just the way they were when I found the place. The walkway was covered with durable, low-nap carpet. The kind that lined the soda-stained floors of movie theaters in the 1950s. It was deep blood-red with a clearly worn path down the middle. The worn path, like the red doors, was there before I arrived. I never met another person in the hallway of doors, and I often wondered how the wear and tear on the carpet happened. But more than that, I wondered where the hallway itself came from. Just a few of the impossible to answer questions that ran through my head every time I stepped foot through one of those shimmering, upturned pools of water.

I walked down the hall, glancing peripherally at the doors. Many of them had towns' names written on them in permanent marker: Murphysboro, IL; Avilla, AK; Bayview, AL; El Paso, TX; Paris, France; Moscow, USSR (which had been marked out and rewritten as Moscow, Russia), and so on. Every door was another gateway to some theater in some town or city. Some doors had huge black Xs written on them—those doors wouldn't open.

If I kept walking far enough in either direction, I'd come to a place where the doors stopped having labels. No towns' names, no Xs. Blank, unchecked pathways that could lead, literally, anywhere.

About two hundred yards from the green door that opened to my theater, there was a door labeled: "St. Louis, Mo. Marcus Ave." That door squeaked and stuck a little, but usually opened on the first try. On the other side, a crumbling movie palace that only had threads of the antique screen remaining, stretched out black and enormous. In the wrong light, it was terrifying. Without my Maglite's glare, only tiny glimmers of light flickered through the collapsing ceiling and the crumbling block walls. The screen that remained hung loosely from the top of the theater, like sheets hanging from the ghosts of movies' past. The disintegrating screen had a few places wide enough for me to step through, and while the gateway opened easily, a chill always ran up my spine when I placed a foot on that old stage.

* * *

Emma

I literally had nowhere else to go, so I walked back to the theater, my body growing weaker with every step. The strange feeling that I was being watched kept me moving, despite my exhaustion. When I got back to the theater, I pried open the ill-fitting glass and aluminum front door. Once inside, I tore into a banana and ate a handful of strawberries. I still wasn't hungry but was sure the weakness I felt was, at least partially, a result of malnutrition. My body seemed to be made of thin, spotty skin stretched over osteoporotic bones. I had no fat or muscle tone. Weak and fading, I choked down another bite and congratulated myself with a sip of water. In the store, when I picked out the bananas and strawberries, I hadn't noticed how aged they were. I thought they'd been fresh, but…now they were covered in age spots.

I bit into a strawberry and got hit with a flash of memory: an old woman sitting in a hospital bed choking down what appeared to be strawberry mush—something like baby food for the dying. It made me gag and almost vomit the fruit I'd been able to get down. Another sip of water washed down the bile in my throat. I tried to follow that memory deeper, looking for anything it could tell me about myself. But when I followed it, my body started to shake, and my head throbbed. It was like those thoughts had been locked away in a leaky vault, accidentally letting out snippets, while keeping the rest hidden from my prying mind's eye. Pushing on that vault's door only made my already sick body feel worse.

I took another bite of banana, but rather than a sip of water, I got another snippet of memory as a reward. A middle-aged man in a filthy white t-shirt, his raw, dark red gums bleeding between each of his rotting jagged nubs. His gums were so swollen they extended halfway down what was left of the man's teeth, like the gums themselves were alive and feeding on his enamel. Again, my body threatened to return the fruit I'd swallowed to the outside world. I forced down another sip of water, set the rest of the fruit on the movie theater's faux stage, opened the cubby under the stage, and crawled back in—a golem returning to its cave.

I pulled the door shut and shoved a screwdriver into the hasp, wondering why there'd been a hasp on the inside, wondering what

I'd needed to keep locked out. I turned on the flashlight and found the bottle of pills in my coat's deep pockets. I took two more Vicodin, sipped some water, lay on the mattress, and pulled the filthy blanket over my shivering body.

I hoped I'd sleep; I hoped I'd wake up and realize it had all been just a bad dream.

Chapter 3

Wyatt

I shined my light on the floor in front of the Marcus Avenue theater's stage, making sure the path was clear. I didn't want to step into a pile of human shit. It'd happened before. The bums who lived in that theater were the filthiest kind—they shit where they slept. The inside of that theater smelled worse than a city park porta-john on a hot summer day.

In the theaters I visited, it was common to come across vagrants, rodents, crackheads, hookers, and everything else that lurks in the shadows. The Marcus Avenue theater, *The Prestige*—the theater I frequented as a child—was no different. When I stepped through the screen, a greasy, disproportionate, fat man shouted, "Where the hell'd you come from?"

I checked my feet, I shined my light in his face and, in my gruff voice, said, "Even I can't answer that one."

The bum stared, mouth half open, eyes wide. Eventually, he said, "This is my theater. Get the hell out of here."

I kept my light focused on him as I walked through the theater. His eyes were glued to me, mouth hanging half open, like I was a ghost floating through his house—but he didn't say another word. I was leaving, and he wasn't interested in pursuing.

Training my Maglite on the floor, I dodged the piles of shit and walked through the back wall of the theater—not the door, but the wall itself, where the cinderblocks had started to collapse and a hole had been expanding for who knew how long. Outside, I started the six-mile walk to Paradise Garden Nursing Home.

Cabs didn't come to Marcus Avenue anymore. When I first started traveling to St. Louis this way, I tried to have one pick me up but couldn't even get a cabbie on the phone. On a naïve day, I tried a city bus, waiting for half an hour at the bus stop, only to discover that the buses didn't stop in that part of town anymore. They just drove by as if I wasn't even there. So I walked. And walked fast. The Goddamned stink of exhaust, trash, and human filth filled my nose like coke fills a frat boy's on Friday night. Dirty streets and overflowing dumpsters completed the city cliché. The closer I got to Paradise Garden, the less it felt like paradise.

Paradise Garden itself was supposedly the crème de la crème of nursing homes, but it was still a Goddamn nursing home. The young lady whose job it was to welcome visitors by saying things like, "Hello, Mr. Gaumond. Can I get you a cup of coffee?" sat there looking at a magazine when I walked in. The nameplate on the table said, "Marcella." Even when I signed in, Marcella sat behind the cheap, oak-veneered desk, ignoring me.

Typical nursing home shit: paid to greet guests, but not paid well enough to actually do the job.

As advertised in the pamphlets, the entryway didn't smell like a nursing home; instead, the aroma of burnt coffee, too much potpourri, and excessively distributed eucalyptus leaves made me want to puke. I walked over to the coffee machine and poured myself a cup. Marcella finally looked up, her face blushing. She must have realized she'd forgotten to do her job. Rather than trying to make up for it with extra kindness, she just stared at me, mouth open, like that filthy, fat bum in the theater. After a few seconds of staring, she dropped her magazine and quickly walked out of the entryway.

What the hell is up with everyone today? I wondered as I sipped stale, room-temperature coffee.

The cheap, round, Roman Numeral emblazoned clock hanging on the wall above the coffeemaker read 11:33. Russell and the rest of the people still strong enough to make it out of their bedrooms would be in the dining room eating ground up meatloaf and pureed peas for lunch.

A lot of people get sick watching their loved ones eat nursing home food, but not just because of the food. It's how they eat that bothers their youthful counterparts. The elderly often miss their mouths, shoving heaps of mashed potatoes all over their chins or cheeks. They chew some and lose some because false teeth that don't fit right aren't easy to use. They get a mouthful and spit it back out because who wants a serving of mashed beets?

Their eating didn't bother me like it bothered others. Could be I saw too much horror for one lifetime. Compared to watching men be destroyed both physically and mentally, watching a group of elderly people eating was a walk in the park. At least they'd made it past their teenage years. At least they didn't die in the mud or the sand in some foreign war.

In the crowded cafeteria, Russell ate like the rest of his peers. More meatloaf and mashed potatoes landed on his shirt than in his stomach. More often than not, when I saw Russell these days, I thought of Shakespeare's famous "All the World's a Stage" speech from *As You Like It.* Specifically the line:

"…Last scene of all,

That ends this strange, eventful history.

Is second childishness…"

Russell used to know the lines well; he once played "Melancholy Jacques" in a community theater production of the show. It was when he was younger and a whole lot happier. Now, Russell sat in an oversized wheelchair, pouring pureed meatloaf all over his bib and sipping orange juice through a bendy straw. I'd give it a 50/50 shot that his diaper needed changing.

He was taking the slow route out of this life. He spent longer in that nursing home than he should have, and I blamed myself for it. Had I known how much longer he had, I'd have moved him to Ely with me. I doubt he'd have liked it; he hated the cold, but when his dementia got bad, I was the only one he remembered.

Twins…go figure.

"Russell," I said, taking an open seat next to my brother, spilling a little coffee on my hand.

"Wyatt? It's been…years," Russell said, struggling to find words he'd spoken so clearly only days before. Despite his mind being soggy, he held out a steady hand. While Russell was suffering from a weakening mental constitution, his body remained strong. He'd been confined to a wheelchair only after a hip-fracturing fall and botched surgery, but his handshake was still solid.

"Years?" I asked, taking his hand like I always did. It hadn't been years; I'd seen him the day before, but when I looked around, I didn't recognize anyone else in the cafeteria. There were usually a few of my brother's compatriots I was familiar with, but all these people seemed new.

"Meatloaf today, Wyatt," a nurse said, placing a tray in front of me. I smiled and slid the tray away. I couldn't eat that shit, but whenever I came to visit my brother, they dropped a tray in front of me like I had to be starving.

Russell pointed at my tray, then his, comparing the two meals, and said, "Damn…blender." Then he pointed to his full set of dentures.

"I know, why do they force you to wear your teeth if they ain't going to let you chew anything?"

"Exactly!" he shouted, slamming his fist on the table, rattling the plastic cups.

"It's so you don't choke," I said, trying to smile.

"If'n I did? What would it matter? I'm dying. Put me…put me on the front lines again. Anything but more…pureed meals…no more having my ass wiped by girls I'd've been chasing a few years ago."

"More than a few years, maybe?" I said, grinning.

"Maybe… Take me…back to our room. I can't eat no more…smooshed shit," he said, pointing at his lunch tray.

I abandoned the bitter coffee and my untouched tray of food, pushed Russell's chair down a green-tiled hallway that opened on both sides to a dozen doors leading to rooms with no windows. Nice for a nursing home or not, it was still like a Goddamn prison. Russell moved his hands to his chair's wheels; so, I let him control the chair under his own power—or at least think he did. At the end of the green hall, we turned onto the elevator that would lead up to his second-story suite. Room 203, to be exact.

"What's the news, Little Brother?" Russell asked as the elevator doors shut, leaving us more privacy than we would have anywhere else in the home.

"I believe you're twelve minutes younger than I am. So that makes you the little brother."

"News!" he barked.

"You're dying and I'm not. Just like yesterday."

"I'm…I'm uh…I'm okay with dying. Never sounds…like you're okay…not dying. What will you do…when I'm gone?"

"Find some other old codger to wheel up and down a shit-stinking hallway, I guess."

"Doubt it."

"Me too," I said as the elevator doors opened, and I pushed my brother into the second-floor hallway. It was exactly the same as the green hallway below, but blue tiled and bright with the sun shining through the windows in the suites. In "paradise" windows also cost extra.

"Wife…that wife of yours?" Russell asked, just as he had every day for the past few years.

"You ask that every day. What do I tell you every day?"

"…Uh…"

"She died, Russell. Years ago."

"Dead? Everybody's dead; what's that make you?"

"The only asshole left from our little troop of assholes," I said, trying to make my voice light. It didn't benefit anyone for Russell to get stressed.

"Could be something…else…something…out there for you. Let me go…forget that Goddamn war…forget it…forget it…and move on."

It seemed simple to forget about the past. All one would have to do is stop obsessing over things he couldn't change. But those were the very things I found myself obsessing over. War? How *could* I forget? I had constant reminders of that war and all the others that followed. I tried to forget, took the medication, did the therapy, but I never forgot a Goddamn thing.

Russell pointed to his bed. I lifted him out of his chair far enough for him to do the rest. He laid down facing a wall with a collage of pictures from his life, our life—many of which I'd taken. A conspicuous black and white, circa 1955, stood front and center like a proud monolith. Russell and I were holding up a tarpon we'd spent the entire afternoon pulling out of the Atlantic; grins spread across our faces like a couple of fools who'd just conquered the world. We felt that way back then. At the time of the photograph, we were in our thirties, had survived The Big One, had our wives, kids, and both of us were making a good living. We were winning.

I hardly remember what that felt like.

Not long before that picture was taken, we found ourselves in Korea, where we made the first good money of our long careers. Though I thought it foolish, Russell followed me there.

He didn't take part in the action like I did. He stayed in safe zones: cleared cities, modest hotels. He was my manager of sorts. I took the pictures; I wrote the stories—or at least roughed them in—he cleaned them up and sold them to the highest bidders. Eventually, he realized what I knew the whole time: he needed to go home. I could mail the stories and undeveloped films to him, and he could work on them in the States. He'd make better sales pitches if he spoke face to face with editors, too.

It worked.

After he went home, our sales doubled, and so did our fees. Freelance used to be a career a good team could live on.

It made sense that I was in the field while Russell did the business side of things. He had the mind; I had the balls. I was the adventurer. I was the one who never seemed to age. The job, being in the thick of it, kept my heart racing, where I liked it, while my unique twist of nature kept my body young enough to keep up with the soldiers I trekked into danger with. The perfect team— brains, balls, unending youth—but sometimes he still came with me; still trekked into unknown lands and dangerous situations. Honestly, I think June sent him with to keep an eye on me if we were heading into really dangerous situations.

"So…the rest of your life…plans?" Russell asked as I adjusted his bed, tilting the top up so he didn't asphyxiate on the bolus of meatloaf still lingering in his mouth. "Tell a dying man you're going to do something great…inspiring."

I didn't answer. He'd asked almost as often as he'd asked about my June. I knew what he wanted to hear, even if he didn't— he wanted me to tell him I'd move on, I'd keep going, I'd keep fighting. I didn't know whether that was true. Rather than keep going down the same conversational path Russell and I had followed a thousand times before—dementia will do that to a person—I dealt a hand of Rummy and waited for Russell to pick up the cards.

"Not playing, Goddammit! I just shit myself. Nurse'll take a…hour…a Goddamn hour to get me to the toilet, wipe me clean, and diaper me. And I'll sleep…too tired. You…coming and going from this…in-between…stop it. There's a job in…St. Louis…photo and interview. Two thousand. Call Hersh for details. You have his number?" Russell said, mixing a twenty- or thirty-year-old memory with confused thoughts from today.

"I've got it, Russell. I'll get the story and films to you this week. Okay?" I said, indulging his delusion. "I'm going to explore some more doors, Russell," I said reluctantly, unsure if he remembered the hallway. Russell always thought we'd find a door that would lead to some other dimension. I tried to tell him that wasn't how it worked, but the older he got, the more he hoped I'd find a door that led someplace where he could be a young man again. Though he was the one dying, I sometimes felt he had more ambition than I did. He always wanted me to do something great, to keep woodworking, keep exploring, keep shooting photos. I may have looked young, but I felt ancient…worn thin, like every bit of my soul had been stretched and tanned in the sun. I was dried up, sour… On the inside, I was older than Russell looked on the outside.

"Yeah? Anything I can sell?" he asked, hope flooding his voice.

"Nothing yet."

"Florida?" Russell asked, pointing at another proud photo on his bulletin board.

"Yep. How could I forget?"

"Mt. Rainier?" he asked, pointing at another.

"The four of us… Yeah. I remember it all."

"When I die?" Russell asked.

"I know Florida, Mt. Rainier, Home, and the rest with Hilda."

"It's for you. Not for me."

I smiled. My brother, even laden with dementia, knew me better than anyone. "I never did anything for anyone but me. You know that better than most. We made a small fortune selling violence like Hugh Heffner sells sex. But I don't think violence does as much good in the world as sex. I should have put down my Leica and picked a different career. You should have forced me to."

"Pay attention to your wife, Wyatt…she's…she's sick," Russell said as he pulled a thick blanket over his chest and closed his eyes. "She's sicker…sicker than sick. She's…she's like Mom was," he mumbled. He knew before I did how sick my June was, how close to death. He'd called me and told me to get my ass home. If not for him, I may not have been there when she needed me most.

"It's okay, Russ. She's all better now. No more pain."

He grabbed my wrist—reflexes still quick as a cat's—and looked me square in the eyes. It was his famous bullshit detector. He always knew if I was lying. But I wasn't. June didn't hurt anymore. She didn't have pain anymore, because she was already gone.

After a second, he nodded.

I helped him roll over onto his side, the way he always slept. I checked his diaper; he was clean. A tear rolled down my cheek as I put a hand on my brother's shoulder. "I'll see what I can do about your last wishes," I said, wiping my eyes and my nose with my other hand. I knew I didn't have long with him. Though his mind seemed stronger than it had in years, *he* was fading fast.

My brother, my twin…my last surviving relative.

What does a man with unending youth and no family do with his time?

* * *

Emma

I woke to the sound of voices; one voice full of anger, the other…fear? Excitement? I couldn't tell; it was strained and hard to make out.

It was coal-dark in my cubby under the stage, and I didn't dare turn on that flashlight. Even a tiny glimmer would stand out like a lighthouse on the edge of a night-darkened ocean. I tried to remember if I'd locked myself in; locked myself away from the confusing world I couldn't quite get a grasp on.

Am I safe in here? I wondered.

Probably not.

How could anyone in my condition be safe? I could hardly hold my body upright, let alone fight off attackers.

Tiny snippets of memories, my likes and dislikes were starting to fill in the blanks in my mind, but one thing was completely clear: since I awoke in that cubby under the stage I was in constant fear. It ached more than my sickly body, or my freezing fingertips. It was a kind of fear that haunted a person, never relenting, no matter how much time passed. But what exactly had caused the spawning of that fear, I couldn't fucking tell you.

"She's here," a man said as heavy footfalls drew nearer to my cubby under the stage. My pulse quickened. Other than one hand instinctively reaching for the bottles of pills in my pocket—a safety blanket of sorts—I was paralyzed.

As the voices drew nearer, I recognized one of them. My stepfather's voice hit me like one of his angry fists had so many times before.

Eddy.

The very name sent shivers up and down my spine, and with those shivers, a rush of memories. Eddy: the villain in all my nightmares, the reason I spent my life in fear was there, in my theater, and he was back to punish me for some unknown offense.

He was never a father figure to me, never showed an ounce of love, but he wasn't terrible until I got a little older. When I was a child, I was simply ignored, but when I grew up enough to have an opinion, to think for myself, the abuse started. Early on, it was just a comment here, an uncomfortable glare there. Then sometimes a slap across the face.

As a teen, my home life started to interfere with my ability to focus at school. I started skipping classes, drinking and staying out all night, staying anywhere other than home, where I'd have to face Eddy. My grades dropped. My teachers' silent glares told me I was "going down the wrong path," but nobody asked questions. Nobody tried to intervene. They didn't do that back then; they just "let the family take care of it." They assumed I was poor white trash like the rest of the white kids from The Valley, and they made it clear that what happens in the homes of poor white trash isn't worth looking into. I was a child brushed under the rug; forgotten by society. It's no wonder I ended up homeless, living under the stage of some abandoned theater…

But that didn't feel right. The details of the life I'd woken up to were close, but not quite accurate. Something buried deep inside my mind told me I'd never been homeless. I'd always had a warm bed.

It was like my mind was mixing details between the life I'd actually lived and the nightmares that'd once woken me from a sound sleep.

Nightmares like Eddy's voice ringing out in the theater as he shouted, "I know you're in here, Em!"

When I was a child, I tried to stay away from him. I'd lock myself in a tiny room down a narrow hallway. A room about the size of my cubby under the stage. It was more of a closet than a room, really. Despite my attempts to stay off his radar, when I got into trouble at school, he'd hit me, usually in the stomach, so the bruises didn't show. Then he'd tell me how worthless I was, how much money it cost to feed me and how he'd have been better off to drown me like the runt of a litter.

And some nights when he'd come home drunk, the single, tolerable sucker punches to the stomach turned into a full-on assault. If my mom was working late—she was a nurse's assistant at the local hospital, which equated to being a maid and bedpan cleaner—he'd take out his anger on me. And the next day, the bruises would tell the whole story of my home life to anyone interested in looking. But again, the school didn't say a word or lift a finger. Not for poor white trash like me.

I remembered walking home from school, sunglasses and a scarf covering the worst of the bruises. I walked head down, shame riddled… And when I got home, I locked myself in my tiny room. I'd installed a hasp on the inside of my door and shoved an old, rusty screwdriver into it anytime I was home. It kept him at bay for a while.

But when he got too drunk, nothing stopped him. Not my mother's screams as he beat her, or my whimpers as I cowered, waiting for my turn.

As I was reliving those memories, Eddy's voice rang out in the theater, drunkenly slurring, "You got kicked out of school again, didn'tcha you little bitch?"

He was out there, just on the other side of my door, getting himself worked up enough to hit me. To kick me. To strangle me until I was on the edge of consciousness, then let me get a quick breath, and start again.

I remembered my boyfriend being there the night Eddy kicked down my door, breaking the hasp I'd allowed to become a false sense of security. I'd gotten in trouble for skipping a whole day of school so my boyfriend and I could go skinny dipping in an abandoned rock quarry, twenty miles away. By that time, the school had given up on me, so I gave up on them. They'd stopped calling home when I skipped. But the school's janitor was a drinking buddy of Eddy's, and at the bar, he'd told Eddy I skipped. He came back from the bar, drunk and angry, and when he pulled into the driveway, my boyfriend jumped out my open window. I wasn't allowed to have boys at home; I wasn't allowed to have anyone at home. If Eddy even heard about me holding hands with a boy, he'd slap me, he'd call me a whore, and warn me that if I got pregnant, I'd be on my own.

That night, Eddy kicked down my door and drunkenly shouted, "You stupid bitch, you skipped school again!"

I screamed, "Stay the fuck away from me!" as I lay back on my bed and got ready to kick him in his twisted face.

When he grabbed my ankle, I kicked, and I made contact, then I kicked again, but I only had to kick twice, because my boyfriend jumped through the window, shattering one of the thin glass windowpanes, and beat Eddy to a bloody pulp.

I remember feeling fear at first, then a sick sense of pleasure as my boyfriend beat Eddy so badly his teeth cracked and broke, and his face turned to mush.

"Em. I know you're in here, girl," Eddy said, searching for me in the darkness outside my tiny cubby under the movie theater's stage. Somehow, my stepfather was back. He was there to torture me. And there was no one to protect me; no boyfriend, no grandma.

My breath was ragged and wet, but my lungs were burning worse than ever. My head pounded; my body sweat and shivered at the same time, like I had a raging fever. I placed my hand over my mouth, trying to silence my soggy breathing.

"You're sure you saw her come in here?" his nasal voice whispered just a few feet beyond my doors.

"Yeah, but that was a while ago. She could'a come and gone," said the other voice. It was familiar too. Feminine, but shaky. I could hear the reluctance in her words. The fear in her voice.

"She could be out drinkin' for hours before she gets home," Eddy said.

"We could just take a look around and see where she's sleeping. Once we know that, we'll know for sure she's in here and we can come back another day," the woman with the shaky voice said. It was almost as if she was trying to persuade Eddy to sleep it off, but she was too scared to say it that way.

"If ya saw her come in here, she's here. Even if she's not here right now, she'll be here. We're stayin' until we get 'er."

"Why don't we—" the woman started but Eddy interrupted.

"Shut up, you stupid bitch. We're staying until we get 'er."

"You stupid bitch…" The phrase was familiar, painful.

I let out a tiny, exasperated gasp as I remembered my mother cowering in the corner while he beat me half to death after I'd gotten a D on a report card at the end of my 8th grade year. I remembered her crying as he took off his belt and slapped it across my back because I asked to be excused from the table without cleaning my plate. She'd been there for almost all of it, an observer, but never a shield. She'd let it happen, because it was either her or me.

Through the crack under the doors, I saw flashes of light moving back and forth across the seating area of the theater.

"Anything?"

"No, Eddy. Can we…"

"What?" he growled back.

"Never mind."

"That's what I thought," he growled. Then a flashlight's beam wisped past my doors, then came back and refocused on them.

I froze.

"The dust around them doors is cleared out; footprints, too. That part of the floor's the cleanest Goddamn thing in this theater." The way he pronounced "Goddamn" sounded like a praise to some horrid god of torture; it made me retch.

"Sure is," the woman said, her voice so uneven I could hardly tell what she was saying.

My body shook uncontrollably as fear, fever, and cold raged through me. I knew I was about to take a beating. And with the state of my frail body, it was likely it'd kill me.

The only thing that had stopped him before was my boyfriend, but I couldn't even picture his face anymore. Couldn't come up with a name. He must have been long gone, scared off by Eddy or the emotional baggage I carried with me.

Eddy and the woman with the flashlight stood only feet away now, flashlight beams shining through the cracks in my cubbyhole doors. "You're not gunna be able to open them doors without breaking 'em," the woman said. It was the same thing my mom had shouted the night Eddy kicked down my bedroom door, then took a beating from my boyfriend.

Eddy didn't answer. He just kicked the center of the doors, the plywood splintering, tiny pieces of wood peppering my face.

"Hey Em, I know you got in trouble at school today. You ready to pay the piper?" Eddy asked as the beam from the flashlight landed on my face, blinding me. All I could see was the huge grin that spread on Eddy's tobacco-filled, swollen-gummed maw. The very same gums I'd gotten a split-second memory flash of earlier. But that didn't seem right either. Everything about this situation seemed wrong, just slightly off-kilter, like the worst experience of my life mixed with an even worse nightmare.

He spat on the floor and asked, "Did you think you could hide from me forever?"

"Fuck you!" I shouted, scooting back into the corner of the cubby.

It's just a nightmare. It's not real, I thought.

I hoped.

"Nasty talking little bitch," he growled.

I backed further into my cubby. But I wasn't just withdrawing; I was preparing for the fight, bracing myself against the back wall. I was going to attack with everything I had and, if I could, run.

"That's a good girl. Just stay there, no need to fight. Nice and easy now," Eddy said, his voice making my skin crawl. I wanted to scream as that nightmare of a man came for me.

He reached his hand out, as if he was going to grab me. He wasn't all the way in the cubby, but he was close enough. I braced my back against the wall and pushed myself out with both feet aimed directly at Eddy's face. I made contact with his scarred mouth. I kicked again and made contact again. Blood from his nose splattered on my shoes. I tried for a third time, but the pills and the sickness had taken too much out of me. I was dead tired. He dodged my final, weak attempt at self-defense.

He grabbed my ankle, shouted, "Stupid little bitch, you're going to pay for that," as he dragged me out of the cubby. In the cold, dark theater he turned me over and, knees first, threw the whole weight of his body onto the small of my back. Air was forced from my lungs, and my back popped and crackled like bacon frying over a too-hot skillet.

I tried to scream, but there wasn't enough air to make a sound. I coughed; red fluid shot from my mouth. I vomited the bananas and strawberries I'd eaten earlier and choked on the vomit.

"Eddy…" the woman's voice begged.

"Shut up, Martha," Eddy growled.

The name hit me harder than Eddy's worst slap. That was my mother's name. That was my mother, with Eddy, standing by, letting this happen…again.

I tried to fight him off, but I was done. The fight was over. He had me, and he knew it. He'd won, and now I was going to pay for whatever offense he thought deserved such retaliation.

"Mom," I pleaded, but Eddy grabbed me by the hair and slammed my head so hard against the concrete I blacked out.

Chapter 4

Wyatt

I climbed through the back wall of The Prestige Theater on Marcus Ave. The sun was high in the sky, and the spring air felt hot. But like the cold, "hot" didn't feel hot anymore. It should have, but since I'd stopped aging, I never felt truly hot, or truly cold. I remembered those steamy summer nights in St. Louis when I was a kid, when the air was so thick I felt suffocated by the humidity, when sleeping became impossible because I dripped with sweat even after the sunset and the temperature dropped, but I simply didn't feel those sensations anymore.

I walked through the theater, dodging the same piles of rubble and shit I'd dodged on the way to see my brother. I hopped back onto the stage, an unknown, nagging urgency pushing me along.

I drew in energy from the world around me; a quiet hum flowed through my arms, through my fingertips, as I touched the frayed and mangled screen. Once it turned from the shroud of an ancient movie screen to a silvery, upturned pool, to intense white light, I turned back to the theater and looked for the bum who'd questioned me earlier, wondering what he'd make of that ethereal glow or of me disappearing through the screen. He wasn't there. The silence in that theater was only broken by the slight electrical hum of the brilliant, bright-white light.

Pushing through that upturned wall of water, I planted my feet in the hall of doors and pulled the Marcus Avenue door closed behind me. When I was young, before I ever found that hallway of doors, exploring had been one of my lifelong goals. When Russell was young enough to do so, we traveled the world together. We hiked the Himalayas, fished the Nile and the Amazon, and visited small towns and large cities on six continents. We became masters of our tiny planet. When I discovered my hallway, it just made adventuring easier.

I don't honestly remember how I found it, or where, or…when. But I've been using the hallway as long as I can remember; searching the world for every meaningful thing it has to offer. But finding something meaningful has been hard recently. My wife and son are gone, my nephew and sister-in-law are gone, and Russell is just days or if I'm lucky weeks from leaving me all alone in this world. You can smell the death on him, permeating around him, like the stink of his rotting insides is leaking through his skin.

Alone again, I walked down the vacant, dimly lit hallway looking for new places, new doors, new experiences. When we were kids, my dad labeled me an adventurer. He said that as a baby, I'd wander off and they'd find me hours later, half a mile away, playing with some stray dog or one of the neighbor's cats. I took on the mantle of "adventurer" with pride. Dad knew who I was before I did.

David Gaumond, my dad, worked long hours, days that started when the sun came up and ended long after it set. But he did it to take care of his family. And when he had free time, which wasn't often, he always spent it with me and Russell, fishing, camping, hunting, teaching us to be self-sufficient. When I was a child, he introduced me to everyone we met as "Wyatt, my adventurous son." I think that label and all the outdoorsmanship shaped me. After the war, I spent years trying to find the feeling I got when just the three of us disappeared into the Missouri wilderness for a few days and the world felt right and there were no worries plaguing us.

I don't think about my dad very often; most of the memories are overshadowed by his last few years—the Alzheimer's years. But in my hallway, with a subtle darkness only broken by the orb-like sconces that lined each side, I still think of him telling me: "One day you'll see the world, Wyatt. You'll see more of it than you want to, but you'll see the good and the bad that most of us never get to experience, too." Walking through the hallway, I was searching for something good. I needed something good to get me out of the doom-mood that had come over me since I left my dying brother's bedside.

On the right side of the hallway, across from a door with a huge X, a blank, blood-red door stood, ominous, like a cobwebbed entrance to a dark basement in an ancient, haunted mansion. A jumbo "Marks-A-Lot" marker lay in front of the unlabeled door. When doors didn't open, I assumed the theater had been torn down or had movie screens too ratty for me to travel through. In those cases, I marked a big black X on the door and moved on. The further down the hallway I got, the older I got, the more X's I drew.

Some doors were stiff, but with a heavy shoulder I could bust through into dilapidated theaters that stretched out empty, silent, dark. I laid a hand on the blank door, and turned the handle, but it stuck when I tried to open it. I pushed again, but the door still refused to open.

Once more, then I'm moving on, I thought as I turned the handle and shouldered the sticking door one last time.

With a creaking of rusty hinges, the door opened to the nearly empty theater. The faint glimmer of a flashlight being jostled around illuminated tiny bits of the crumbling building. I took a silent step through the wall of water onto an unremarkable, two-foot deep, black stage. A lot of theaters used to be built with stages. It was an architectural aspect that carried over from playhouses. This theater was strikingly similar to my own, even if in later stages of deterioration.

Along with the glimmering of a shaking flashlight, I heard an animalistic shout from a deep-voiced man, and the unmistakable sound of a woman gasping, choking, whimpering. The whimpering was silenced by a wet, meaty thud and a roll of odd, restrained sobbing from another woman.

Violence was so thick in the air you could smell it. Fear, blood, and hate have their own odor, like rotting garlic and formaldehyde.

It got my heart racing before I even knew what was happening.

Outlined by a flashlight's dim glow, I could see bits of the scuffle as it took place in front of me. A man straddled the unconscious body of a young woman. He'd wrapped a massive hand around her throat and was choking the life out of her. I'd seen something like this before, but…it'd been a long time.

I watched, taking advantage of the fact that no one knew I was there. The man kept wiping blood from his nose with one hand and strangling the girl with the other. When the girl's face went slack, he let her breathe, but only for a second before he started squeezing again.

The other woman, the one holding the flashlight, continued that odd, restrained sob.

I couldn't help thinking of my June. Her stepfather was terrible to her the same way this shit-bird was being horrible to the girl he straddled on the floor. My wife, June, had been beaten by her piece of shit stepfather, too. He'd beaten her so badly she carried the scars the rest of her life—scars both physical and emotional. She was just a teenager when I put an end to it, though. We'd been making out in her bedroom, thinking her stepfather would be at the bar until the small hours. But when he pulled into the driveway, I jumped out the open window. If he'd caught me there, he'd beat her. He'd scream, "Whore," or "Slut," as he choked her. She told me all about it. And it made me sick to my stomach. She was such an innocent thing. And so beautiful. How could anyone want to hurt a person like that?

Something in me was feeling brave that night, all those years ago, and rather than running like I normally would have, I waited under her bedroom window, listening to make sure he wouldn't hurt her. I don't know if it was the tensions of The Big One building, or if I was just feeling protective of a girl I was starting to care about, but I can honestly say, as I sat under that window, part of me hoped he'd come for her, and part of me prayed he'd just leave her alone.

"Shut up, you stupid bitch. Stop fuckin' crying!" the scumbag shouted, his voice echoing in the empty theater. He wiped snotty blood from his broken, scarred face, looked back at the girl on the ground and when she breathed, he squeezed her throat again, slowly choking the life out of her.

"Eddy, stop," the woman with the flashlight sobbed.

Eddy? That was my June's stepfather's name. Ironic, since I'm about to kick the shit out of this asshole, too, I thought.

Eddy let go of the girl on the ground, started to stand, and the woman with the flashlight took a step back. When he was all the way onto his feet, he pointed a finger in her face and said, "Shut the fuck up, you stupid bitch, or you'll be down there next to her!"

The woman didn't argue. She just took a step back and then another. But she didn't go far. Just far enough to be out of his reach.

Eddy knelt back down to choke the girl some more, and my heart kicked into overdrive. I was still a little amped up from those shit-birds insulting my wife that morning, and I was ready for a fight. I doubted this "Eddy" would give me any trouble. He was fat, sloppy, and based on the blood pouring from his nose and gums, he'd already taken a few blows. But there was always the possibility of danger. Like a cornered animal, sometimes an injured man makes the most violent and rash decisions.

I liked my chances of knocking this tub on his ass before he laid a finger on me, though. And I could already tell I liked this poor, injured girl. She had to be the one who'd bloodied his nose—which meant she was a fighter! Eddy outweighed her by at least 75 pounds, but she fought anyway. That's bravery. That's the kind of spirit I admire.

And though I didn't know her, I knew I'd have died to get her out of the torture she was about to endure. I'd have died for anyone suffering at the hands of an asshole like Eddy, but something about this girl was special.

I remember how her stepfather's abuse affected my June. Nightmares haunted her sleep from the time she was a kid until she died. She was always scared. Scared he'd come back. Even after he was dead, she was afraid someone else would take control of her the way her stepfather had. A lifetime of fear, all spawning from one man's abuse.

The sobbing woman let out another subtle protest as Eddy choked the girl on the floor. He looked up at her, the glimmer of her flashlight shining directly into his eyes, distracting him.

In movies, the hero always talks to the criminal. They exchange taunts and stories, and then the fight commences. This wasn't a movie. I wasn't a hero; I was just angry. I let my Maglite slip in my hand, so I gripped the narrow end of it. It was one of those big Maglites that cops carry; the kind that double as a club. I squatted a little and jumped off the stage, launching myself toward Eddy.

When I landed, I was almost within arm's length of that disgusting slob. He stopped choking the girl in the sudden commotion, wiped his nose with one hand, and reached into his pocket—presumably for a knife—with the other. His companion kept shifting the flashlight back and forth between me and Eddy.

I took a short step toward Eddy, clicked on my light, and shined it in his eyes for a second. He pulled out the knife he'd been digging for and, still kneeling, swiped it at me. But before he swiped, I turned off the light and sidestepped. He couldn't see anything. I moved one more step to the side and shone the light in his face again. And again, he swiped the six-inch blade in my direction. He was faster than he looked, but he was severely disadvantaged, bleeding, and blinded in the dark theater. I shined my light in his eyes again, and he lurched toward me, jabbing the knife in my direction. I took one step to the side and brought the Maglite down on his face. It was a single hit. A single, skull cracking hit that broke the head off my light. His body crumbled to the ground like a sack of meat. No muscle resisted the fall.

Eddy's partner kept pointing her light toward me. The beam from that light, which wasn't strong to begin with, had dimmed to a flickering sepia tone, like an antique projector playing slow-frame movies. All the sobs had finally disappeared from her voice as she asked, "Eddy? Emma? Eddy?"

Eddy was down. My light was broken, and if the woman ran, she could easily get out of the theater before I cared to catch her. But she didn't run; she just stood there, shining her light on me. And then I realized she wasn't a threat; she was another victim.

Though Eddy wasn't a threat either, an old bloodlust came over me. Hate made my face turn hot and my fists clench. I thought of June, of her stepfather, and I felt the obsolescence that I'd been carrying with me since June died melt away. Before I knew I was going to do it, I grabbed Eddy, dragged him away from the girl, then beat his scarred face bloodier than it already was.

It was an animal inside me I only lost control of a few times in my eighty-eight years. Every time that monster took over, it scared the living hell out of me. I saw it for the first time when I beat June's stepfather half to death. I beat him so bad his face was scarred for life afterwards, and he needed dentures—but he never got them. He just let the rotting nubs of his broken teeth fester in his swollen gums.

I saw it in The Big One when I was in a prison camp filled with Americans; American Jews were targets often selected to be beaten and abused by Nazis. A man named Hersh, a man who became a lifelong friend of mine, would have been killed had I not stepped in. I fought four Nazis to the ground before a fifth hit me in the back of the head with his gun, knocking me out. The next few days were the worst of my life, but I don't regret what I did.

As I beat this piece of shit to a pulp, the monster inside me came alive, and I reveled in the blood that splattered from his face onto mine.

"Kill him! Please!" the woman yelled as she dropped her flashlight. It rolled down the theater's tile floor and stopped against the girl's limp body.

I heard the woman's rapid footsteps as she ran from the theater, and I kept going.

I stopped hitting Eddy sometime after that and checked to see if he was breathing before I did anything else. A shallow but consistent breath filled his lungs. It came out raspy, like I'd broken a few ribs… *To hell with him, he deserved it.*

The bastard was bleeding profusely, but not so badly that it'd kill him. Physically, he'd be fine. He'd definitely have some new scars to deal with, though. He'd probably need a few new teeth, too. I didn't know if I wanted to kill him or not. Part of me said, *Yes. Kill that piece of shit. Nobody will miss him.* A bigger part of me thought about how much the three men I killed in The Big One haunted me. I didn't want another face staring out of the dark. I didn't need any more death on my hands.

I stood, took a deep, somewhat satisfied breath, gave Eddy one more quick kick to the ribs, and stepped toward the unconscious girl on the floor. "You awake, girl?" I asked, pulling my shirt up and wiping the blood off my face.

She let out a groan that almost sounded like an answer.

"I gotcha. You're going to be okay," I said, kneeling beside her. I used my shirt to wipe her face, picked her up, cradled her like a baby, and laid her on the stage.

"Hrmnmm," she mumbled as I laid her down. She tried to fight, but there wasn't any fight left in her.

"Don't worry, kid, I'm not going to hurt you," I said as I went back for the woman's flashlight.

With the dim flashlight in my hand, I stepped onto the stage and energized the screen. I had to squint against the bright light filling the theater. I grabbed the girl and walked her through. In the hallway of doors, I laid her down again, slammed the door shut and labeled it "Eddy."

Once we got into the hallway of doors, even with the heavy coat—a coat that looked just like my old Army coat—I could tell the girl was thin. Her skin was yellowing, and when I pried open her eyes, they were foggy, jaundiced. At the very least, she needed sleep, fluids, food, and a bath—she smelled like it'd been months since her body had seen fresh water. She reminded me of a Jewish girl I found in a collapsing building during The Big One. She was so malnourished she could hardly stand. She must have been hiding—Anne Frank style—while the Nazis destroyed her city. Her body looked like leather laid loosely over a skeleton. It was the same way my June looked in the last days of her life. The same way this girl looked.

I couldn't tell this girl's age; she was too ragged, but I could tell she needed a hospital immediately. I thought about taking her right back through the screen and finding the nearest hospital. I wasn't sure what situation had gotten her into trouble with that man and didn't want that trouble to come back to kill her, though. She was a damsel in distress, so I had to be her knight in shining armor. If that meant taking her to the hospital, that was what I'd do, but not in her town. I had a dozen doors that opened to theaters within a mile of a hospital. I could get her to any hospital in the world if I needed to, but when I saw the girl's waxy, yellowing skin and bloodshot, green eyes, one specific hospital came to mind.

My wife suffered from addiction much of her life. She didn't know I knew that, but I did. Hilda, my brother's wife, kept an eye on June and let me know how she was doing when I was away working. There'd be times when I was on assignment that I'd go a month without talking to June, but I'd talk to Hilda or Russell three or four times over the course of that month. Hilda took care of my June—she was June's best friend from the time they were kids. After Hilda and Russell lost their boy, it gave Hilda something important to do.

I always assumed Hilda knew everything about June, about the way she grew up, but I never asked. It was obvious that Hilda knew that June's addictions—all the alcoholism and pill popping —kept her demons at bay. And, for the most part, June functioned fine through it all; she never got a DUI, endangered our son (that I knew of), or got so drunk or high she couldn't walk, talk, or think. But when she got cancer the first time, an overdose nearly killed her. It wasn't just the booze and the benzos; it was booze, benzos, and opioids. She'd burn through prescriptions faster than she could get them filled, and she bounced from doctor to doctor, getting more drugs. She survived the overdose, then made it through her second round of chemo, then the doctors told her the cancer was in remission. It was like an unexpected gift from some higher power, and the day she realized she was going to live, she stopped it all—cold turkey. Those few years between her cancers were the best of our marriage. We traveled, we laughed, we ran our old movie theater; we truly fell in love for the first time since we were kids.

Then, driving through Canada on a cold October night, over a decade after June's first cancer went into remission, June coughed—just once—and blood spurted from her mouth onto the dashboard of our old Corvette. I took her to the first hospital I found. She never made it back home.

In the last few weeks of her life, my wife's waxy skin had been much like this girl's. And now that I was thinking of June, I couldn't get over how much this girl reminded me of my wife, right after we got married. Filthy and emaciated as she may be, if she put on forty pounds, she'd be the spitting image of a young June.

I tossed the girl's frail body over my shoulder and walked toward the door that opened into my theater. Ten doors down from my green door, there was one labeled "Trois-Rivières, Quebec." About three blocks from that theater was the hospital where June died, only a few weeks after her diagnosis. Lung and bone cancer. Of all her addictions, smoking had never been one, yet she died of lung cancer…I guess you never know what'll get you.

I hated hospitals, but the doctors and nurses at Trois-Rivières took good care of June. They cared for her like she was a friend, not a number, not a dollar sign, not an experiment. I felt some kind of protective instinct toward the girl I found in the theater, and I wanted the same kind of treatment for her. I sat her down in front of the "Trois-Rivieres" door, and pushed it open.

I lifted the girl into my arms, like a baby—God, she was light. She stirred, but she didn't say anything. The Trois-Rivières theater was empty, as usual. Who knew how long it had been shut down, but the owner, like June and me, had kept the old building in good condition. The black theater was colder than the hallway of doors, and I stepped onto the stage and turned on the sobbing woman's flashlight. I thought I should be able to see my breath, but I couldn't.

"Where are we?" the girl grumbled, somewhere between awake and dreaming.

"Relax, you're safe. I'm just taking you to the hospital," I said calmly.

"No hospital. Please. I hate the fucking hospital," she said, breathing into my face. Her hot, sick breath smelled of blood.

"You need it. There's something wrong with you."

"I'm fine. I just need someplace safe to clean up and rest," she said, her voice anything but fine.

"Nope. Hospital," I said, stepping further into the theater.

Her eyes widened as she took in the scene. "This isn't my theater."

"I know. I'm taking you to a good little hospital I know of. Then, when they say you can go home, I'll take you back home."

"No! Eddy's there," she said. Her weak, slow voice was too soft for it to come out as anything but a whisper, but I could tell she meant it as a scream.

I carried the girl out the side door of the theater and headed down the alley. The night air had a sharpness to it, and I could feel her shiver in the Canadian breeze.

"Not back to Eddy," she whispered again.

"I won't take you back to him, but you're going to see a doctor. I'll come check on you in a few days," I said, carrying her out of the alley, onto the street that would lead us to the hospital. The wind was stronger and sharper than it had been at home, and the sky looked like it would open and drop a foot of snow at any moment.

"What's your name?" the girl whispered as I carried her down an icy street beside a crumbling brick building.

"Does it matter? I'm helping you; no strings attached." I didn't know why I was playing coy with her. But I did know my response to her question was at least partially flirtatious. Maybe it was the injured puppy look in her eyes when she tried to focus on me; it was the same look June often gave me during those last few miserable weeks of her life.

By the time we reached the front desk in the ER, the girl had passed out again. I told the welcoming committee, "I found this girl a few blocks from here."

A nurse came up behind me with a wheelchair, said something in French, and motioned for me to put the girl in the chair. I did. But as soon as I let go of her, I wanted her back in my arms. Holding her made me feel something I hadn't felt in a long time. The Brazilians have a word, "Saudade." It's used to describe the feeling of homesickness, longing, nostalgia, and sadness all at once. Our impersonal North American temperaments don't have a word that is exactly synonymous with saudade, but that's how I felt when the girl was pulled from my arms. Her being taken away was like reliving all my greatest losses at once. I was homesick, and that girl was home.

"You okay, kid?" I asked as the nurse lifted the girl's feet onto the chair's leg rests and the girl's eyes flickered open.

"I will be, boy," she replied, a hint of playfulness in her hushed voice. It brought an honest to God smile to my mouth— June used to call me "boy" when we were young and playing. I used to call her "kid." For a second, I felt like my wife was there with me. Like I wasn't going to be alone anymore.

"I'll check on you in a few days," I said, not sure what else to do for her.

"Promise?"

I nodded, and I knew I would. I'd follow that girl around like a lost puppy, even if I didn't know why.

* * *

Emma

I watched as the man who saved me walked out of the hospital. His physical attributes were…odd. He carried himself like a young man, with broad shoulders and a straight spine. He was clearly tough enough to handle Eddy and carry me who knows how far to a hospital, but despite his appearance and physical ability, something about him seemed old—like he'd simply been around longer than most people. I remembered my grandmother using the term "an old soul" about my father. Like he'd been on earth, reincarnated so many times that his soul had grown old and tired, even if his body was young and strong.

I tried to call out to the man as he was about to turn the corner at the end of the hallway, to thank him for saving me, but my voice stuck in my throat. Everything I'd held in reserve I'd used to fight Eddy. My tank had run dry. My nerves were shot. So, I closed my watery eyes as the nurse wheeled me down a yellow hallway with a glossy white floor. The sterile smell and coldness of the place were unmistakably those of a hospital. A hospital where, for some reason, everyone spoke French.

Where am I? I wondered. But even as that thought crossed my mind, something else, something invasive, something terrifying, came to me. A memory that couldn't be *my* memory; yet…somehow had to be.

There was once an old lady, sick like I am now, in that same French-speaking hospital. She'd coughed up blood in a car, on a cold night, and a man brought her here—the same man who'd just walked away. But when he brought her here, he was much older.

I knew I was sick and possibly an amnesiac, but I wasn't delusional; there simply was no mistaking the intensity in his eyes. It was him. The same man, but he was younger now. At least forty years younger.

Again, things weren't making sense. My mind or the world was playing tricks on me.

But, more pressingly, there was a hot, liquid feeling in my lungs, like I was trying to breathe under boiling water. Like I was huffing in tiny, razor-sharp bits of metal. It was the same pain that tormented the old woman who'd once died in this hospital. And as I felt that pain, I felt the old woman's fears, too. Just like me—she'd suffered abuses, torments, addictions, and losses. Based on the way I looked, she was old enough to be my grandmother, and she'd died at least a decade before, but I knew we shared death—my upcoming and her past—in the narrow hallways of that generic, French-speaking hospital.

The same way I'd known I was sick, the same way I'd known it was my stepfather in that theater, the same way I'd known that the old woman in the Piggly Wiggly was my grandmother, I knew I was reliving this old woman's experiences.

But I also knew this was all an illusion of some sort.

Nothing was quite what it seemed, but the details were close.

The nurse continued to speak to me in French as she rolled me down the hallway, but I could neither understand her nor respond to her. Even if I knew what to say to her, my body wouldn't have had the energy to speak. I was deadweight. I was like an octopus out of water, jelly without a jar.

The nurse rolled me into a small room with a bed, a tiny desk, some medical equipment, and a stack of intake paperwork. Behind the desk sat a woman in a pair of sensible slacks and a white button-down shirt.

"Anglais?" Button-Down asked.

"Yes," I groaned, hardly opening my mouth as the nurse who'd wheeled me down the hallway left the room.

"Name?" Button-Down asked with a syrupy French accent.

"Emma," I said. My mind was starting to fill with an odd spattering of details about the old woman who'd died in that hospital, and without having my own memories, I used her details to answer questions.

"What happened to you?" Button-Down asked as the nurse returned with a plastic tote full of supplies. She leaned me up, helped me into the bed, pulled my ratty old coat off, and slid an automatic blood pressure cuff around my emaciated arm. As the cuff did its job, she slipped a digital thermometer under my tongue.

Around the thermometer I mumbled, "My stepfather was beating me. Maybe he would have killed me. But the man who brought me here saved me."

"Should I call zhe police?" Button-Down asked as the nurse's thermometer beeped, and the blood pressure cuff cut the circulation from my arm.

"No… That man won't bother me anymore. How did I get here?" I asked, more to myself than to the nurse. It was an odd feeling, I remembered the man carrying me through a theater into an alleyway and down a snow-covered street, but I also remembered the older version of that man driving me to the front doors of this hospital and laying on the horn until a team of nurses ran out the front doors and helped me into a wheelchair.

"A man brought you here. He just left," Button Down said as the other nurse showed her the thermometer. "Bad news, Emma, you have a high fever, 104. You also have veezible symptoms of jaundice, you're extremely underweight, and I don't need a stethoscope to tell your breazhing is…ragged. We're going to get zhe doctor. She'll run some tests. What medications are you taking?" Button Down asked, pen in hand, ready to take down notes.

"Vicodin, Meprobamate, and Chlorambucil," I said, still unsure what two of those drugs were. Vic and I were old friends, though—I was sure of that.

"I'll get zhe doctor. Don't move," Button-Down said as she and the other nurse walked away.

I lay in the bed, shivering, my head throbbing, and my lungs raw. *Shock?* I wondered as I lost control of my shivers. My body thrashed on the narrow bed. Even while my body shivered so badly it felt like I was seizing, my mind sifted through the old woman's memories. The old lady had died just a few doors down from here. She started on the cancer ward, but after she refused chemotherapy, she was moved to general admittance. She was here for weeks before she had a stroke. She had lung and bone cancer, and she was coughing blood and lung tissue for the last few weeks of her life. She nearly drowned in her own fluids, but then the stroke hit her like a freight train. Her mind still functioned enough to know what was happening, but not enough to communicate that she knew. It was a horrible death.

"Emma," a woman's voice rang out as the curtain separating me from the rest of the hospital was pulled back. I recognized the doctor as soon as I saw her. She'd taken care of the old woman.

But the doctor hadn't aged a day.

This couldn't be real. It had to be a delusion. An illusion. A hallucination. Anything but real.

I tried to smile, but I continued to shiver; my teeth chattered together as I shook.

"Cold?" the middle-aged doctor, who looked like a soccer mom and sounded like East Coast-American, asked. I tried to nod, but my body shook so hard I couldn't control it. The doctor looked out into the hallway and said, presumably to a nurse walking by, "Infirmière, va chercher une couverture chaude s'il te plait." Then back to me she said, "I'm Dr. Shale. The nurse is going to get you a warm blanket. Can I take a look at you?"

"Yes," I said as I thrashed about like a fish out of water. I didn't know where my body had gotten the energy to do so; only moments before I'd been too weak to cry. Dr. Shale held my thrashing body, making sure I didn't slip off the bed. Button Down came back into the room and started filling in information on my chart.

"We'll need to take some blood. If you can't stop the shivering, we'll have to strap you down," Dr. Shale said.

My stomach felt sick. I was freezing cold. My lungs burned, and when I coughed, blood splattered onto my face.

Is that enough fucking blood for you, Doc? I wondered.

The wave of shaking peaked about the time the French-speaking nurse returned with the hot blanket. The warmth gave me a momentary refuge from my aching, tired body, easing the tremors. But that relief only lasted long enough for them to insert an IV catheter, take some blood, and hook me up to a freezing cold bag of saline.

Dr. Shale shined a flashlight in my face, touching the bruise on my forehead—which I'd completely forgotten about. It didn't hurt and…didn't fit with these memories. It was like my mind was mixing one set of memories with another. I remembered, as a little girl, falling off my bicycle and busting open my head. I'd hit the crumbling concrete on our street, and my head had split like a rotting melon. But we didn't go to the doctor—too expensive. We just wrapped gauze around it, cut the top off a pair of stockings, and stretched them over my head to hold the gauze in place. I remembered it, but I didn't know if those memories were mine or the old woman's. I couldn't seem to differentiate between the two.

Dr. Shale asked, "Emma, you have a high fever, but that's not from your head injury. How long have you been sick?"

It seemed like I'd been sick for a long time. A decade at least, but I just shrugged.

"Why are you on the Chlorambucil?"

I shrugged.

"When was your last dose?" the doctor asked, slight panic in her voice.

"I don't know. Maybe this morning. That man who saved me… He might know," I chattered, the tremors in my muscles running at full pace again, as the cold IV fluid poured into my veins.

"Okay. What was his name?"

I shrugged.

But I knew his name: Wyatt. He was the old woman's husband.

"Okay, I'm going to give you a shot for the pain. It'll help you relax, too. Stop those shivers. Then I'm going to see if I can find your health records. What's your doctor's name? Where do you live? And do you know if you're allergic to anything?"

"I don't know about allergies. I live in The Valley… Mill Creek Valley, Missouri. My doctor's name is Dr. Robinson," I said. Again, they were the old woman's memories; I knew they weren't right, but they were the best answers I had.

"Okay, that's a start," Dr. Shale said. "We'll get you cleaned up and run some scans. If you knew what kind of cancer you had—"

"Lung and bone cancer," I interrupted. It seemed right, because that's what the old woman died from.

"Smoker?" Dr. Shale asked.

"I never smoked, but my grandmother and stepfather did when I was growing up."

"Okay," Dr. Shale said as the nurse hung a bag of antibiotics and the doctor gave me a hit of morphine. Relief washed over me. I didn't know how badly I needed that shot until they poured that liquid warmth into my veins.

They ran tests for hours. I felt like a piece of worn-out luggage at an airport. With every test they asked more questions, questions I couldn't always find the answers to. But the more questions they asked, the more I knew. Each question gave me another bundle of memories from the old woman who'd died in this hospital. They were her details, not mine, but I was sure that whatever ailment I had was the same as what she'd died of. I felt that connection all the way down to my cancerous bones.

Between tests, I slept, and I dreamed horrible things. I dreamed of addiction, of depression, of a dead child, of an absentee husband. I dreamed of the life she'd once lived—or at least parts of it.

Chapter 5

Wyatt

My curiosity about the girl got the better of me and, without understanding why I was doing it, I felt an absolute need to go back to her theater. She was more than just intriguing; she felt like hope bundled up in a frail, helpless package—hope that I'd have something to live for once Russell passed.

With Eddy's partner's flashlight in my hand, I stepped through the door and jumped off the stage, looking for the place I'd left Eddy's unconscious body. The inside of the theater was stark black, with just that dim flashlight illuminating the vast emptiness of the room. I moved the flashlight around until I found the shimmering slick of Eddy's blood on the concrete floor, but that asshole was nowhere to be seen.

I guess he lived, I thought as I shined the flashlight around the theater, looking for any of the girl's things.

Like so many of the theaters I visited, it was disheveled. Seats strewn around, damaged and rotting. Ceiling panels warped and drooped. And, not entirely uncommon, there was a small cubby under the faux stage; much like the cubby in my own theater. Also like the cubby in my own theater when June and I purchased the old building, this theater came equipped with a filthy squatter's mattress and a worn-out blanket. I sifted around carefully; I'd seen used needles and other paraphernalia in many of the theaters I visited and didn't want to stab myself. All I found in that cubby, though, was an almost empty pill bottle. Chlorambucil: the same stuff June took when she had cancer the first time.

The drugs, the theater, the cubby, even the girl's name and looks were starting to make my mind ache. It was almost too much. The whole scene had an impossible déjà vu quality I couldn't stomach. I hated that feeling—like you should know something or like you've done something before but just can't remember it. It terrified me, made me think I was getting my brother's and father's disease.

I backed out of the cubby and felt a spidery tickle climb up my back. Between the chill in the air, the faint smell of blood and mildew, and the darkness that almost completely engulfed the theater, I couldn't help thinking about my first real fight. I'd been in Europe for twelve days, ten of those on the beach in England, waiting for transport to France. On my second day in Sainte-Mere-Eglise, France, we were taking cover in a burned-out building, waiting for the mine crew to give us the all clear. I snuck across an alleyway to the building next door; it was more complete than the one my division was in, but it didn't have power, and it was as black as night in there. It was strictly against the rules for us to leave our crew, but I had to shit, and I had a real problem shitting in front of people. I hadn't had a good shit in two days, and I took the opportunity to get some privacy.

As I was wiping my ass, a German with a long knife came at me with my pants down and my hand between my legs. It was so dark in there I couldn't see where he came from, but I could hear the rustle of his gear as he charged me. I dropped the toilet paper and reached for my gun, but he tackled me to the ground, and we fought, struggled, fought, struggled until neither of us had any strength left. His knife cut through my coat in two places, a stinging wetness spreading across my back, leaving permanent reminders of that day on both my coat and my skin. They were my first scars of war, but not my last.

If Russell hadn't disobeyed orders and come looking for me, I believe that German would have killed me with his knife. By the end of the fight, he had me down and was slowly pushing the blade closer to my chest. My strength waned, and I was just about to give up, when Russell showed up out of nowhere, turned on his flashlight, and kicked the German in the face with his heavy combat boot. The Nazi bastard spat a mouthful of blood, and Russell gagged and puked, dropping his flashlight on the ground. Russell never had that killer instinct, and it's not like the movies. The hero doesn't always overcome his weaknesses. After the war, Russell wouldn't even clean the fish we caught or the game we killed. He didn't have the stomach for blood; I envied that my whole life.

With my brother gagging in the corner, and the German spitting and coughing as he tried to get back up, I regained enough energy to get on my feet, pull my pants up, and grab my rifle— which I'd laid on the floor when I was shitting.

The Nazi had overcome the pain of Russell's kick, and he was stumbling his way toward my brother, who was still puking his guts up. I took aim in the dim light and pulled the trigger. The Nazi fell to the ground and grabbed his throat, trying to stop the bleeding.

I picked up my brother's flashlight and shined it on that Nazi's face as he took his last breath. I wish I'd tended to my brother first. Then I wouldn't have seen the life fade from his eyes. It was my first kill, and it has haunted me ever since. Over the years, I've thought about that kid a thousand times. I've wondered if that German soldier had a family, a wife. Wondered if he wanted to be a father or was already a father. Wondered if he had a garden or watched the same movies I watched. It's no easy thing, killing a man. It gets under your skin, haunts you, steals away part of your soul—your innocence. Of all the nightmares I've seen in this world, the horror in that man's face, as the light faded from his eyes, is the one thing that keeps me up at night.

In my mind, he and I were very similar. If Russell hadn't stepped in, the Nazi would have won that fight, and I would have died. We were evenly matched. Two young men fighting for what they believed was right. I regretted killing him, not because I sympathized with his cause, but because I knew, had he been born in a different country, had he been shown different propaganda, had he followed a different religion, he wouldn't have bought into Nazi ideologies. I regretted that we had to go to war, to fight to the death, like animals. I regretted that his life, like so many others, had to be cut short. Knowing that what I did was necessary, not just to save my life, but to stop the spread of evil didn't make it easier. Any man with a conscience will tell you the same. We may have won the war, but the cost was greater than those who never fought would ever understand.

Unlike that first German I killed in The Big One, I never reflected on what I did to my June's stepfather. What I did kept her safe. I went to the war just a short time after I saved June from him, and though he never bothered her again, he'd done enough to haunt her the rest of her life. A man like that deserves no mercy. He wasn't hurting her because he believed in something—regardless of how wrong that something was. He didn't believe in anything; he just liked to hurt people. And like June's stepfather, what I'd done to Eddy, the piece of trash whose blood I was straddling in that dark theater, wouldn't haunt my dreams. He was the same type of garbage June's stepfather had been: the type you don't think about after you've tossed it away.

Once I got my head clear and saw that Emma hadn't left anything important in that theater, I energized the screen and walked back down the hallway of doors, into my theater. By the time I got home, my legs were weak. It had been a long time since

I'd carried a fallen soldier out of the trenches. And while Emma was a lightweight, moving her to safety had taken its toll on me.

I turned the shower on straight hot and washed the rest of that bastard's blood off my hands and face. The sight of blood running down the shit-stinking shower drain made me queasy. I saw too much blood in my life. I saw too many friends die; too many family members die. Every death, bloody or not, leaves its mark. The world is a violent place, and I'd been witness to some of the worst of it. It turned me into something I didn't want to be. As a kid, I was a joker, an adventurer, a conqueror of feats small and large. As an old man, I was the kind of person who took a sick type of pleasure in beating an asshole half to death.

It hadn't always been that way, though. After I killed that first Nazi, I cried myself to sleep for a week. It was only out of sheer exhaustion that I ever slept. Russell made it through the entire war without killing anyone. He'd shot at a few Germans, but either his aim or resolve was off. I had three confirmed kills. Three men died because I was there. The guilt I felt for killing those men faded when I went to Korea to shoot with a camera. I saw more death in Korea than in Europe because I was looking for it. Later, in Nam…what was left of *me* faded away. Violence became part of me. The goofy, fun-loving me melted like so many napalm-soaked soldiers.

Though I felt sick in the shower, after I dried off I took a shot of Jack, then another, then another; the sickness started to pass. I reminded myself that the past was the past. That I did what I had to do. I did horrible deeds for what I'd deemed at the time to be good reasons and maybe, just maybe, the good things outweighed the bad. If I ever did die and had to answer to some white robe-wearing God, I'd tell him I did what I thought was right.

But I doubted he'd accept that answer. I doubted there was a spot behind those pearly gates for a man like me.

When the *Jack* settled my nerves, I heated up a frozen Salisbury steak TV dinner and put *The Sting* on the projector. I went to my favorite recliner in the center of the theater, ate a few bites of the lukewarm, flavorless dinner, set it aside, and imagined my wife's cooking. The perfect scald to a medium-rare steak, the crispy edge on her fried potatoes. I missed her food but missed *her* more than anything.

I leaned my chair back and passed out before the first reel change.

* * *

Emma

When I awoke the next morning, little of the young, sickly girl I appeared to be, remained. Though I still looked young, I didn't feel young. I felt ancient, and my mind was filled with memories that belonged to the old woman who'd died in that hospital. I felt…worn down by the lifetime of memories that had filled in the sprawling gaps in my mind. I knew about the weeks the old woman had spent in the hospital right before her death. I knew about the pain as cancer spread to her bones, pain she covered with excessive Vicodin use. I remembered her hiding the pain and the cancer from her husband. But more than anything, I remembered the fear she felt.

The old woman…June…had lived her life in fear. So, I lived in fear.

As I lay in the hospital, remembering the end of her life, I knew my own death was coming. I felt it deep in my core. Time was short. More than short, past due, and the bill collector was on his way. The old woman lived on borrowed time. After her first cancer diagnosis, the doctor gave her a ten percent chance of living another year. Five percent chance of living two. But she'd lived ten years before the cancer came back.

Ten years of constant fear that it'd return, worse than before. Every little mole that looked off, every little bone-deep ache from standing on concrete and serving popcorn for five hours, every raspy breath screamed, "You're dying!" But those ten years had also been some of the best of her life. Wyatt had been there for her in ways he'd never been before. They'd been true partners. She'd been sober and clearheaded, and she'd dared to believe she was happy, dared to believe she was in love.

But when June died, she was ready. She was tired of being afraid, tired of waiting for those aches or raspy breaths to be the first signs of something worse. June knew nothing could be worse than the pain and fear she'd already lived through, and she was ready to let it all go.

Along with the details of her life, I knew details of her husband's life, too. At his core, he was a good man even if, until the end, he wasn't always there for her. Despite that goodness, he had demons, both violent ones and sorrow-filled ones that lurked just behind his eyes. Demons he fought to keep locked away, but demons that, in moments of tension, sometimes slipped beyond his grasp. A whiskey bottle thrown against a wall; a chair smashed against the floor. And an apology—always an apology—followed by a hasty return to whatever war was currently brewing.

She'd accepted Wyatt's demons for what they were, without judgment. June had her own share of demons. Demons *he'd* accepted for what they were, without judgment.

Her husband, Wyatt, had spent the bulk of his life on the battlefield, and while he knew his career choice was dangerous, he was okay with it. He actually expected to die on assignment, on the battlefield, in the jungle, or in a war-torn city. He'd warned June over and over again that his "next assignment was dangerous." And he'd remind her about his life insurance and his safe deposit box, and the money Russell set aside for their retirement. She knew, not because he'd blatantly told her, but because of the reminders he always shared right before he left on assignment, that he expected to be collateral damage to some foreign war.

Maybe he even longed to be.

But as he sat beside his wife, watching her die, all the rigidity in his eyes softened, then faded. June knew that he finally understood he'd outlive her, and he didn't know how to deal with it. It tore him up inside, because he was old and getting more and more forgetful, confused, lost. Without June, the only person he'd have left was his twin—and Russell was fighting his own battle against dementia. And once Russell's mind was completely gone, it would leave Wyatt on his own for the first time in his life.

It nearly drove him insane. He was a soldier—a warrior who wished he'd have died in battle rather than growing old and watching his loved ones slip away slowly, painfully. In the back of his mind, I think he felt cursed, because he didn't die young and strong like he'd expected—like he'd wanted. Instead, he'd grown old and tired, and, worst of all, afraid. And though the old woman knew how to handle fear—she'd been afraid most of her life— the concept was totally foreign to him.

"Emma? Are you awake?" Dr. Shale asked, interrupting my exploration through this twisted world I was trying to navigate.

I nodded.

"We've got the results from your bloodwork. It's cancer, like you thought, and…it's not good. We've been in contact with your oncologist in St. Louis. He says you had leukemia ten years ago but have been in remission until a few months ago. He said you knew about the lung cancer and knew it had spread into your bones but refused chemotherapy."

I was familiar with the details Dr. Shale gave me. They were the same details she'd once explained to the old woman. And like

June, I zoned out as Dr. Shale spoke, because it was irrelevant. All of it was irrelevant. The only possible relevance her ramblings of medical jargon and treatment options held was a reminder that time was short. If I followed the same timeline as June, I only had days before the inevitable stroke would destroy what was left of my mind. Days to figure this all out.

The IV dripped.

Dr. Shale talked.

My stomach churned.

My lungs burned.

My bones ached.

And I closed my eyes waiting, anxiously for Wyatt to return. He had to come back for me.

Chapter 6

Wyatt

The next morning, I followed my typical routine. Push-ups, sit-ups, a ten-mile run, breakfast, and a trip to my brother's. I thought about the girl, Emma, as I walked from The Prestige on Marcus Avenue to Paradise Garden. I wondered how she was doing. Wondered if she was awake; how the head injury was feeling; how many stitches she got. I wondered about the sickness she was clearly suffering from.

And I felt guilty for not being there.

If I felt guilty, it meant I cared. Other than Russell, she was the first living person I'd cared about since my wife died. I didn't know what struck me about her. Maybe it was her hopelessness? Or her suffering? Maybe it was because she reminded me of June. But something…

When I got to my brother's, my concern for the girl disappeared. As soon as I saw the look on Nurse Hope's soft, khaki face, I knew something was wrong.

"Mr. Gaumond, do you know what happened this morning?" she asked gently, taking my hand in hers.

"What's wrong?" I asked, my heart beating too hard and too fast, an odd pain running down my left arm. I knew this day would come. I knew Russell was near the end, but that didn't make it easy.

"Do you know where your brother is?"

I shrugged, mouth open, unable to talk.

"He was taken by ambulance to the hospital. I can get you a ride if you want to visit him…to say goodbye."

"Please do," I said, my voice even more gruff than usual as I held back tears.

She didn't hesitate. She picked up the phone and dialed. A bit later she said, "Your ride will be here in ten minutes, Wyatt."

"What happened?" I asked.

I wasn't ready to lose my brother, my one remaining constant in life. He'd been with me since we were born. We'd been through everything together. I just wasn't ready to be completely alone. Possibly even scarier was the potential that I'd be alone on this planet forever. How much longer would my unaging body hold on before Father Time realized he'd forgotten about me?

Nurse Hope said, "Early this morning, on the two o'clock rounds, the CNA on duty—Davie—saw your brother out of bed. He was…urinating in a trashcan in the hallway. These kinds of things happen; people get confused. Davie waited until Russell finished to approach him. When he did, Davie asked him if he needed help back to his bedroom. This was the first time any of us had seen Russell walking since his hip surgery. Davie said your brother seemed steady on his feet, but that his words were jumbled. 'An incomprehensible mess,' according to Davie."

I grimaced, and Nurse Hope placed a hand on my shoulder.

"Should I go on?"

"Yeah…" I said.

She nodded and said, "Davie asked him if he was okay, but your brother's words came out even more jumbled. Davie also noticed that the left side of his face was slack. That's when he called 911. Before they got here, Russell collapsed. Davie had to start CPR to keep him going."

"It's definitely the end, then?" I asked, making a fist and shaking out my hand in a lame attempt to relieve the horrible pain in my arm and pressure in my chest.

"I can't tell you that for sure. But he's on a ventilator and, at his age, in his condition, it's unlikely he'll come back from a stroke of this…magnitude," she said.

I cared for my wife through her cancer and the stroke that finally destroyed her mind. After that stroke, when she was awake, she drooled, spat, scratched at nurses…she was hateful. Luckily, she wasn't awake often. When she tried to talk, her voice was garbled and unclear, but when she'd scream, her meaning was as clear as a freshly washed windowpane. In confused grunts, she'd scream, "Fuck you!" at nurses trying to take her vitals. She'd scream, "No!" as they tried to pump more drugs into her IV. She'd scream, "Just let me die!" as doctors discussed her treatment plans with me. After the stroke, the doctors told me she still had complete brain function; she'd just lost her ability to speak. Even if she couldn't say it, her frustrated grunts made it clear what she wanted. I knew my wife well enough to know what she wanted, too. So we stopped all treatment. I brought in Hospice, and they helped ease her through the last days of her life.

From the time she coughed up blood in our old Corvette, to the few days after her stroke, when her body gave up, I held her hand. I read Agatha Christie to her because she loved a good mystery. I watched her dwindle to a skeletal eighty pounds. Her yellowing-waxy skin hung from her body like a worn-out suit. The whites of her eyes turned grey, her skin tore, and bruised at the slightest touch. Then one night, she simply disappeared. It just took a little longer for her body to realize it.

"Your ride's here, Wyatt," Hope said, tapping me on the shoulder.

"Thanks," I said as I rushed out. I could feel the strength in my legs give way as the pain in my chest grew. But, as I always had before, I soldiered on.

The ride Hope got for me was a nursing home minivan, complete with wheelchair lift and the Paradise Garden crest emblazoned on the side. A man with a cigar sat behind the wheel. The cigar wasn't lit, but my grandpa's smell filled the air. Sitting there on the vinyl seat in that nursing home van, I could all but taste my grandpa's rich tobacco smoke and heavy aftershave.

"St. Alexius Hospital," I mumbled to the driver, still trying to shake the tingling out of my hand.

"Sure," he said. "Somebody sick?" he asked as he pulled the minivan onto the street.

I grunted, "Brother," but didn't engage any further.

I witnessed my loved ones pass from this world into…whatever comes next. My estranged grandfather, who died over a steak dinner when Russell and I were just kids, was the first death I saw. My mother, who I loved dearly, went a few decades later. The cancer ate her away in two and a half months. My father, who died when I was fifty-seven, followed. He suffered from the same kind of dementia that took Russell's mind from him. The whole time I watched my dad weaken from an intelligent, hard-working and even harder-headed man, into a lump of living flesh too confused to know his own name, I prayed I'd never get that horrid disease.

I loved my parents, and when they died, a part of me died, too. There would be no more Cardinals games for "just the three of us boys," a phrase my father used to explain to my mother, wife, and sister-in-law why they couldn't go to the game with us. No more fried chicken and affectionate doting from my mother. There'd be no more rabbit hunting trips or "cold ones" on the front porch as our family watched the sunset, reminiscing without saying a word. There'd be no more fatherly advice or motherly scrutiny.

I knew shortly after my mother died, and I stopped aging, that I'd have to suffer the loss of every one of my family members. And I did. And while losing my grandfather was bad, each loss after his has been infinitely worse. Grief compounds, grief lasts, grief builds. Every new loss brought back all the old losses—the old hurts. I saw hundreds die in war, but they weren't my family. Maybe seeing all that I saw made it worse for me. Maybe it intensified my own pain. One thing was for sure though; I wasn't ready to lose Russell. I wasn't ready to be the sole custodian of all those losses—the only enduring memory of our lifetime.

When we pulled into the circle drive in front of the hospital, the minivan driver said, "Good luck wich yar fatha," which hit me like a brick to the face. My mom and dad died in that hospital, too. My dad lived at Russell's nursing home but had been transferred to the hospital with double pneumonia. Dad looked, and God, now that I think about it, smelled like Russell. Dementia put him in the nursing home. Heart disease killed him. Russell's degrading state, it seemed, was a repetition of my father's death. Difficult as it had already been, the van driver's verbal screw-up made everything so much harder.

My knees shook and the pain in my chest grew as I walked toward the huge information desk in the entryway of the hospital. Two elderly nuns sat behind the desk answering questions. I didn't want to talk to anyone; I just wanted to get to my brother's room. But I could wander around St. Alexius for hours without finding him. I stepped up to the semicircular Formica desk and said, "Russell Gaumond."

"I'll fetch a room number for you. Just a second," the nun said. She was probably around my age but looked like a relic from some long-forgotten civilization. She talked to me like she was talking to a six-year-old who'd get a sucker if he behaved in Sunday school.

"Family?" she asked as she flipped through a three-ring binder at a slug's pace.

"Twin brother," I mumbled.

"Room 3254. If you go down the hall to the elevator, and go up to the third floor, then go to the right, you'll see the 32-Wing."

I grumbled a quick, "Thanks," as I rushed down the hallway.

My insides were turning to water, and my body felt like rubber. I couldn't catch my breath, and my left arm… I didn't even know if I'd make it to his room. I walked, oblivious to the rest of the people crowding the overly busy hospital, down an all-white hallway with brighter than average lighting at the end.

The tunnel is opening, I thought, but I didn't know what that meant. I'd never been religious, and all those stories about a tunnel of light leading you to heaven seemed like utter bullshit to me. Made-up stories that are simply there to help people accept death.

I boarded the elevator with a dozen doctors, patients, and visitors. None of them had smiles on their faces. For a moment I lost track of my thoughts and found myself wondering about the girl I'd helped the night before. And then I thought about my June being in the same hospital where I'd dropped off that girl.

When the elevator dinged on the third floor, I got off, read the sign at the crossroads of the two hallways, and headed to the right, to Russell's room.

My chest hurt so badly by then that I considered asking a doctor for help.

But still, I pushed forward.

If I died right then, it'd be a gift.

But I didn't.

I pushed on.

Russell lay in a hospital bed, tube down his throat, thin gown covering his upper body, his face slack and expressionless like all the muscles had given up their fight against gravity. His chest rose and fell with the mechanical consistency of the ventilator.

"Russell," I said, tears welling up.

He didn't move, not even his eyes.

I pulled his chart off the end of his bed and started reading through the tests they'd completed. MRI, CT scan, and EKG all showed that he had suffered a severe stroke and that his heart had stopped. He was revived by the EMTs, who brought him to the hospital, but as soon as the "plug" was pulled, whatever remained of my brother would be gone because his mind and body had finally lost their war against time.

"Mr. Gaumond? Wyatt Gaumond?" a tender, feminine voice asked from behind me as I looked through the chart.

"Yes."

"*Paradise* said you were the only living relative."

"Yes," I mumbled, still looking at the chart.

"You know about his DNR, then?"

"I was with him when he signed it."

"I know we broke protocol, and we should have let him go, but we didn't realize until after we had the ventilator in place that he'd signed a DNR. After that, we wanted to give you the opportunity to say goodbye before we removed the vent. There's nothing else we can do… I'm sorry, sir."

"When will you do it?"

"As soon as you're ready."

I hung the chart back on the end of the bed, pulled up a chair, and sat next to my brother for the last time. "Give me a few minutes, please," I said to the nurse or doctor, or whoever it was that was standing in the doorway like Lurch.

"Of course, sir."

My brother knew almost everything about me, so I didn't have any last-minute secrets to confess. I didn't have much news to share with the man I spent eighty-eight years with. Instead, I told him, "I saved a girl's life last night, Russell. God, she looks so much like a younger version of my June. She's got the same name, too. Well, first name anyway. And she's sick like my June was at the end. So, I guess I've found something to do with my time. I'll take care of your remains, like you wanted," I paused, took a deep breath, and let it out with a wet sob.

"Thanks for always being there, Russell," I added before I stood and walked out of the room, wiping tears from my eyes. I motioned for the woman who'd been standing just outside the door to come back in.

"Are you ready?"

I nodded, hiding my tears and holding my aching chest.

I might just follow you down that tunnel, Russ. Maybe I'll see you on the other side momentarily.

She walked into the room. My brother's chest rising and falling with that unnatural rhythm. But it was time to let him go, to let him find whatever peace awaited those who traversed across that final plane.

"Okay. Once I shut off the vent, it will be very quick," the doctor said.

"I've seen it before."

"I'm sorry," she said. She shut off the machine and disconnected the hose from Russell's throat tube. His chest stopped rising and falling. He never even opened his eyes. I held his clammy hand as I watched him slip away. It was peaceful, calm, none of the fear I saw in those poor soldiers who'd died too early.

Russell had lived a full life, a good life.

His time had simply come to an end.

* * *

Emma

D r. Shale hung a fresh bag of clear liquid on my IV stand and connected the tube to my arm. It was cold going in, but they always were. It was one of those things chronic patients grew to hate. As the liquid poured into me, I couldn't help but wonder why they didn't heat the damn stuff up? How hard would that be? Then, as opposed to freezing, the IV fluids would feel like stepping into a warm bath, and right then I'd have killed for a warm bath.

"You doing okay, Emma?" Dr. Shale asked as she made notes on her clipboard and checked all the sensors and monitors hooked up to me.

"Cold," I said, my teeth clattering. But there was more to it than that. The cold was real, but at the same time felt…manufactured, like the weird, radiating heat from those fake fireplaces. Your mind thinks it's warm, it feels warm, but it doesn't warm you like a real fire. I knew I wasn't there to enjoy myself; hospitals aren't a holiday, but everything I'd experienced since I woke up was, in a way, a replay of the worst things that the old woman, June, had lived through. This freezing IV bag was just another hell she'd endured through her first round of cancer and again in the last days of her life.

"I'll get you a warm blanket," Dr. Shale said. "Do you have questions for me?"

I'd had access to June's memories for a short time, and I'd seen her life. Seen horrors no one should have to live through; I'd felt the persistent, nagging fear that followed June since her childhood. But I'd seen beauty in her life, too. Beauty, and joy, and hope.

Her memories were jumbled in my mind, as if all the pictures in the photo album of her life had been dumped into an empty cardboard box and shaken up. I tried to put the pieces of her life into some comprehensible order. But they had no order, no consistency. I had memories of childhood right next to memories of her child. I saw memories of her husband and memories of her best friend, Hilda. But one glimpse would be of Hilda and June as teens; the next would be of an older version of Wyatt returning from some battle-torn country with a bag of undeveloped film and a handful of notes scrawled across crinkled, yellowing paper.

There was no clear timeline, which made deciphering June's reality impossible. Everything that'd happened since I woke in that theater was like a fever dream, like the last bursts of energy coursing through a dying mind. Maybe I *was* just that old woman, confused and at the end of her life. Maybe Wyatt was right beside me, holding my hand, but my mind had broken, and I couldn't feel him anymore.

Maybe death was already in the room with me, and I just needed to give in, so he could take me home.

Maybe. But none of that felt right. What felt right was that I'd been somewhere else, some other plane of existence, and for some reason I was given leave to come back to this plane—a short leave, but leave, nonetheless. I was here; I had to do something, and I had to do it quickly, because my body, soul, essence— whatever you wanted to call it—was fading fast.

Did I have questions? You're fucking right I did, but I didn't think Dr. Shale would be able to answer most of them.

"Emma, do you have questions for me?" Dr. Shale asked again as she brushed a loose strand of hair out of my eyes and put an electric thermometer in my ear. Her warm hand on my clammy skin was the most comforting thing I'd felt since I'd been back. Though most of the memories I'd relived were of June's worst moments, Dr. Shale's touch reminded me that not everyone was a monster. Now that I had more details, I knew that June liked Dr. Shale because her caring energy reminded June of her grandmother.

"How much time do you think I have?" I asked.

"One can't know for sure, Emma, but I'd say time is short. You've got advanced cancer in your bones and…" Dr. Shale went on, talking through the details of my disease, but I let my focus fade and eased into the soothing tone of her voice—practiced and intentionally designed to ease patients into the worst news they'd ever get. And as I eased into her soothing tone, I thought of June's Grandma.

Her house was just a few doors down from June's when she was a kid. But unlike June's house, Grandma's was nice, clean, recently painted on the outside and the inside could have been a *Good Housekeeping* cover from the 1940s. Grandma always had warm snickerdoodles cooling on her bubblegum pink stove. The smell of cinnamon and sugar filling the house, masking the stale cigarette stench. When June stayed at Grandma's, she had her own room—an actual room, not a closet-sized space she could hardly turn around in—and Grandma would give June milk and cookies for supper. She'd let June hide out while Eddy slept off another night of heavy, fury-inducing drinking.

Once, when June was in Jr. high, and Eddy was on a week-long bender, and looking to stretch it out another week, Grandma packed her up and drove her all the way out to Colorado, to camp in a hidden bend beside a river swollen with ice-cold water from the spring thaw. As I lay there in that hospital bed listening but not listening to that practiced, soothing tone in Dr. Shale's voice, the memories of June's life became so real I could almost smell the fresh spruce scent as the sun warmed the needles scattered across the ground. I could hear Grandma's soothing, nonjudgmental tone as she taught June how to start a fire, how to build it so the smoke would blow away from their tent, how to clean the innards from a trout so they could roast it on a spit.

She didn't know it until years later, but Grandma had to sell her TV and cash in a savings bond so she could afford to take

June away for that week. So she could keep June safe. But Grandma would have done anything to keep June safe. That kind of love isn't something you can remember without feeling the intensity of it. And while June wasn't sure her mother ever actually loved her, she knew Grandma loved her more than anything. And as I remembered June's Grandma, my heart filled with undeniable joy; a feeling so opposite the fear I'd been experiencing since I'd woken under that stage in the theater that words couldn't describe it.

My mind shifted to the old woman at the Piggly Wiggly after I'd just woken up in the theater. I knew it was June's Grandma. Same cotton-ball haircut. Same warmth. Same overly white dentures. She'd been there, and then she'd disappeared.

Real or delusion? I wondered as Dr. Shale's voice stopped, clearly waiting for a reply.

Her hand swiped another loose strand of hair off my forehead, and she repeated, "Does all that make sense, Emma?"

I nodded, feeling the same kindness that had lived in June's Grandma radiating from Dr. Shale. She truly cared, and that was a rare thing. If you weren't looking for it, you'd forget that type of kindness existed in this world.

I didn't know why I was there. Why I was filled with June's memories. I didn't know why I was being tormented by half thoughts and confusing timelines, but it seemed, maybe, there was still something to fight for.

"Okay, Emma. I'll send a nurse with a warm blanket. If you need me…just press the red button," Dr. Shale said, taking a step back from the bed.

When Dr. Shale left the room, the coldness that had surrounded me since I'd woken in that theater returned, like an arctic blast of frigid air. And with that coldness, a bone-deep ache that made it seem like the pain would never end. And with the physical pain, came fear. A fear so ingrained in June's life that it made me feel I was sinking into a black sea of icy sadness. A sea so deep it would swallow me whole, and I'd never feel true happiness again. I'd never feel anything but physical pain, loss, sadness, heartache, or, at best, a grey neutrality induced by heavy drug use. As long as I was here on this plane, I knew I was destined to suffer.

And maybe that *was* my purpose. Maybe that's all our purposes. Maybe we're just here to suffer, to learn how to cope with whatever life throws our way, but to endure the suffering we're given a peppering of joy to season the pain.

Chapter 7

Wyatt

"Ken," I said, holding my hand out for a shake. On the way out of the hospital, I ran into the mortician our family had used since my nephew died in Vietnam. Ken was a good man, a quiet man that didn't ask questions like: "Why haven't you aged in 40 years?" He just did his job. I needed him to do that job as quickly as possible. I wanted to get Russell's remains spread before the overthinking side of me started down memory lane. The dark cloud caused by the idea of distributing my brother's remains was threatening to strike me down with a thunderbolt. I needed to act before that thunderbolt hit me and the long depression I knew was coming set its vicious claws on me.

"Wyatt," Ken said, giving my hand one of those sympathetic handshakes, where the person places their other hand on top of yours and just holds it there for a few seconds. "So, so sorry for your loss. He died an old man and lived a good life. Who can ask for anything more?"

I nodded, thinking in rapid fire about all the losses I'd been through with Ken. I felt my eyes start to glaze over as they did when I was about to dig deep into some horrid memory. With great effort, I stopped myself from delving into whatever hell my mind had in store for me.

"Look, Ken, I was hoping—"

Ken held up a bony, calloused old hand. "Your brother's remains will be ready tomorrow afternoon. Do you prefer a specific type of receptacle?"

When he said the word "Receptacle," I felt something inside of me shutter, like a door to some hidden part of my mind closing abruptly.

"Cheapest, sturdiest *receptacle* you've got, Ken. It doesn't matter what it looks like; I'll be taking him back to some of our favorite places to lay his ashes to rest. But I don't want to break the damn thing and spill him all over my knapsack," I said, glancing over Ken's shoulder. His hearse was parked just a few spaces from where we stood. I wondered if he had Russell loaded yet or if an assistant was inside, getting my brother's body.

Over the last few years, whenever Russell's mind was at its sharpest, we talked through what he wanted done with his body. Russell chose to forgo the hubbub of a funeral, saying, "Nobody but you would be there. Our family's gone, and our friends are all in homes like this one or worse. If your old bones can get you there, burn me up and scatter me at our places. You know the places. Save just a little for home and a little for Hilda, too."

I had years to prepare for that day, but like every loss I'd been through, his death came quicker than I expected.

"We have a selection of brass Roman Urns that will be both inexpensive and appropriate for travel. A screw on top is suggested if you will be taking Russell to multiple destinations for placement," Ken said, his choice of words always funeral director proper.

"Okay. Brass, screw on top, fine," I said, putting my hand out to shake with Ken one last time. In some ways, he was like family. Ken saw me at the worst times of my life. He saw me break down more than once. And I think at one point or another he saw the demons inside me.

Ken took my hand in his, placed his other hand on top of mine and looked into my eyes. "Again, Wyatt, I'm sorry for this loss. I hate to see you go through this alone. But it seems you'll outlive us all."

"Seems that way," I said. "Tomorrow? Three o'clock?" I was putting a time crunch on him. Cremations usually took much longer, or so Ken told me when we originally spoke about Russell's wishes.

"That's fine, Wyatt. We'll have Russell's remains prepared for you," he said, letting go of my hand.

Ω

The Paradise Garden minivan was waiting for me. While that seemed as odd to me as Ken showing up to pick up Russell before I even had time to walk out of the hospital, I wasn't one to quibble over oddities. I *was* a living oddity, after all. The same cigar-chewing driver helped me into the van and drove through the city, back to Paradise Garden, where I was greeted by a host of sniveling nurses. Hugs and handshakes were meant to keep me strong as I went to clean out my brother's room—I knew those vultures, though. They appeared to be upset but would have some other old codger in there before the day was over.

I gathered the framed pictures of us and of our family, wrapping them carefully in some of my brother's clean shirts—twenty-year-old rags so threadbare they were nearly transparent, but, according to Russell, were "the most comfortable." I packed the wrapped, framed pictures of our lives, pictures from dripping jungles in Thailand, and fishing charters in the Gulf of Mexico. Pictures of Russell, Hilda, June and I in the mountains when we were still just kids. I shoved them all into Russell's suitcase—an Italian leather bag he had carried since the end of The Big One.

On top of the wrapped pictures, I loaded unframed snapshots from the collage on his bulletin board. I couldn't pull the Goddamn tacks quickly enough to get the photos down without having to look at them. The images of our lives splayed out on glossy photo paper cut like knives. We'd been linked, joined, one, since before we were born. Together, we outlived our marriages, our children, our families—we outlived all those smiling faces that stared back at me as I pulled picture after picture from his collage. Even at the end, when his mind was mush, we could finish one another's sentences. You can't buy that kind of closeness.

Now it was gone.

Ken's words echoed in my head: *"He died an old man and lived a good life. Who could ask for anything more?"* But as I thought of Ken saying that, another man's visage came to mind. The in-house priest at Russell's home. I didn't know him, never even shook his hand, but thinking back, Ken's face, a face I'd once known so well, was completely gone from my mind. All I saw was Father Curt. Father Curt in his black polyester shirt, with the white hashmark of his clerical collar poking out at the neck.

I tried to clear my mind of that dreamlike nonsense and went back to Russell's bulletin board. His passing made me think back to the dozens of conversations we had about what came after this life. As kids, we'd lay out under the stars beside a dwindling campfire and ask one another: "Do you really believe in God?" and we'd both giggle. When we were young and hopeful, those conversations were young and hopeful; naïve. We'd both agreed that God was watching us, protecting us, and He'd continue to do so as long as we prayed.

I lost my faith in God long before Russell, but after his son died, Russell's faith quavered, then collapsed. Later, as we strolled moonlit beaches in far-off countries, after we'd both agreed that God was dead, we'd ask each other about the soul. "Does it exist?" or "Does it live on forever?" and "If there's no God, where does it go?" We'd talk for hours under the starry sky about what could be on the other side of that last doorway… But we never got answers.

Those are the questions you never get an answer to. Not while you're alive, anyway.

I wondered if those questions had been answered for him now that he was on the other side. I looked down at my hands, still those of a young man, and wondered if I'd ever get to visit that last doorway.

I pulled the final few photos down, stacked them neatly in Russell's suitcase, and tightened the leather straps. I sifted through everything else, throwing most of it in the trash. I still hadn't unpacked the boxes of the rest of my family's things. Boxes upon boxes were stacked in my living room, waiting for my emotions to settle so I could open them; my family's lives waiting to be reviewed, remembered and finally set to rest. But I couldn't let them rest. I still loved my wife, my son…the others. And looking back was simply too painful. So those boxes sat, untouched, just like that awful box with the red stripe in the projector room.

Russell's things would be just another box—or suitcase in this instance—stacked in the corner, waiting for me to sift through and decide what should be kept and what should be thrown away. But I had time. Time was always on my side. I could let Russell's dust settle before digging through his past.

"You know you're not supposed to be out of bed," Hope, my favorite nurse, said as I tossed the last few greeting cards into the trash. She stood behind me, leaning against the wall, her hands in the pockets of her flowery scrubs. She was a pretty girl, probably around twenty-five or thirty. Her short, boy-cut hair emphasized her long neck and prominent cheekbones. Soft, warm skin was highlighted with just a hint of rouge but no lipstick. She was pretty, not gorgeous, but the lighting made her honey-brown tone seem perfect. If I had my Leica, I'd have asked for a photo.

Instead, I asked, "What do you mean 'not supposed to be out of bed'?"

Ignoring me, she said, "We're going to miss him, Wyatt. He had personality. It wasn't always the best personality, but he was full of it. Some of the people who come through here are…their minds have gone, but their bodies keep moving around. Russell wasn't always sharp, didn't always know who we were, but he was always funny. He was a flirt, but he never got handsy. He was a good man. We miss good men when they're gone. I'm so sorry for your loss, Wyatt."

A tear was threatening to fall from her left eye as she spoke, and I realized it wasn't just a courtesy comment. She meant what she said. I was surprised that these people could feel anything after the number of souls they'd seen crossing over. But she felt it, and I really wished I could capture that moment with my camera.

Old habits…

"I'm going to miss him too," I said, feeling like my chest was being stepped on by an elephant. The pain in my arm hit again, only worse. My chin shook as I tried to catch my breath. I *was* being crushed by that unnamable weight. I tried to hold back tears, but with a gasp and an explosion in my chest, they came anyway. I felt myself sinking to the floor.

Hope's clog-covered feet clunked against the asbestos tiles. She wrapped her arms around me as I melted to the ground. She held me, and I cried like a child whose puppy had just died. I cried like I hadn't cried in years. I cried until my nose was full, my breath became ragged, and my heart felt like a wet rag being twisted in a giant's hands.

She whispered, "It's okay, Wyatt, you can let go."

She held me and rocked me like a baby.

I closed my eyes, and I let go.

* * *

Emma

I slept, dreamed, awoke, had my vitals taken by a drowsy French-Canadian nurse, slept, dreamed…and so on. When I dreamed, I dreamed about Wyatt and June as old people. I dreamed about how Wyatt never left June's bedside when she was dying of cancer. And how she could feel his presence even if she was too tired to open her eyes or reach her hand out to him.

I dreamed about hiking in the mountains with their long-time traveling companions, Wyatt's brother, Russell, and his wife, Hilda. Wyatt and Russell were twins, identical in so many ways, but Wyatt was a brooding old man, with sad eyes and an unstable temperament. Russell smiled genuinely as he helped his cane-wielding wife to the small summit of the emerald green mountainside. June was jealous but felt she didn't deserve a man who smiled. She deserved a man who brooded and lost his temper, because she, too, was a brooder.

The four of them had been there, to that mountain, together, as young people. And they went back a lot. It was where June fell in love with Wyatt for the first time. They'd already been married for years, but his extended stay in Europe during WWII kept them separate for much of that time. When he was away, he'd write, and she cherished every postcard he sent, but he didn't send them often.

Alone in a cramped apartment with junk furniture, no money for clothes, or food, June was constantly under pressure, but she never asked for her mother's help. She never once talked to her mother after she left their tiny bungalow—after Eddy and Wyatt's altercation.

She thought about her mother, though. She wanted to ask her, "Why did you let Eddy treat me that way?" Wanted to ask her, "Why were you such a fucking coward?" After being a mother, June knew the lengths she'd have gone to in order to keep her son safe; why hadn't her mother done the same for her? Was there something wrong with her?

At one point, as June was trying to make the 42 cents she had left—pennies and nickels tossed into a warped paper cup on the counter—last another two weeks before Wyatt's next paycheck, she almost asked her mother for a loan. Just five dollars to get her through. But if she asked for help, it would be like admitting defeat. Instead, she became a "Rosie the Riveter." It was the only time in her long life that she held a full-time job; it was the only time she needed to—Wyatt took care of everything on the financial side, once he returned. But while he was in WWII, she worked at a munitions factory in the heart of St. Louis. It was hard work, but somehow, at the end of the day, when she'd come home covered in the smell of hot metal and gunpowder, she felt accomplished. She felt like she'd done something worthwhile. She felt proud.

On that mountain, as Wyatt and June walked two paces away from one another, Russell and Hilda walked hand in hand. It made sense. Wyatt and June kept secrets from one another. They'd been married for nearly sixty years, and she never once told him she worked during WWII. Wyatt had the old-time notion that women should stay at home and that, financially, men should take care of their families. His father had kept his mother from working outside of the home throughout the entire Great Depression; Wyatt took great pride in that.

June kept secrets from him, secrets that could have damaged his ego, and she knew Wyatt had secrets, too. But she didn't need to know what they were. She really didn't care. They were partners, and while their self-centered, impulsive, childish notions of love waned shortly after their marriage, their mutual respect never faltered..

On the side of the misty mountain that day, a rock slipped from under June's foot, and she almost fell, but Russell, the smiling brother, caught her hand even as he held his wife's.

Wyatt rushed over, something almost like concern in his voice as he asked, "Are you okay?"

"I'm fine, Wyatt. Just slipped on some loose rocks," she said.

"Be careful, kid, don't want to lose you to the volcano," Wyatt said, trying to smile as his brother smiled, but it wasn't real. He'd seen too much, done too much, felt too much to be sincere. It was something he and June had in common, and maybe that's why they worked as a couple—neither of them could feel like normal people felt. And maybe their abnormalities and their history kept them bound to one another.

Is that all love is? History, comfort, and balance?

"Emma? EMMA?" Dr. Shale said, shaking me awake.

"What?" I said, my voice clear of all the raspiness and gruffness that had distorted it since I'd woken up in that theater. I sounded like a teenager again.

"You were dreaming. How are you feeling?"

I lifted my arms, stretched my feet, took a deep breath. My lungs felt alive again; there was no raspy, gurgling wetness in them. My body felt…relaxed. Good. I looked at my hands. The sunspots and frail skin had been replaced by smooth, fresh, ivory-colored flesh—like that of a child who's never had a sunburn. I was young and healthy. As time passed, rather than stepping closer and closer to death, my body felt younger, stronger. It was like time was running in the opposite direction since I'd arrived at the hospital.

"Surprisingly, I feel good," I said, smiling at Dr. Shale.

"Then you're almost ready to go. You just need to wait a little longer," she said, then she winked, like she was in on some massive conspiracy that I was about to be part of.

Chapter 8

Wyatt

The next afternoon, I picked up Russell's remains from Ken's funeral home. As much as I didn't want to let him go, I was anxious to start the impossible task of scattering my brother's ashes. I knew the places he wanted to visit one last time. Important places. Places he'd been truly happy, if only for a moment.

When we were younger, we traveled together often. As photojournalists, we saw the world together. From continent to continent, country to country, we saw everything from Kenya to Cambodia. But it was our private life, our vacations, that stood out in Russell's mind.

In the hallway of doors, there was a red door with black letters that read, "Key West." I found the door on my first visit to the hallway. Florida had always been a popular vacation destination for our family; even my folks loved the beach. Regardless of the war we were covering, the financial strain we were under, or the assignment I was on, from 1946 until Russell couldn't walk, we went to Key West every May for tarpon season. It was one of the first places he mentioned when, after he got too old to travel, we started talking about our "Best days." Everyone has best days, days they know, as they're happening, they'll remember forever.

Every time we went tarpon fishing was like a shadow of the first time… Most things in life are like that. Drugs never feel as strong as the first hit; killing never feels as bad as the first kill; love never feels as intense as a first love—love so strong it hurts deep down. That was how we felt the first time we went to Key West, when we were still twenty-somethings. It was a perfect sunny Florida Keys day. Water so deep blue it was like sitting atop an infinite liquid sapphire. There was just enough breeze to keep the sweat at bay. We had cold beer in a cooler, and the fish were biting faster than we could reel them in. Mid-afternoon, Russell snagged a two-hundred-pound tarpon that wrestled him for hours. I offered to take a turn at least a dozen times, but every time I reached for the rod and reel, he recoiled. "No. Goddammit. This is my catch!" he'd shout; "hands off!" he'd shout. After a while, I reached for the rod and reel just to mess with him.

His hands bled from the struggle, but he wouldn't give up. As the last glimmers of sun reflected off the blue waters of the Atlantic, the tarpon surfaced close enough for me and the captain to pull it into the boat, but we couldn't even lift the damn thing. I had to hang from a canvas harness off the jib crane to get a rope through the fish's gills. The captain used the hand-cranked jib crane to get the tarpon out of the water. When the eight-foot fish hung over the edge of the boat, Russell laughed. He wiped his bloody paws on his white shirt, leaving copper streaks down the front. And he laughed. For a while he didn't say anything; he just laughed.

He laughed so hard he crumpled to the ground.

It was infectious, and soon the captain and I laughed, too. I laughed like I hadn't laughed since before The Big One.

It was a massive catch, possibly a record breaker for that area, but Russell's reaction to it, his childlike happiness, was the real prize. When his laughter died out, he held out a raw, bloody, blistered hand to me and said, "Help me up, Wy. Let's get a photo and turn that thing loose."

I took a few pictures of Russell standing next to his catch. Then the captain took a few of both of us, still laughing. Russell lowered the fish to the water, stroked its silver-scaled body and cut the ropes that held it. About fifteen feet from the edge of the boat, the fish's tail fins splashed as it dove into the blackening ocean.

"Well?" I asked like I always did when I couldn't quite tell what Russell was thinking.

"I believe I could die a happy man now," he replied. I had no doubt that he meant it. We sat our poles down, flopped our bodies into a set of fold-up lawn chairs on the stern and sipped cold beer until the wind turned prickly. It was one of those days that you want to relive, but no matter how often you try, it's never the same. It stood out as the best of the hundreds of days we spent together in the Keys. A perfect day.

Russell's urn in hand, I walked down the hallway of doors, and noticed, perhaps for the first time, that the hallway of doors was like a basement: always the same cool, moist air, always the same smell. I assumed I was the only one able to manipulate it, but why, then, was there a pathway down the hallway's carpet that seemed to be getting increasingly more worn out with every trip? Maybe, as Russell suggested more than once, it was all in my mind, just a way to organize the paths I took through my infinite life. I never could make that stick, though. If it was in my mind, just a construct of an overactive imagination, how could I bring people through it?

When I opened the Key West door that afternoon and pushed through the silver screen into a water-damaged theater, warm air hit me like a slap in the face. The salty smell of the ocean seeped into the disintegrating theater. It wouldn't be long before that door would no longer be accessible. More and more theaters were decaying. Fewer and fewer doors were opening to my strange magic.

The Key West theater had been there for as long as I could remember. When the theater was still open, Russell and I would sneak in for the late show after a day of fishing. We'd watch a film and, as the theatergoers left, we'd hide out behind the screen, like a couple of ornery kids. When the coast was clear, we'd walk through the screen into my hallway. Now, that once grand theater was only a crumbling semblance of what it had been. Like the rest of my world, I supposed, the theaters of old were going the way of my family. The silver-screen movie palaces were replaced with multi-show megaplexes with cheap PVC screens. The old palaces that offered one movie, twice a night, were a rare thing. Those with screens made of silk and silver were even rarer. The Key West's screen was more than half gone; a ragged mess of strings and tears that hung like an ancient death shroud. For now, though, there was enough screen left to step into the darkness of another collapsing memory, another failing pathway.

When I arrived at The Key West, the rear door of the theater was already hanging partially open. Metal on metal screams cried out in the Floridian breeze. It was dusk when I got to the beach Russell and I had frequented throughout our lives. It had been abandoned by most of the sunbathers and vacationing families. A single girl—hands wrapped around a bottle of *Jack*, sunburnt butt cheeks hanging out of a bikini that had ridden too far up her crack—lay in the dwindling light. She'd passed out on a long beach towel, and her friends had left her there. *Friends.*

I looked for a second at her burned butt cheeks—the red skin angry and puffy. She had a mole on the left cheek, just like my June. I wondered, as I removed my leather shoes, laid them on the boardwalk, and walked across the sandy, man-made beach, how long it would be before her burnt skin would blister. June used to burn like that, and I could tell that the next twenty-four hours would be miserable for that poor girl. Not just because of the hangover, either. That skin would tingle, and sting, like a thousand tiny bees attacking her at random intervals.

I rolled up my jeans and waded, ankle-deep, into the salty water. A tiny wave splashed my legs, soaking the cuffs of my jeans. I unscrewed the top of the brass urn that held Russell's remains, stood in the water, feeling the faint waves crest across my legs, and said, "Here's to tarpon fishing, cold beer at sunset, and a lifetime of memories," as I dumped about a quarter of Russell's ashes into the water. For a few seconds, I considered dumping the rest of him in, just to be done with it. He wouldn't care; he was gone.

Rituals that surround death aren't for the dead, though. They're for the living, and I needed to spend a little more time with him. I needed to visit our favorite places and remember everything we did together. I needed to remember how we conquered the world. I needed to remember where we came from. I needed to remember *him* most of all because memory was all that I had left.

I walked back to the edge of the water, sat in the sand, and listened to the waves crashing down on the break some unknown distance offshore. The first time I'd heard that sound was in Europe. Of all my memories from The Big One, I thought of my first visit to the ocean nearly as often as I had nightmares about my first fight. Russell and I had been sent to some English beach town to await orders. A few ambitious military men set tents up on the beach for themselves and others awaiting orders. A beach that should have been filled with laughing children and scantily clad women was mostly filled with fresh American soldiers, like the two of us, waiting to enter the horrors of battle. That's what we did in that war, we waited, we fought, we marched, we waited, fought, marched… On that beach, as the sun burned our skin almost as crispy as that young, bikini-wearing girl's, hundreds of soldiers waited. Russell and I walked to the beach's edge and looked out over the English Channel for the first time. In the grey English weather, it seemed endless. The waves crashing down were so loud they drowned out the constant chatter of the soldiers.

I sat there holding my brother's remains and remembered simultaneously the hundreds of nights Russell and I spent on this beach in the Keys, and others like it. Drying my eyes, I recapped Russell's urn, put my shoes on, and walked back to The Key West theater. As I walked, the sand in my shoes rubbed my feet raw—like slow-motion sandblasting. That annoying pain got worse with every step, and I couldn't wait to get home. To take a shot or three, take a shower, warm up the projector, throw on a movie, and pass out.

In the hallway of doors, I lingered at every door I passed, thinking about things I did in each place. Murphysboro, Illinois: Russell and I started our freelance career in that small, inconsequential town in the southern part of the state. We'd been sent to cover a tornado. There was minimal damage — a few roofs taken off, a few signs toppled over. *The St. Louis Post Dispatch* gave us a $50 advance. We got one picture and a fifty-word article published: our first article. The $50 advance, which was all we got out of the story, hardly covered the gas, food, and time.

Every door had a story; every door had a memory.

Rather than go back to my theater and drink myself stupid, I sat Russell's urn down near the green door, the door that led to my home, and walked to the "Trois-Rivieres, Quebec" door. When I stepped into that Canadian theater, a rush of northern air hit my sea-soaked pants. They were frozen to my leg hairs, tugging on them with every step, before I got out of the theater. More snow had accumulated on the greying mounds that lined the roads and sidewalks. The sun had fallen below the horizon, and the streetlights cast long, sepia shadows from high-pressure sodium bulbs.

In the hospital, the smell of disinfectant and warm air was a welcome change from the ice-covered city just beyond the dual sliding doors. Where an information desk with two nuns had been in my brother's hospital, here, a simple list of patients and room numbers lay on a rectangular table. I looked for all the "Emma's" on the list. There was only one, though. "Emma June Gaumond" was listed for "Room 235."

Seeing my wife's name listed in the hospital registry, like it had been when she was dying, gave my heart another painful rush. But I brushed it off; the girl, Emma, had to be confused. She didn't know who she was, so she'd given them my wife's name. The only question was: *how the hell did she know my wife's name?*

Walking down the hallway, toward room 235, I tried to remember what room my June died in. 235 seemed right…but again, it seemed impossible.

In that room, Emma sat alone behind a partially closed curtain, dim light filtering through, illuminating her face like an angel's. An IV stand with three different bags hung, dumping who knew what into her veins as she shivered under a layer of blankets. Her skin looked much clearer than it had when I found her. It wasn't yellow and spotted like it had been, but it was still thin, like an old woman's. Her hair was auburn, about shoulder length, and now that she was clean and healthier, I saw just how beautiful she was. I hadn't noticed how well her strong jawline, high cheekbones, and delicate complexion worked together. Despite her beauty and youth, something about her looked ages older than she could have been.

I interviewed a lama for a story back in the '70s. He talked about soul ages; something about the number of times a person comes back before they reach enlightenment. I didn't take any stock in that, but if I had to guess, if that lama saw this girl, he would say her soul is old and her body is young.

Her eyes were closed when I sat down in a metal fold-up chair beside her. I didn't touch her even though I had an urge to. I just sat there quietly ruminating on the overwhelmingly intense sense of déjà vu. I could think of nothing but my wife, dying in that hospital, dying in that wing with a similar trio of bags hanging from a looming IV stand. I couldn't help but think of this girl's name, her high cheekbones, and her pale skin. The sunburnt girl's butt, back in Florida came to mind, too.

Something funny was happening…

Hearing concerned voices in the room next to us, I couldn't stand letting her think she was still alone. She must have heard them talking, crying, laughing as she lay there, dying. To be alone in such a situation was beyond unfair… I took her hand, and when I did, a strange coursing of energy ran up my arm, through my chest, and stretched heart muscles that hadn't been stretched in a long time. I felt her. I felt the goodness in her. I felt the fear, the anger, the hate, the abandonment, and the losses she'd suffered. I felt the confusion. She hurt like I hurt; she hated like I hated; she loved like I loved.

For the briefest of moments, I forgot my brother.

* * *

Emma

I knew he was there as soon as he walked into the hospital. Not the room; the hospital. I could feel him through the walls and the doors, through the elevators and all the medical equipment that was supposed to keep people alive. I knew he was there, and his mere presence was like a long, deep breath after nearly drowning.

When Wyatt sat down, I kept my eyes closed, feeling his warmth. It wasn't the same warmth I felt when Dr. Shale touched my face or when June's Grandma held her in her arms. His presence was more like a promise of warmth, the first glimmers of a lighthouse spotted from a distant ship about to come to port after months at sea. His warmth started to pull me out of that utterly confused state, and the memories I'd been trying to shuffle through started to come into sharper focus.

I kept my eyes closed as he sat there, quietly worrying over me. It reminded me of how June felt, how Wyatt made her feel as she lay there dying. He wasn't Russell, the brother with quick quips and a constant smile, but he was there when she needed him. And right then, *I* needed him as much as she ever had.

He shifted in his chair beside me, but I kept my eyes closed, pretending to be asleep. Not because I didn't want to talk, but because his presence made me feel…at ease. There are certain people who make you feel better, safer just by being there. In June's life he'd been one of those people and now, for me, he felt just the same. A light on that dark, distant shore. A light drawing me to safety.

"Hey, man," I said after a while.

"Hey, kid. How are you?"

"Better. Yesterday was tough, though."

"For me, too," he said. The shaking in his voice told me he was more broken inside than I'd gathered—broken, twisted, and confused.

"What happened to you?" I asked, trying to make my voice young, vivacious…maybe even flirtatious.

"My brother, Russell, died," he said matter-of-factly. It seemed like he wanted to say more, but he just kept his eyes glued to the floor.

"Jesus. I'm sorry," I said, squeezing his hand.

"What happened to *you* yesterday?" He asked.

"I found out I have lung and bone cancer," I said, holding back the rest of the details of my time in the hospital. I didn't want to sound crazy. I added, "Thank you for saving me," looking him in the eyes for the first time.

He gave me a smile so forced it seemed like his skin might crack from the effort.

"Do you know what you saved me from?" I asked.

He nodded, but I doubted he had any idea. People who haven't lived through that kind of abuse don't know what it does to a person. He may have known the mechanics of it, but he didn't know the torment that would've followed.

"Eddy, he's my stepfather," I said, keeping things in the present tense, because that's how Wyatt would be thinking of them. "He…tortured me, beat me, made me afraid of everything when I was younger. I ran away with my boyfriend—who's now my husband—but he's in the Army, deployed overseas. Eddy must have found me and… Well, when I ran away, my husband beat Eddy pretty badly, and with my husband out of the country, I guess Eddy finally worked up the courage to take revenge," I said. It felt like some of those details were still wrong, somehow, but that they were what Wyatt needed to hear.

Wyatt closed his eyes and took his hand away from mine. I could feel a change in him; he emotionally withdrew. I went on, "I'm from Mill Creek Valley. The doctor said she contacted my oncologist in St. Louis, and somehow, now, I'm in Quebec."

He waited for an actual question, so I kept talking. "How did I get from Missouri to Quebec without any memory of it happening?"

"Have you ever been to an ocean?" he asked, crossing his legs. He did this without adjusting his balls as I saw Eddy do my entire childhood. Instead, Wyatt grabbed my hand again, wrapping it in his, keeping it safe, warm.

I could have told him about the hundreds of days he and June spent together on beaches around the country; instead, I stuck with the life she'd lived before she met Wyatt. I said, "Yeah, my stepfather took us to the Gulf of Mexico when I was in Jr. high. He said we were going to visit his family, but we never visited anyone. We never went on vacation before or after that. I think he pissed off the wrong guys and was hiding out for a while."

Wyatt sort of glared at me out of the side of his eye, then nodded and asked, "You remember the sand?"

I closed my eyes and thought back to June's childhood. I could almost feel the sand rubbing her skin as she walked to the car in her worn-out Keds. "Yeah. It got…everywhere. It sticks to you like glue after you've been in the saltwater. Then it rubs you raw, and the salt burns."

He nodded, adjusted his feet, slipped his right shoe off, lifted his leg up to the side of my bed, and showed me his foot.

"Okay. Your foot's sandy and a bit raw. So?"

"I was in Florida less than an hour ago."

"Uh-huh," I said, confused.

"My brother and I used to go to Florida every spring to fish. I just spread some of his ashes there, in the Atlantic."

"Uh huh," I grunted, still not quite sure what he was saying.

He put his leg on the edge of the bed. "Feel the bottom of my pant leg," he said.

I let his hand go and touched his pant leg. "Wet."

"Right. Salty wet. Smell."

I did. The smell of the salt water was awash with memories: beautiful days relaxing on beautiful beaches. But also sunburns. Hangovers. And heat so intense it seemed you'd cook from the inside out. "Salty, so?" I asked, grabbing his hand again, wanting, needing, human contact.

"I'm a fast traveler."

"'Fast traveler,' what the fuck does that mean?"

He smirked at my cussing. "I may show you sometime. But for now, it just means I'm different than the rest of these people," he said, waving his free hand around at nobody. "But you're different too, you know?"

I stared at him, cautiously wondering what he thought he knew. But he didn't go on; he was waiting for a response, waiting for me to ask him something. "I'll bite, different how?"

"When you touch my hand, it's like…I feel connected to you. I don't know…connected to your emotions, thoughts," he said. I must have flinched because he quickly added, "Don't be afraid, kid. I'm not going to hurt you. If I wanted to hurt you, I'd have left you back in the theater in…Mill Creek Valley?"

"Mill Creek Valley, right," I said, wondering why he couldn't remember where he found me.

"Mill Creek Valley… I remember that place, but…"

I raised my eyebrows.

"Never mind. It's in St. Louis, right? Just a neighborhood," he said. And after he said it, June's memories confirmed it.

I nodded. "St. Louis, born and bred," I said. When I said it, I got a glimpse of a crumbling, Depression-era neighborhood; a tiny, poor city within a city. I saw ragged brick streets filled with kids—most of them black, all of them poor. I saw June playing in those streets with other kids. I saw her shopping at a bookstore in a blue dress. Blue, my favorite color. The more I thought, the more those disorganized old photos in my confused mind fell into place. I almost had a clear timeline of June's life, but still didn't quite have the details sifted.

I also saw Wyatt holding June after he saved her from her stepfather. Bloody fists wrapped around her. Reddish-brown stains on his white button-down shirt bleeding onto her blouse. I saw him in a rage after he returned from the war, an emotionally damaged man, I saw him as a broken man trying his best to overcome the lasting effects of so much violence, and I saw him as an old, tired man holding his dying wife's hand. He was ingrained in everything, every memory, from the night he saved her from Eddy until the night she died. But he didn't define her. He *completed* her.

He was right. Whatever was going on between us was special. I needed to keep hold of him. I needed his touch, so I squeezed his hand again, and he smiled.

Was that a real smile?

Is any of this real?

"You know I'm not here to hurt you?" he asked.

"I know you're not. But *you're* hurting. Your brother?" I asked, my eyes getting heavy as the unmistakable effects of drugs—drugs I didn't remember being given—wore me down.

"Yeah…my brother. My twin brother."

"I'm so sorry," I said, thinking about Russell, the brother with a real smile, the laughing brother.

"Have you ever lost anyone?"

"Other than myself?" I asked, my voice drowsy and fading quickly. "My father died before I was born. My grandfather, when I was young. I knew little about either. I lost my grandmother, who meant more to me than anyone, at an important time in my life. She died just before my senior year of high school," I said, relaying more of June's memories. "I was the one who found her… Years later my mother died—but I hadn't seen her in so long it wasn't like a real loss," I said, as I closed my eyes. I didn't mention June and Wyatt's son. Instinctively, I knew I couldn't get into that right then, because he wasn't ready. He didn't know I knew everything about his wife, and if I told him, I'd lose him. And I couldn't lose him.

Besides, I was ready to sleep, to curl into the warm safety net of Wyatt's presence. I wanted to dream of better times.

I fell asleep with his hand in mine and dreamed of a husband who went months without contacting his wife. A husband June was in constant fear of having lost. Of a husband that sometimes scared her. I dreamed of Wyatt as the old woman remembered him. And in those dreams, I felt comfort, love, fear…a lifetime of emotions bundled up into a single stream of consciousness.

Chapter 9

Wyatt

"Sir?" a woman's voice came from the door behind me, startling me awake. I'd drifted off at some point, entranced by the calming effect of Emma's presence. Half asleep, in an uncomfortable chair, I let her hand go for the first time since I'd grabbed it. I stretched my aching body—thinking of all the hours I spent in that hospital, in uncomfortable chairs, beside my wife—and headed to the door to talk to the doctor.

"Yes?" I said quietly. I had no idea what time it was, but the hallways were dark, and the hospital staff moved like ghosts in the night. All except Emma's doctor; she was lively, and her eyes had a faint glimmer in the corner, reflecting a desk light from the nurse's station.

"Are you a relative of Emma's?" the doctor whispered.

Knowing hospitals had strict rules on visitors, I nodded and asked, "You're her doctor?" I already knew she had to be. She was the same doctor who'd treated my wife all those years ago.

How long had it been? Ten years? Twenty? Why couldn't I remember anymore?

Oddly though, Dr. Shale didn't look a day older.

Was she like me? Unaging? The same sort of immortal that has to suffer through a lifetime of losses alone.

"I'm sorry, yes, I'm Emma's doctor. Dr. Shale," she said, holding her hand out to me.

"Wyatt Gaumond. How's she doing?" I asked, shaking hands with her as if we'd never met, as if she hadn't watched me watch my wife die. As if we hadn't embraced and wept when June finally crossed over.

"The cancer is…beyond treatment. We may be able to slow it, but without a lung transplant, she's got little chance. And the board won't approve of a transplant into a patient with cancer…I'm sorry, Wyatt. She doesn't have long."

"I understand. My wife went through this very same thing a while back."

"Emma will be ready to go home, to live out the rest of her time, but she'll need someone to help her through it. Will you be the one who takes that role until Hospice is needed?"

"Yes," I said without hesitation, even though I knew what it meant. Another person to love, care for, and watch die. Another box to add to the pile. Another crack in my broken heart.

"Good," Dr. Shale said. Then she went into a long explanation of all the things I'd need to do for Emma over the next few weeks. I didn't listen to all of it. I just kept looking over my shoulder at the girl in the hospital bed. I still couldn't get over how much she looked like June. Even the faint unevenness of her eyebrows as an almost indecipherable scar peeking out from her hairline, pulled her right one slightly higher than the left. June's scar went deeper into her scalp, leaving a kind of cowlick in her hair that she always complained about, even though no one could see it. She claimed it was from a bike accident when she was a little girl, but I was pretty sure Eddy was responsible for it. I wondered how far back that scar on Emma's forehead stretched.

Dr. Shale wrapped up with, "Does all of that make sense?"

"Of course. I'll pick her up tomorrow."

"Okay. Thank you for being here for her. It's good to see she's not going to go through this alone."

"I'll be here," I said, thinking back to the same conversation I had with Dr. Shale about my June when she was dying. We'd made a plan to get June back to Ely, but the day we were supposed to head south, she had the stroke. After that, we decided she'd stay in that hospital until her body gave out. It wasn't long…

Ω

The next afternoon, after spreading more of Russell's remains, and crying myself snotty again, I dropped my hiking gear, snowshoes, knapsack and Russell's urn off at the Ely theater. I grabbed a garbage bag of clothes I'd gathered from June's dresser, then headed to Quebec.

"Hey, man," she said as I sat beside her, dropping the bag of clothes on her inclined bed. Her tone improved, even from the day before. Her skin looked even better, and there was more light behind her jade-green irises. She was only covered by one blanket now, and her shivering had completely stopped.

"Hey, kid. Do you know my name?" I asked, pretty sure she didn't.

"Wyatt," she said.

"How'd you learn that?"

"The old woman. You took care of her in this hospital."

I stared, my mouth hanging open like a Goddamn moron's. Eventually I coughed out a gruff, "What?"

"I had a dream about you, Wyatt. You took care of the old woman in my dream, now you're here to take care of me. Dr. Shale says you're going to take me home with you."

I glared at her for another second, not sure how she could have known about my wife, about me, but then I realized Dr. Shale had to have told her everything. "Yeah," I said, "I'm going to take you home. And your information from this 'old woman' in your dream is correct: my name is Wyatt." I stuck my hand out. "Nice to meet you." It was a weak pretense, but I had this unending desire to touch her.

She shook my hand, and I felt that electric charge between us. But less intensely than the previous day. Instead of elation, I simply felt relief from the nagging tightness in my chest and the tingling down my arm.

As we held hands, she said, "Wyatt fits, you know? Like a hero from the old west, here to save all of us damsels from monsters."

I smiled and nodded. June had once said something very similar.

She added, "Where've you been today, Wyatt? You look like you're dressed for the mountains." I clearly was—red and black checkered flannel shirt tucked into insulated denim; hiking boots, and a sock cap—I could have been Paul Bunyan.

No reason to lie, I was about to show her how different I was from the rest of the world. I was hoping to learn more about how she was, too. How she knew about my wife. How she knew about me.

"I started the day in Ely, Minnesota. I was in Mt. Rainier National Park at lunch. I scattered some of my brother's ashes, and now I'm here, in Quebec with you."

"Do you have an airplane?" she asked.

"No. I have other means of travel. I'll show you how I get around once we get out of here."

* * *

Emma

"Why Mt. Rainier?" I asked. I remembered their trips to Mt. Rainier, but I wanted his details to fill in the blank spaces in my mind. I still couldn't quite put all the pieces together...

"Shortly after Russell and I returned from The Big One—that's World War II to most people—we headed on a cross-country camping excursion. Both of us had been married right before the war. I left my wife in a shitty apartment, just a bed, wood stove, community bathroom, and an old bucket for a nightstand. We'd been dating just a few months when Russell got called to Europe; of course I couldn't let him go alone, so I signed up, too. June was only seventeen when we got married, but her stepfather was abusive, like yours, and I couldn't stand the thought of leaving her in that house with him. So, I stole her away, married her, and dumped her in that shitty apartment for years. I felt so bad about it, but at least I knew she was safe from Eddy.

"Other than the monthly bills for the apartment, food, electricity, etc., Russell and I had saved our service pay throughout the entire war. We came home with nearly eight hundred dollars each—big money back then. We had this absurd notion that we'd be able to pay cash for houses when we got out. We were stupid kids with stupid dreams. A set of twins unable to cut the damn cord, placenta, or whatever it is that twins share in the womb that makes them so close in life. We had a notion of living right next door to one another with our wives and unborn kids."

I laughed, not because it was funny, but because he was telling it almost exactly like June remembered it. Just from a different angle. Like when you look at someone's profile compared to when you look at them straight on.

He didn't get distracted when I laughed, just squeezed my hand a little tighter and went on. "Our parents were victims of the Great Crash in 1929. They saw what it did to the country, to their families. My dad lost the farm, so to speak. Long story short, it made us…thrifty."

"I bet."

He nodded and plastered on that forced, fake smile. I nodded back, urging him on. I could listen to him tell stories for the rest of my life—as short or long as that may be. He was a good storyteller, but what really made it interesting was how he added details June missed or forgot.

"When we got back from the war, our wives were dying to get out of the city. My June kept telling me, 'We'll buy a house when we've got kids. Right now, I just need to get out of this fucking town for a while.' She was a cusser, my wife; loved the 'F' word. Honestly, I kinda loved that about her… Without asking our wives their thoughts, Russell and I used a portion of our savings to split the cost of a car and a small camping trailer. We thought we'd do the western U.S. that fall. Figured we'd hunt for food and camp where it was free. Going that way, it wouldn't cost much, and if we kept a good pace, we could see the whole western side of the country before winter.

"When we pulled into the parking lot behind our shitty apartment building with the car and camper, we both knew our surprise wasn't what our wives had envisioned. They'd been planning their dream trip for months. They dreamed of the Florida Keys, nice hotels with room service and pools with bars built right into them. But once we had the camper, reluctantly, they agreed to our trip. But I think they would have agreed to anything to get out of St. Louis for a little while."

"How old were you? What year was it?" I asked, still wanting to fact-check the details in June's memories.

"We were released from duty in July 1945, so we probably took off in mid-September of that year—which would have put us in our early 20s. We traveled from St. Louis west through Missouri, Kansas, and Colorado. Outside of Vail, Colorado, we stopped for a few weeks to explore the Rockies before moving north through Wyoming, Montana and then heading west again, to the very northwestern edge of the country. We went to all the parks, saw Old Faithful, glaciers and glacial lakes, and more wildlife than you could see in any zoo back then. I probably took a thousand pictures on that trip.

"After the Allied powers freed us prisoners from the Stalag, the powers that be replaced my gun with a camera. Even though I'd gotten a Purple Heart and spent longer than I cared to think about in a prison camp, they didn't send me home. The Government taught me how to photograph the war for 'archival purposes.' And I shot thousands of pictures the last few months I was in Europe. They didn't let me keep any of the photos, but I did keep my cameras. The U.S. Army gave me a shitty PH501. I found a Leica, which was a far superior camera, on a dead German. I used it for the next thirty years."

He stopped, wiped a tear from his face, shook his left arm and took a deep breath. He didn't say anything as he tried to fight back whatever was clawing at his insides. I knew the feeling—June's emotions were working on me, too.

I squeezed his hand and smiled again, trying to give him some footing to climb out of his emotional hole.

He blew his nose and was about to start talking when Dr. Shale walked in. She grinned, handed over a clipboard full of paperwork and a few white paper bags full of medication.

"Sorry to interrupt, but you'll need to fill out these forms and leave them with the nurse. Your medications are in these bags. I've got you scheduled for a checkup one week from today at eleven AM. Your pills all have directions with them. If you need more pain medication, just call. Questions?"

"No. Thanks, Dr. Shale," I said, smiling at her. It was the same awkward smile I'd shown Wyatt earlier. I couldn't quite tell if it was a fake smile, some Midwestern courtesy thing, or if I really was happy. Either way, I felt a million times better than I had when Wyatt brought me to Quebec. I surely didn't feel like I was dying of cancer. In the library of June's life, this more resembled the way things played out the first time she had cancer, rather than the second.

Maybe time wasn't as short as I thought.

"Okay. I'll see you next week. Rest, Emma!" Dr. Shale said, waving on the way out of the room.

I nodded to Wyatt, wanting to hear the rest of his story. With June's memories and his voice, it was like reading a book and watching the movie at the same time. "What happened in the Northwest?" I prompted.

"By the time we made it near the west coast, it was starting to turn cold. Our intentions were to head south along the coast to the southern border, then back east toward home. We just wanted to make one more stop before we moved on. Mt. Rainier. Do you know it?"

"In Washington," I said.

He nodded. "Before the war, neither Russell nor I knew about that place. Before the war, we didn't know much of anything. A young man in our battalion, Henry something or other, said he climbed this 14,000-foot volcano in Washington. Hell, growing up in the mid-west, we didn't even know there were volcanoes in the U.S. We were so close, we just had to see it.

"After a long day of driving and hiking, we parked our Chevrolet Special De Luxe woodie in one of the empty campsites—we had our pick of any spot in the park since nobody else was there. It was dark by the time we got there, and after we unhitched the camper—a little Trotwood that didn't even have a bathroom—we were too tired for anything else. We didn't even break out the cards for one of our nightly poker or pinochle games."

"You play pinochle? I play pinochle," I said. "My grandma taught me when I was younger." Playing cards was something I loved to do with Grandma. She knew every game there was and, though she said she didn't, I knew she let me win. Not all the time, but sometimes, so I'd stay interested.

"Maybe you and I can play when we get home. I haven't had a good game in years."

"Sure, Wyatt."

"Deal," Wyatt said, smirking at his stupid pun. It was one he and Russell threw around when they were still young enough to get together to play a few hands over beer or whiskey.

He went on with his story. "When the four of us woke the next morning, I could see my breath *inside* the camper. Russell tried to start the propane heater that had served us through the coldest nights in the Colorado Rockies, but he couldn't get it to light.

"'Tank valve must be closed,' Russell said, clearly suggesting that I open it. 'I'll get it,' I said, sliding out from under the mountain of blankets June and I shared. The frosty air hit me hard that first morning. When I opened the door, the sight of all that snow hit even harder.

"I called my brother over to the door. He stepped one big step across the camper—that's how small it was, one big step from our bed to their bed, one big step from their bed to the door—God it was small," Wyatt said, shaking his head. "'Jesus,' Russell muttered when he saw the fifteen or more inches of snow that had accumulated through the night. I'll never forget the look on his face. Shock, horror, then realization. We were stuck. I wouldn't have tried to take that craggy old road down the side of that mountain in a tank with that much snow on the ground, let alone pulling a camper in our old Chevy with worn-out tires.

"When the women crawled out of bed and saw what we saw…well…Hilda nearly broke down. She'd been growing more and more weary with every new town we visited. June, being stronger willed and having less of a gilded past, was quick to calm her companion. But that didn't mean she was happy about the situation. I thought Hilda would kill us all before winter was over. But whenever she got too worked up, June calmed her down."

"The *winter*? You were there the whole winter; I'd have slaughtered the both of you," I said, but I knew it wasn't true. That winter was one of the happiest of June's life. No kids, no jobs, no worries other than food. She had all the people she loved in one spot. She'd never felt so whole before, and until her son was born, she didn't know there could be any feeling richer than that.

"We deserved it, too," Wyatt went on. "We were stupid for getting caught in that situation. We holed up in that Goddamn camper for four months. When the snow melted enough for a plow to get through, we slid down the mountain pass, finally heading south. Four months in a space about the size of this hospital room, with four twenty-somethings… It was one of the hardest winters in my life, and, oddly, one of the best. There weren't taxes to pay, factories to work; no war to fight, or friends to watch die; no money to be made and not much to be spent. Every day was a new trial. A new test. Everyday Russell, Hilda, June or I had to overcome some impossible challenge. Whether it be figuring out new ways to cook rabbit and snow soup or raccoon and snow soup or, if we were lucky, deer and snow soup, or figuring whose turn it was to hike six miles into town to get the propane tanks filled. It was all a struggle.

"But after the war, it was a nice type of struggle. A nice change of pace. Just the four of us against nature. Just another day living like our great-grandparents had. And we knew if it got really tough, we could have hiked out of camp, got jobs in town, and spent the rest of the winter in a hotel room. But we didn't. We wanted to make it on our own. To prove we could conquer the world.

"From then on, Russell and I visited Mt. Rainier at least once a year. We hunted there in the winters. Fished there in the summers. Hilda and June went too, but not as often as me and Russell. It was one of our favorite places in the world. Part of Russell belonged there. So, I took him for one more hike up the mountain."

"How many places do you have left to…um…distribute your brother's remains?" I asked.

"Just two. Both in St. Louis, our hometown. It's going to be hell. He's been in my life since before I was born. When my wife died…he became my life. I just don't know how to say goodbye."

"I'm sorry, Wyatt," I said, because I didn't know what else to say. June hadn't lived to see Russell's death, but when Russell started to show signs of dementia, she saw it wearing on Wyatt. When the cancer came back, and she knew she didn't have long, she was terrified of what Russell's death would do to Wyatt. Terrified it would completely undo the man he'd been.

Chapter 10

Wyatt

Emma pulled the curtain and changed into June's clothes, then filled out the paperwork so she could leave the hospital. She had to sign a book's worth of garbled, legalese documents before we could go. It was just like when June was discharged from the hospital in St. Louis, the first time she had cancer.

Emma was up and moving around like the healthy young woman she resembled, not the dying person Dr. Shale claimed she was. She slipped into her filthy Army coat—a coat that looked really familiar, yet somehow foreign, like it was something I should have recognized, but just couldn't place it in my mind. She gathered her things, bags of pills in each hand, book of signed documents tucked under her other, and moved toward the door. She dropped the paperwork off at the counter, and we walked from the hospital to the theater in the cold, mid-afternoon Canadian breeze. She walked steady and strong whereas only a few days before I had to carry her like a baby. Those few days in the hospital had changed her so much it was hard to fathom.

As she walked beside me, wearing June's clothes and that dirty green Army coat, I couldn't help noticing how much more she looked like my June, now that she was healthier. The briefest moment of panic crossed my mind when I wondered if this girl was somehow related to my wife. An unknown cousin, a niece from some sibling or half sibling June's mom had given up for adoption… Really, I knew nothing about this girl, only that I had to take care of her. I felt a kind of parental responsibility toward her. Only 'parental' isn't quite the right word…

Silently, we headed down the empty alleyway behind the theater, snow swirling in the gusty wind; puddles of brown muck splattered against the walls and dumpsters. I motioned for her to follow me to a pair of heavy steel doors that led into the dark, cold theater.

"Why another theater?" she asked.

"You'll see."

"What's in there—a teleportation machine?" she asked, a little uncomfortable laugh slipping from her lips.

I laughed, too. She wasn't far off. "This is the way home," I said, opening the door, letting her see the pitch-black room. I could see confusion and fear wash over Emma's face. She did not want to go in there. Who could blame her? Only days before, she'd nearly been beaten to death in a building just like it. "I know it's weird," I added as she hesitated by the doorway, "but it's the quickest way home."

I stepped into the shadows, silently urging her to follow me.

* * *

Emma

Nothing I'd remembered since Wyatt dropped me off at the hospital hinted that this was right. Not knowing what was beyond those doors scared me. Not knowing why we'd need to go into that abandoned theater scared me.

What was the connection between us and these theaters?

Yes, he and June spent a lot of time in theaters. Movies were one of his only non-alcoholic escapes from the horrors he spent his life chasing, but at the same time, running from. He and Russell would watch any movie on the screen when they were younger. As he aged, and the horrors he was trying to escape started showing up on the silver screen, he got a bit more choosey, but he always loved the movies. He loved the moment the room went dark. He loved the anticipation while the opening credits scrolled across the screen. He loved the hour and thirty minutes with no other responsibilities.

As Wyatt disappeared into the darkness of that cold, Canadian theater, I stepped back. For the first time, it was clear that something was wrong with Wyatt. Something was different from June's memories. He was…like a shadow of the man she knew—blurred around the edges, slightly out of focus, a little off kilter. I wanted to trust him, because she'd trusted him, but I was growing suspicious of him.

"Don't worry, Emma," he whispered from inside the pitch blackness, a faint blur of his face hardly visible. "You're safe with me." His voice remained smooth, easy. But I knew that whatever this was, it wasn't going to be easy.

"I'm not worried," I lied. "Just not sure what to expect when I step through that doorway. How *are* we getting home?"

"Trust me," Wyatt said calmly. "I'll keep you safe." He stepped back into the light, motioning me toward the open door of the theater. His voice was still easy, calm; the way you'd talk to a scared dog.

"Come on, kid. You can do this," he added.

"Kid?" He'd called June that. Even when they were old together, he called her that, and for some reason that eased my mind.

"Okay," I said.

"Okay." He showed me a flashlight, then held his other hand out to me.

When I finally suppressed the fear that had me paralyzed in that cold alleyway, I grabbed his hand and stepped through. He pulled the door shut, leaving us in complete—you can't see anything even an inch in front of your fucking face—darkness. While June's life experiences told me I should have been afraid, in the split second between the door shutting and Wyatt clicking on his flashlight everything changed.

I saw June die.

I heard sobs from Wyatt as her monitor went bleep, bleep, bleep…bleep…bleeeeeeeee—then a rush of commotion as nurses stood over her, calling time of death and whatever else doctors do when an ancient, cancerous old woman dies.

After they cleared out, Wyatt stayed, holding her hand until her skin went cold.

Then…nothing. Peaceful nothingness. Dark, quiet, like that theater.

And then a light so bright and rich and full of hope that *I* knew *I* had nothing left to fear. *I* knew everything that could hurt had already happened. And the light absorbed *me* and then…

Then I came back. I appeared in that old theater, under the stage, confused, in pain like I had been just before I'd died. Thin and starving, but so sick I couldn't eat. And finally, I understood that this wasn't life, that June's life…*my* life had already ended. And this was something else entirely.

This was…

Wyatt clicked on the flashlight and said, "Up there." I opened my eyes and saw he was pointing his flashlight at the ragged old movie screen. "That's our way home."

"How?" I asked as he led me through the crumbling building toward the stage.

"I can travel through movie screens. You mentioned a teleportation machine. Well, it's kinda like that but only through these old screens."

"That's…"

"Impossible?"

"Yeah," I said, "impossible." But impossible things had been happening since I woke up sick and cold, under the stage of that old theater.

"My brother told me it was 'Impossible' when I first told him, too. But once I showed him it was possible, he never questioned if I could do it again. In fact, he never questioned how I do it. He only asked where we could go."

Wyatt helped me onto the stage and then touched the screen, turning the crumbling silk into an odd, upturned pool of liquid. After a few seconds, the pool of liquid turned so bright I had to squint. It was the same powerful light I'd seen shortly after I'd died, and after a few seconds I was entranced by it, in awe of it, and I couldn't take my eyes off it.

"So, where do you want to go?" he asked.

Chapter 11

Wyatt

"Home," she whispered. She didn't meet my eyes as she said it, keeping hers trained on the movie screen. Despite her obvious distrust, she moved to touch the pool of shimmering silver-white light. When she got close, her eyes glimmered, full of life and hope and awe, as she stared at the pearlescent glow.

"Okay. Home it is. Ready?" I asked, stepping closer to the screen, holding my hand out to her.

After a moment's pause, she overcame her doubts and fears, grabbed my hand, took a deep breath, and nodded.

I stepped in; she kept hold of my hand and followed.

On the other side of the screen, she let go of my hand and looked herself over. I don't know if she was expecting to be wet or dirty or what, but after she looked to make sure none of that watery white light had left its mark on her, she said, "Doors." She looked down one side of my hallway and then the other. "Infinite doors?"

"I don't know how infinite they are. And I don't know how to explain *what* they are. Russell once suggested they're all in my mind. It almost makes sense. Except…"

"Except, how could I be here if they're all in *your* mind?"

"Right."

"Where do they go?"

"Each door goes to another screen. Another theater."

"All over the world?"

"Yep. Some are labeled. Some aren't. The doors with X's no longer open. The green one there," I said, pointing a few doors down and to the left from the one we'd just used, "that's home. Your theater, your hometown, is that way," I said, pointing in the opposite direction.

"Are they organized in any way? Like, geographically?"

"Not that I can tell. They seem totally random. Like thoughts bumping around in a drunkard's head. That may be why Russell says—used to say—'it's all in your mind.'"

"How far can you go?"

"I've been to six continents," I said. She smirked; an odd, knowing look sneaking into her eyes. "I still haven't found a doorway to Antarctica; doesn't seem likely that I'll find one now. Sad, too, it's the only continent I've never visited. I'd still love to get there."

She smiled. Again, it seemed like she thought she knew something I didn't. But then she grabbed my hand and looked back down the hallway toward the green door, toward home.

"There are some limiting factors, Emma. So, I can't just take you anywhere. For instance, I can only go to theaters built during a certain era. 1920s to the early 1970s, far as I can tell. Most of the doors don't work now. Just another problem with the 'construct of the mind' theory. If they were in my head, wouldn't I only have doors that worked?"

"This is…totally surreal. I mean, I'm here so I kind of believe it, but at the same time I don't fucking believe it."

"Imagine how I felt the first time I walked into this," I said, but even I didn't remember that. I didn't know if it was so long ago that I couldn't remember, or if I'd just visited the hallway so many times that it'd been washed out in my head.

"Shall we?" I asked, gesturing for her to move toward the green door. When she did, I followed her, opened it, and we stepped into my theater.

* * *

Emma

I gawked at the theater, mouth open, like some kind of moron. *I* knew that building intimately. *I* remembered it—not June... *me*. Wyatt and I saved the old theater from demolition in the early 1990s. We did what we could to remodel the inside, making it more comfortable than any regular theater, and cheaper to run, too. Thinking we'd never sell more than a hundred tickets, we put in a hundred leather recliners rather than old-style movie seats. I remembered that we got mostly new furniture for our house when we moved to Ely. "Smarter to buy new than move the old," Wyatt said.

When we moved into our house in Ely, we'd fallen in love with a pair of La-Z-Boys we purchased from a small, family run, furniture store in town—Anderson's Furniture. When we talked about chairs for the theater, and started pricing typical theater seating, we both agreed that recliners were a better option—they were the same price and so much more comfortable.

I never forgot the look on Dale Anderson's face when we went back a few weeks after we bought the first two recliners and Wyatt said, "We'll take a hundred of those recliners, all black. Leather."

Simultaneously, I had a flash memory of the day, over ten years after we'd opened the theater, that I told Wyatt it was time to close it down. My cancer had relapsed, but I didn't tell him that. Instead, I convinced him to close the place down, so we could travel. He'd been all over the world, and I'd only been in parts of the U.S.

We left for Niagara Falls on a sunny Tuesday morning. My lungs felt like I was breathing fire, but I was as excited as a kid on Christmas.

I never made it back to the theater, though. I died on that road trip…died in that French-Canadian hospital just five weeks after we'd hit the open road.

Looking around the theater now, I realized that many of the details weren't quite right. Like the strange, blurry feelings I got around Wyatt, the theater was just slightly off kilter. What he'd *created* was a blended version of all the places we'd lived throughout our lives—all crammed into the theater we'd loved so much. I tried to decide which details were right and which details had been altered since the older versions of us had taken to the open road. The upturned bucket beside the bed he'd been using as a nightstand was wrong. It was the "nightstand" I used in our first apartment. It wasn't the one me and Wyatt had in our later life. When we moved to Ely, one of the few pieces of furniture we brought was the oak and granite nightstand Russell made for Wyatt on their 65th birthdays. It was a yearly joke for them—they'd each make a piece of furniture, identical to the other's, based on a design they came up with together and trade them. Wyatt would never have given that nightstand up. But now, instead of that beautiful piece Russell made, a dented metal bucket, the very same dented metal bucket I'd used when Wyatt was in WWII, sat beside the bed.

"Confusion breeds confusion," I murmured to myself.

Wyatt ignored my mumbling and said, "It's not much, but you're welcome here as long as you're interested in staying with an old man like me."

Old man? Does he know he's old, too? Does he know this is all wrong? I wondered as he helped me off the edge of the theater's stage.

I let go of his hand and walked toward the back of the theater, trying to see what other details were off. There were the recliners, of course, and they were all in the right places. In the back, though, there was a basic kitchen, a couch, some boxes—boxes that made my heart skip a beat—and a king-sized bed crammed into a large open area we used to let people set up lawn chairs in, if we ran out of regular seating.

So many details had been recreated from different parts of our lives together. The couch, for instance, was the couch we had when Wyatt Jr. was young. When Wyatt brought that couch home, I thought it was a good choice, because if Wyatt Jr. puked on it, a vomit stain probably wouldn't even show against the horrid floral pattern. We threw that couch away at least thirty years before we moved to Ely. We'd replaced it with a denim-covered hideaway sofa and, later, other sofas—roughly one per decade. That couch being in the theater was just one of the many impossible details he'd gotten wrong when he created this…*memory? Hell? Purgatory? What exactly is this place?*

Wyatt caught me staring in the direction of the couch, which sat only feet away from the bed, and said, "One of us will have to sleep in a recliner or on the couch. I don't expect to share the bed if that's what you're worried about."

"That's not it," I whispered. The more I looked around the old theater, the more disturbed it made me feel. He'd created a sort of museum of our lives, set up on bits of used furniture placed around the theater to remind him of every home we ever shared. Even parts of the floor were the same as the hardwood floor he'd laid in our house in St. Louis—the house we spent most of our married lives in.

"Yeah? What were you thinking?" he asked, unable to see my expression in the dim light.

"It's familiar. Like home, not that old theater where you found me, but my home, home," I said. I wanted to confront him about the theater. I wanted to tell him who I was. I wanted to tell him about our lives together, about my death. But I was scared to go too far with him. In the hospital, when I'd suggested that I'd dreamed about his wife, the dark look in his eyes scared me. Wyatt wasn't a verbally expressive person unless he was drunk or mad; then, he could get a little mouthy. But his eyes, if you knew what to look for, could tell you everything you needed to know about him. And I was an expert at reading those eyes. If I pushed too hard, I knew I'd see a side of him I never wanted to see; a side of him I'd spent a lifetime trying not to awaken.

"There's just something I love about this old place, too. It feels like home, like you said," he said. "After my wife died, I considered moving back to St. Louis to be closer to my brother, but I just couldn't leave. This is the only place I feel comfortable anymore." He led the way into the kitchenette, and, like a proper gentleman, he pulled out a red vinyl and chrome chair and asked, "What do you want: coffee? Tea?"

I sat and gawked, somewhat disbelievingly, at the tiny kitchenette. It was a miniature, disorganized and run-down version of the kitchen at our house in St. Louis.

Waiting for an answer, he stared directly into my eyes with a familiar intensity. In the past, that glare had been unsettling at times, terrifying at others, and sometimes the intensity in his eyes aroused me.

That intense gaze only started after Wyatt came back from WWII. He wasn't the same laughing, joking man he had been. But that was common. A lot of veterans weren't quite the same after the war. The look in his eyes as he stared over our old kitchen table at me was as easy to read as a book. He was lost in a stress memory—that's what the doctor called them, "stress memories." I knew that unless I wanted an ugly response, I shouldn't interrupt him. But I didn't take my eyes off him. I wondered what country he was in; what memory he was reliving.

Eventually, he shook his head and said, "Sorry, I don't mean to stare, but you look like someone I loved very much. I noticed it before, but in this lighting… Sorry. Tea? Coffee?" he asked again.

"Tea, thanks," I said, pulling my chair closer to the red Formica table—the first table we ever bought. We'd gotten it secondhand at a yard sale for twelve dollars. And we kept it for half of our married life. Until Russell made us an oak table for their 55th birthday.

I slipped off the heavy green coat, hung it over the back of the chair, laid my hands in my lap and took a deep, soothing breath as he got the kettle going for me and the coffeemaker going for himself. The coffee maker gurgled and spat its steamy water through finely ground beans. The smell was intoxicating. I never did like the taste of coffee. Even with a lot of sugar, it just seemed bitter, but the smell always made me feel good, calm. Like sitting by a fire with an Agatha Christie novel on a cool fall night.

The tea kettle popped and crackled on the stove like they do when they're warming up, but otherwise, the room was filled with eerie silence. Like the odd silence after the theater emptied for the night. After the roaring of the movies, the laughing, gasping, or crying of the crowd, that silence was powerful. Silence that could cut you to the bone, like those long cold winter nights on Mt. Rainier.

While Wyatt diddled around in the kitchen, I thought of the night we reopened the theater in 1990. We'd planned a huge "Grand Re-Opening" night with free coffee, soda, and popcorn. Wyatt must have thought a thousand people were going to come because he brewed coffee for hours before the night's activities began. We'd scheduled a screening of *Lady and the Tramp* for the six o'clock show and *Casablanca* for the nine o'clock. To my surprise—but not Wyatt's—the theater filled up for both shows, the coffee warmer nearly ran dry, and the popcorn machine popped all night long.

In the first month of being open, we ended up making just enough money to cover our expenses. By the end of the fourth month, though, we'd recouped all our losses on the recliners, the reels, and the repairs to the three antique projectors. We were having fun, too. I don't remember another time in our entire life that Wyatt had that much fun without his brother.

Russell had been Wyatt's grounding pole. If he was there, Wyatt felt good enough to enjoy himself. If he wasn't, Wyatt wasn't the Wyatt I'd loved. It's why we bought houses next door to one another. It's why we went on all our vacations together. It's why, whenever there was a problem, I had to get Russell on my side if I wanted to convince Wyatt of anything.

We'd tried to get Russell to move to Ely with us, but for the first time in their lives, Russell and Wyatt parted ways. Wyatt pleaded with his brother, saying, "I can't stand this city anymore, Russell. It's not the same as the city we grew up in. I can't stand living here…where every stone in every building holds a memory of some grander time in my life. I lost my son; you lost yours. Your wife is gone. Come north with us. We can still start over."

Russell's mind was starting to slip by that time. Nothing like their father's quick descent into hell, just an extra pause here, a confused look there, mixed-up facts everywhere. It was just the beginning of Russell's slow walk toward perdition.

Though Russell refused to follow us north, it wasn't like Wyatt stopped visiting. He flew to St. Louis every Monday and stayed in Russell's room at Paradise Garden until Wednesday afternoon—the theater was only open from Thursday night to Sunday night. Every week, for nearly ten years, he made the trip. It was the compromise they'd come to. A compromise that made me a half-time wife. But I was used to that; I'd rather have a good Wyatt half the time than a brooding, irritable Wyatt all the time.

As he sat down in one of the red vinyl and chrome chairs around that old table and poured coffee for himself and tea for me, I asked him, "Your brother, how did it happen?" It was a detail I really didn't know. Russell had outlived me.

"He was old, sick. He…stroked out," Wyatt said without looking up at me.

"I'm so sorry, Wyatt. You were spreading the ashes today and you still came for me?"

"Yeah. Can we not talk about this? How about a film? I can get the projector running. When's the last time you saw a film on an old-fashioned screen?"

"Sure, Wyatt, whatever you want."

"And a shot of whiskey?"

"Or three," I said. Drinking and tiptoeing around Wyatt felt natural. Like the rhythm of our lives was playing out in real time.

He smiled, then. "A drinking, cussing woman? I love it!" he said as he brought out a bottle of Jack. He poured a shot into my tea—a hot toddy, my evening drink—and a shot into his coffee, then said, "Go get a seat. I'll get a movie on the screen."

I knew if I took that first drink I wouldn't remember the rest of the night—because I wouldn't stop at one. It was how I spent so many nights when I was alive. It wasn't just the booze, though. I had pills and took them religiously. Self-medication got me through the hardest times in my life. So, I sat the drink aside because now that I knew who I was, what I was, I had to figure out why I was back."

I couldn't do that if I was drunk.

Chapter 12

Wyatt

I woke before the sun came up. With everything hanging over my head, I was amazed I slept at all. But something about Emma's faint snores was like a Siren's song softly compelling me to sleep. When I climbed out of bed, I went to the front of the theater, near the screen, and got into my workout routine: push-ups, sit-ups, and a ten-mile run.

When I got back, Emma was already making breakfast. Dancing to her own music in an oversized T-shirt of mine and a pair of slippers that once belonged to my wife—slippers with little dogs embroidered on them; slippers that hadn't seen the light of day in at least twenty years. I don't even know where she could have found them. She ran a wooden spoon across a cast-iron skillet, scrambling eggs. Another skillet sizzled with the unmistakable sound and smell of bacon. Coffee, black, thick, like molasses, ran through the coffeemaker. A hideous pink ceramic teapot that belonged to June's grandma sat steeping on the table.

God, she was just like my June—she even moved the same, shaking her bony ass in awkward little shivers as she danced from one skillet to the other.

"Good morning," she almost sang as I walked into the kitchen and got a glass of water from the sink.

"Morning. Sleep well?" I asked, fighting the urge to grab her by the waist, lean her over, and kiss her hard on the mouth. I knew it was a reaction to how much she reminded me of my wife, but it was a hard one to overcome. Like my body's appearance, my sex drive was still that of a thirty-five-year-old's and despite the cancer eating her from the inside, her body was…perfect. You couldn't tell she was sick at all. The sick spots all over her skin had disappeared while she was in the hospital. Her cheeks and breasts had filled out. Her curves were an hourglass. Her eyes were full of light, and as I watched her, I instinctively glanced around the room for my camera.

I had thousands of pictures of my June, mostly still on films that had never been printed. Part of me wanted to tear open the boxes that stored my archived negatives and start searching for pictures of June at Emma's age. I knew if I took pictures of this girl and set them beside pictures of my June, nobody, not even Emma, would be able to tell the difference between the two.

"I slept well, Wyatt," she said. She added, "You snore like a grizzly bear." She looked at me for a split second, smirked, then turned back to the stove.

June again: playful and demure at the same time.

I took a step back, restraining myself. "I didn't used to sleep well either. After my wife died, I think I spent five years without sleeping more than a few hours a night. That's why I exercise so hard. If I miss my run, I don't sleep at all. Too many nightmares."

"You've been out running in that?" she asked, motioning toward my torn-up sweatpants and holey sweatshirt. "How cold is it out there?"

"Not so cold. Like an Alaskan spring. But my body adjusts quickly. After a few seconds, it doesn't even feel cold out there. It feels…neutral…neither hot nor cold. Perfect for running."

"I think I'll take your word for it."

"My wife would have said the same thing. I'm going to take a shower before breakfast. You need anything?" I asked out of courtesy; she'd clearly made herself at home and knew her way around a kitchen.

She shook her head, smiled, and went back to cooking.

I headed to the shower but took one more glance at her before going down the hallway toward the bathroom. It was undeniable; she was like an exact copy of my wife—just younger.

I turned on the shower, letting it get as warm as possible while I got undressed and slipped on my shower shoes. I let the tepid water run over my back, trying not to think about the girl dancing around in my kitchen, but rather about the day's tasks. This was the end of Russell's earthly existence. Today, I'd spread the rest of his remains and all that would be left were my memories of him.

I needed to prepare myself for what I'd feel when I sprinkled him onto his lawn in St. Louis and finally buried the rest of him on his wife's gravesite, but I couldn't quite focus on anything except Emma's presence.

I dried off, dressed, and made my way back toward the enticing aroma of breakfast. But didn't go into the kitchen quite yet. I stood outside of Emma's eyeline watching her as she moved around the tiny room, washing, drying, and oiling the skillets she'd used for breakfast. I longed for the touch of a beautiful woman. For the touch of my June. I didn't know how much I'd longed for it until Emma was there, looking so much like my wife I doubted a younger me would be able to tell them apart.

But I forced myself to remember she was too young for me. I was eighty-eight and she couldn't have been more than twenty-five. She may have looked like my wife, moved like my wife, sounded like my wife, but she wasn't my June. She was just some girl I'd vowed to protect.

"Smells great," I said, finally stepping into the kitchen. I sat down at a table full of food and drinks.

"My grandma taught me how to cook. She was more like a mother to me than my momma ever was."

June felt the same about her grandmother. Another coincidence… They were adding up. There were too many to take lightly. But I didn't have the mental energy to process that yet. I'd deal with Russell, then I'd figure out this girl.

* * *

Emma

Wyatt stared at me as I pushed the food around on my plate. I may have been feeling better, but I still had no appetite. *Do…people…in my condition even need to eat? Is that food even real?* Even though I hadn't eaten anything other than a few bites of banana and strawberries in that old theater, I hadn't lost any weight. I'd actually gained weight, especially in my chest and butt, since Wyatt dragged me to the hospital.

He shoveled another mouthful in, made a few pleasurable groans as if he hadn't eaten a good meal in years, and said, "Tell me about your family."

I looked at him, but his eyes were on his plate. I couldn't tell if he was baiting me, wanting me to tell him about *our* life, or if he still didn't realize who I was. When I stepped into that dark theater in Quebec, it all came into focus for me, but I was sure Wyatt's mind wouldn't come into focus without being hit with a sledgehammer of evidence. He'd built this world, this illusion, and without self-realization he'd be stuck here forever.

To answer his request, I thought about my childhood and said, "You met my stepfather. Imagine that man's wife. She was the definition of white trash. Cigarettes always hanging out of her toothless mouth, messy hair and sloppy clothes; uneducated, drunk, angry—that was my mom.

"Grandma was sweet and tried her best, but when I saw how hard she took the stories I told her about my home life, I stopped telling her the horrible things Eddy did and said. I stopped showing her the bruises. Grandma was my dad's mom, and she hated my mom and Eddy, but she stayed nearby to help me in any way she could. I loved her; of all my blood relatives, I *only* loved her. And when she died, when I was in jr. high, I felt completely alone for the first time. That's when I met my friend Hilda at school. She'd been in a private school until seventh grade, but the private school didn't go all the way to eighth grade, so she had to go to public school. She was a bit of an outcast, like me. And she was a little socially awkward, but she came from a good family. We hit it off and were inseparable for the rest of her life."

"'Her life?' She passed?" Wyatt asked.

"Yeah. She died a while back," I said, completely unsure how long it had been. When I died, she'd already been gone eight years. I had no way of determining how long ago that was; how long Wyatt had lingered here; how long I'd been gone before being thrust back into this pain-filled world.

"I'm sorry. Loss like that is impossible to deal with," he said. I don't know if he was trying to show empathy—if he even knew how—or if he was just trying to trade stories. But he went on with, "My son was a gay in the 1960s. Well, he was a gay his whole life, but he was in high school in the late 1960s. High school was horrible for him—not that I was there for a lot of it, but June told me all about it. He suffered from a constant barrage of boys dunking his head in the toilet, boys slapping his ass in the locker room, boys snapping towels on him. That poor kid went through hell. Wyatt Jr., that was my son, never told us he was gay, but he never married. He moved to New York for college and had a 'roommate' for his whole adult life. I knew. His mom knew. He knew we knew. We just never had that discussion. It's one of those things I wished I'd done but didn't get to. I should have told him it was okay, that we didn't care as long as he was happy."

As he talked on and on about our son, my eyes wandered to those boxes in the corner of the theater. I knew one of those boxes had "Wyatt Jr." written on it in black marker. I knew his things were in there. Everything that was left of him was either in that box or in the projector room, where Wyatt and I had decided to keep our valuables.

I looked back at Wyatt. He was holding a fork with eggs and bacon on it, just a few inches from his mouth; he'd paused, frozen up, as if lost in another of those stress memories. But as he froze there, he'd changed. The crow's feet around his eyes were more emphasized—like he'd aged a decade in a few seconds. But more shockingly, a collection of scars suddenly covered his chest, his arms. I remembered them; they'd been there when he came back from WWII, but until he started talking about Wyatt Jr., his face had been young, and his chest had been free of those ghastly marks. It was like thinking about our son filled him with so much pain that his body started to show signs of it. Again, none of this made any sense, but somehow…somehow it felt right. Felt like progress toward some unknowable goal.

We only ever had a single "conversation" about those scars, but it was an enlightening one. It was the night he and Russell returned from the war. His mother and father had a "Welcome Home Party." Family, friends and of course, Hilda and I were there. Wyatt seemed to be his old self—for the most part—maybe just a little quieter. Russell, too. Both boys seemed happy, laughing, joking—still very much like the kids they were when they left. He held me close to him the whole night. He kissed my cheek, the back of my hand, and when no one was looking, the side of my neck. He whispered love into my ears and grabbed my butt when he thought he could get away with it. I wanted him; needed him. I was still just a kid, and in the flurried days before he'd departed, I'd welcomed Wyatt to our bed as often as my body could handle. And when he'd been away, I'd longed for that fullness between my legs, the throbbing thrashing of sweating bodies. I could hardly wait until the party ended to unbutton his shirt and lift my skirt.

After the party, we went back to our shitty apartment, and the kissing turned to heavy petting. Then he laid me down, but when Wyatt took off his shirt, I recoiled at the scars. Not because they were hideous, but because of what he must have suffered through. I swallowed back my immediate revulsion and ran my hands over his chest, feeling the keloids from burns and the recessed areas where his skin had been peeled away with knives.

"What happened, Wyatt?" I'd whispered.

"War happened. Goddamn war happened!" he'd shouted.

I kissed a particularly large scar across his left pec; he jerked away and shouted, "Don't touch my Goddamn chest. Ever!" He stood, walked across the room, poured himself a full glass of cheap whiskey, drank it in its entirety without coughing, then slammed the glass down so hard it shattered. When he pulled his bloody hand away from the shattered glass, I saw the *look* in his eyes for the first time. He'd done a great job covering his changes at the party, but while he stood there, staring off into the distance, blood pouring from his palm, I saw what he'd become. Growing up with Eddy taught me how to keep hidden when I needed to. And it taught me when to speak and when to hold my tongue. I just lay there in bed, half dressed, watching Wyatt stand statue-still, staring into nothingness.

He later apologized, but he never told me the story that went along with the scars on his chest. I had to hear the truth from Russell years later. The word "torture" doesn't do justice to what happened to him. But it was the only word that described it.

Since he saved me in the theater, I felt mostly at peace around Wyatt. There'd been just that one sharp, little glance in the hospital when I'd first mentioned the dreams about "the old woman who'd died there." Seeing those scars across his chest and the emphasized crow's feet around his eyes brought back hidden fears I had suppressed my entire life. I knew he'd never intentionally hurt me; I knew he loved me, but I spent my life holding back around him. I'd worried I was one question, one wrong phrase away from turning my knight in shining armor into a monster like my stepfather.

If he did snap, I knew he'd never take pleasure in hurting me. But I had waking nightmares about him slapping me or throwing a glass at me, or maybe even a bottle. None of it ever happened, but I always half-expected it. I lived sixty years waiting for Wyatt to snap and for the abuse I'd experienced from Eddy to reappear, but at the hands of my husband instead. Seventy-seven years of fear and anxiety. It was no wonder I drank too much and took too many pills.

Shaking off those fears, memories, I asked, "How old was your son when he died?"

"Wyatt Jr. died of the virus in 1989. His *roommate* died a year later. He was thirty-nine… Thirty-nine years… What a short life. So much wasted potential… He was an amazing guitar player. Played Carnegie Hall. Played Royal Albert Hall. Played his way around the world, really…"

I kept my eyes off his chest and mumbled an obligatory, "I'm sorry." I was sorry. That kind of loss left its own scars. But while I was sorry for his loss, I also remembered that while Wyatt stood stoically beside our son's grave, I'd collapsed the day we buried him. I didn't think I'd ever get off the ground. Didn't think I wanted to. I'd wished I'd die so they could just flop my corpse into the hole with my son. I lay there in the dirt that would soon be covering our son's coffin and wept. And Wyatt stood beside me, emotionless. Now, though, his aging eyes were filled with tears as he remembered our son.

He wiped his nose on a napkin and admitted, "It's been a while since I thought of my boy. Death seems to bring up regrets, though. Regrets like never telling someone how much you love them, or how proud you are of them, or how you'd wished you'd spent more time with them. Those are the things that eat at you as you age. I have a lot of regrets like those," Wyatt said. "Too many. So many… I don't think I was a good man. Russell, Wyatt Jr., Russell's son, Jeffrey, they were good men. And they're gone, and I'm still here…"

He looked up at me, stared into my eyes for a moment. The intensity behind his gaze flickered like a candle in a breeze. And everything that I'd once feared, all that blustering anger just beneath his scarred exterior…faded. I understood it was just pain and sadness. I never really understood him when I was alive, but now I saw his pain for what it was. He ran from his demons most of his life, and when he wasn't running, he suffered in silence. His outbursts, his angry jabs, his snarls, they weren't meant to hurt me. They were just responses to emotions he didn't know how to handle.

As I stared at him, seeing him as if for the first time, Wyatt growled, "What kind of balance is this God of theirs trying to establish? By all rights, good men like my brother, my nephew, and my son should still be alive, and leeches, like me, who made their living on the suffering of others should be in the ground. This is my punishment for not doing better, being better."

Starting to feel like a broken record, I said, "I'm sorry, Wyatt. If there's anything I can do…"

He dropped his eyes back to his food and said, "Today I'm going to St. Louis to scatter Russell's ashes and I'm wondering what things will come up a year from now, ten years from now that I forgot to tell him. There wasn't a lot left unsaid between my brother and me. But now that they're gone and I've had time to think on it, there are things I wish I'd told some of the others. I wish I'd told my wife how proud I was of her. I should have told her how sorry I was for scaring her. That I never meant to remind her of that monster she'd grown up with. That she'd been a saint to put up with me. I should have told my son…so many things…"

I squeezed his hand. What else could I do? I couldn't offer any true relief for his regrets; in his eyes, I was just some girl, some girl he'd found in a theater. Until he realized who I was, I couldn't help him. I couldn't ease his mind.

"All of my family is gone. And I'm alone and full of regrets… With you being sick and all, it's probably too much to ask, but… I need someone to come with me today. To lend me their strength while I scatter my brother's remains."

I squeezed his hand again. He needed me to go, and I would go. Not because I felt like I had to, not because giving in to him had been the rhythm of our lives, but because in this world where nothing seemed to make sense, Wyatt was my only constant. I don't know what happened after I died. I don't know what that bright light that seemed to absorb me was. I just knew that I was back and that my return wasn't without purpose. I wasn't here just to suffer alongside Wyatt; there was something I had to do. Some greater reason for my existence.

"Yes, of course, I'll go, Wyatt."

Chapter 13

Wyatt

There's something to be said about the simple act of cleaning without getting in your cleaning partner's way or them getting into yours. As Emma and I washed, dried, and shelved dishes, we danced steps of the tango, the waltz, and the foxtrot. We danced around the kitchen like we'd been doing it for years.

I never spent much time helping June in the kitchen. Looking back on it, I realize it was unfair that I expected her to do it all. She took care of our son, our house, me, and did it all without objection. She was a modern woman; she had her own ideas, thoughts, complaints, and she expressed them when she felt she should. But I know she held back around me. I hate to admit it to myself, but it's an undeniable fact that she was, at times, afraid of me. Even thinking about that stings. So I packed those thoughts away, crammed them down into the vault full of information I'd rather not remember.

As Emma and I danced around the kitchen, a flurry of dishes and silverware going in their respective places—she seemed to know where they belonged without me telling her—I regretted not spending more time doing that with June. The simplest things in life are the things I miss the most about her. A subtle glance over her shoulder as she crawled out of bed in the morning, making sure I was looking—making sure I never stopped looking. Our hands brushing up against one another's as we both reached into the popcorn bucket at the same time. The lingering smell of her hair conditioner after her bath.

These were the things that made a house a home, that made being alive a *life*. And since she'd been gone, I'd been homeless. I had a roof over my head, a bed to sleep in, food and shelter…but I didn't have what I'd had with her. And I didn't realize what I'd been missing until Emma brought that spark of life back into my theater.

After we cleaned the kitchen, I showed Emma to a box of June's clothes, so she could pick out something to wear. I didn't expect to see her in June's favorite jeans from the sixties. They hadn't been worn in forty or fifty years, but June kept them. She wasn't a pack rat, but there were a few things she just never could let go of. They looked good on Emma. A perfect fit, really. Her shoe size must have been the same, too, because she had on a pair of June's hiking boots, and a dark brown sweater. She'd left that filthy old Army coat hanging on the back of the dining room chair and replaced it with one of my wife's denim jackets, a peace sign patch stitched to the breast pocket.

Again…if I had my camera…

I handed Emma an extra flashlight and hopped up onto the stage. Emma clicked the flashlight off and on, off and on. Its batteries weren't fully charged, but there was enough juice to get us through the day. She hopped up onto the stage behind me, and kept clicking that light off and on, off and on.

Nervous, I thought. But that was probably a projection of my own feelings. Part of me knew that once we walked through that screen, nothing would be the same. I just assumed it was because we were going to spread Russell's remains.

Emma grabbed hold of my hand, and I squeezed hers. "The theater we're going through isn't in the best neighborhood," I told her before I touched the screen.

"What does that mean?"

I glanced back over my shoulder and said, "Just stick close to me."

"I'm not afraid of some scumbag in an old theater, Wyatt? You've already proven you can handle something like that," she said. I shined my own light in her face and saw the smirk.

"Yeah. I remember," I said, the horrified sounds she made as her stepfather slapped her, choked her, then smashed her head to the floor still rang loudly in my ears. "I just wanted you to be forewarned. This isn't a good neighborhood anymore. A girl looking like you may draw some unwanted attention."

"Looking like me?"

"Beautiful," I said, but I took my light away so I couldn't see her reaction.

"Thanks, Wyatt," she said, then, in the most June way possible, she added, "Let's get this show on the fucking road."

I glanced at her, smirked, then laid my hand on the theater's screen. She put her hand on my shoulder as the silky silver turned into a wall of brilliant water.

We took a simple step forward and were reborn into the hallway. Though the hallway was endless, at that moment none of those other doors mattered. We headed straight for the Marcus Avenue door, my gateway to the west.

"How many have you visited?" she asked, shining her light down the hallway at the red doors graffitied with my poor penmanship.

"I don't know. A hundred. Two hundred? Maybe more."

"There have to be thousands of doors here. Hundreds of thousands," she said, a hint of excitement in her voice.

"Yeah," I agreed. Her estimate was probably a bit low. But at least half of the doors I'd tried didn't work. I never ruled out the possibility that some of the doors were another kind of portal. I just had no idea how to open them. I also remained open to the possibility that Russell had been right; that this was a construct of my mind. If that was the truth, though, why were there so many doors? Why so many non-functioning doors? Did each door represent a possible portal that, had I made a different choice at some point in my life, would have been one of *my* doors?

Were they a reflection of the ambitiousness I felt when I first stepped into the hallway? A young man's hall, full of hopes and dreams? Now, though, an old man's hall full of lost possibilities, regrets…and no second chances.

I had no answers for the millions of questions that had to be running through Emma's head. Questions I'd struggled to answer most of my life. Metaphysics was never a strong suit of mine. Russell liked all that New Age shit, but I was a lot less of an abstract thinker than he was. I was goal-oriented. I saw what needed to be done, did it, and handed the results over to Russell so he could polish it with the artistic flair I never had.

Maybe once we got through this, if she lived long enough, she'd explore more doorways with me, and we could talk about the how and why of it all. Maybe she'd have some ideas.

* * *

Emma

We moved through the hall, unevenly spaced round light fixtures making it just bright enough not to need the flashlights. It seemed dimmer this time than it had before. I was more aware of the impossibility of the hallway's existence this time, too. Yes, I'd died and come back—which was

144

impossible. Yes, my husband had reconstructed details of all our previous houses in our old theater and somehow didn't recognize his wife—which seemed impossible. But places like the hallway of doors didn't exist. Not even in books, horror movies, or nightmares. As far as I knew, a place like that had never even been considered, and yet there we were. Me, some kind of ghost, Wyatt…something I couldn't quite name.

Passing a doorway that said *Pripyat, USSR,* I realized I was afraid. I accepted that the hallway scared the fucking shit out of me. Wyatt, while comforting in so many ways, scared the shit out of me, too. Not because I thought he'd hurt me; I knew he never would. I knew he'd do anything to protect me, but because he seemed unstable—which made everything we were doing uncertain, unclear.

My confidence was drained more and more with every step further down the hallway. As if we were walking over some ancient covered bridge that shook under the weight of heavy footfalls and creaked in the wind, I kept waiting for the world around us to collapse. Or for the floor to give out as I timidly placed my old boots on the worn carpet.

When Wyatt stopped at a door labeled "Marcus Avenue" and laid his hand on it, I stepped up behind him and grabbed hold of his jacket.

He glanced back over his shoulder at me, then tried to push open the Marcus Avenue door. But it stuck. He had to throw his shoulder into it three times before it finally gave.

"I've used that door almost every day for years. It just keeps getting harder and harder to open," he said, looking back at me.

"Should we keep going?" I asked, worried about what would happen if that door didn't open when we tried to go back to Minnesota.

"Yeah. With Russell gone, this may be my last trip home for a long time. I'm not willing to say 'ever' because my wife and son are there, under six feet of Missouri clay. My parents and nephew, too. And of course, my sister-in-law. What's left of Russell will be there soon. My whole family buried and scattered; lost along this tiny path of my unending life," he said as if he'd practiced it. It was poetic but didn't fit—it sounded more like something Russell would have said. Russell spent his career bringing Wyatt's heartless, emotionless stories to life. He was the real writer, but he couldn't have gotten those stories without Wyatt's observations. Wyatt saw everything, everywhere— I guess that's why it seemed impossible that he didn't see me.

"Okay, Poe," I said, trying to lighten the mood.

He didn't respond. Instead, he turned to the open door and said, "Get ready for a smell. Dodge the piles of shit and don't touch anything, ever."

"Jesus, really?"

"Don't step on any newspapers on the ground, either. They're probably covering piles of shit, too."

"You're joking, right?"

He smiled and shook his head. "You may have been homeless once, but you were homeless in a small community with people you knew. Not all of them were great people, but there weren't many theater-dwelling crackheads using your home as a shithouse, either. Here, the situation's different. People here are like rabid dogs, just looking for something to bite. There are also self-designated businessmen willing to sell anything or anyone they can, especially attractive young women like you. It makes me sick to think of the danger I'm putting you in; so, stay close and don't look at anyone."

Sick or not, though, he held his hand out to me, leading me through the door.

Unlike our theater, this place was in ruins. A huge portion of the roof and two of the four walls had started collapsing. Hazy, gray Missouri sky filtered into the crumbling building, casting skeletal shadows on blackened walls. Gusts of heavy wind blew trash and dust into dirt devils. But the bums he'd been so concerned with had vacated the building; apparently more afraid of the falling roof than the fresh spring air.

"What *is* this place?" I asked as we hopped off the stage into a post-atomic bomb blast of chaos.

"Tread lightly and don't fall," he said, pointing a dim flashlight at piles of drying human shit and dirty syringes that lined the building's debris-covered floor.

"I'm fine, Wyatt," I said, trying to catch my breath as I looked around at the rusted, rotting roofing materials that'd crushed rows and rows of theater seats. I looked back at the screen and the stage, and I realized where we were. Wyatt had taken me there on our first date. I looked back over my shoulder, and though the curtains that once hung, framing the movie screen, had long since rotted away, I remembered them. Thick, velvety gold and black. I remembered the ceiling's lights, now scattered in the rubble around my feet, as they'd once looked. I remembered the carpet…the same carpet that lined Wyatt's hallway of doors.

On our first date, we saw *The Wizard of Oz*. That first glimpse of color on the screen when Dorothy woke up in Oz was like magic. Wyatt had already seen it twice—with other girls—but it was my first time seeing it. And it was…memorable. So much so that we showed *The Wizard of Oz* every summer in our theater. After a few years, it didn't draw the crowds like it did at first. It seemed everyone had already seen it, had their own copies of it, or just weren't as interested in the classics anymore.

But the last time we showed it, in 1999, on the sixty-year anniversary, we threw a costume party. Free admission if you were dressed up. I dressed as Aunt Em, Wyatt as Uncle Henry. He spent two months letting his hair grow scruffy for the costume party.

"Careful over here, kid, there're some used needles," he said, bringing me back to the now. I wrapped myself around him like I had the night we'd first gone into that theater together. It was so long ago, yet still so fresh in my memory.

Chapter 14

Wyatt

I warned Emma about the rusty building materials and drug paraphernalia scattered all over the ground. A slip and fall on that fragmented metal or a junkie's used needle, and she'd be right back in the hospital. This time, a potential bacterial infection running through her veins as God only knew what coursed through her dying body. The girl had late-stage cancer and was in enough trouble without that nastiness. With her compromised immune system, a small scrape here or cut there and she was as good as dead. There was no way I could have faced another loss right then, so I kept my arm out, ready to grab hold of her as she stepped over piles of junk.

"I'm fine, Wyatt," she told me, but she kept ahold of me as we moved through the theater. I tried not to show it, but the self-assuredness in her voice made me laugh. June would have had that same tone.

I looked back over my shoulder, just checking on her, and got a good look at the silver screen we'd come through. With the morning light shining on it, I saw the terrible shape it was in—probably the worst I'd ever been able to travel through. I don't know what happened since I came to get Russell's remains, but most of the roof and two of the four walls of the theater had caved in, taking most of the screen with them.

I tried to imagine The Prestige Theater as it had been when we were kids. Russell and I would beg our parents to take us to the show there. Friday nights, opening nights for new movies, were the hardest to miss. More often than not, we'd stay home, listening to the radio or reading books we'd already read a dozen times, knowing that other kids were seeing new pictures on the silver screen. Some of the other kids would come in on Mondays blabbing about the new movies, ruining the endings for those of us who hadn't yet seen them. But our father, who'd actually grown up wealthy, became a product of The Depression. He couldn't fathom letting go of a quarter for his kids to see a "moving picture," forget about another quarter for popcorn and sugary snacks. It didn't matter that he had the money to send his kids to the show; it only mattered that during the Depression there were times he didn't have a quarter for food, let alone entertainment— so he hoarded it. When our father died, we found money stashed all over his house. From dollar bills shoved into the pages of every book to nickels and quarters shoved under the insoles of his worn-out work shoes. In the latter part of his life, he'd amassed a small fortune in squirreled-away money.

By the time we were in high school, Russell and I worked whatever odd jobs we could to save up for Friday night dates. We saw every new show on opening night for two years straight. We usually went to the same theater Emma and I were wading through, back when it was more than a pile of rubble. But sometimes we went up north to meet girls from the other side of the tracks, where the school districts changed, and girls didn't know our reputations. The Prestige Theater was once a grand movie palace complete with plaster-sculpted walls, chandeliers, and gilded seat frames—gilded with real gold leaf, not paint.

The theater on the other side of the tracks was built cheap, like the houses that lined the main streets in the poorest parts of the city. But even cheap theaters back then were something to see.

Quality craftsmanship. Art Deco was still thriving when most of them were constructed, and every Art Deco theater had awnings, fluorescent lights, wildly ornate carpets. They were a work of art. Not like today's cold, sterile buildings with vinyl seats and smooth tile floors.

Those nights at the movies made Russell and I feel like we were stepping into someone else's life. Each week, a new story, a new girl, a new character to emulate. In that sense, the theaters themselves were like my doorways. They were an escape from the humdrum reality of life.

Nearly tripping over a vent pipe that had cluttered the aisleway, I flashed back to a time in France, when Russell and I hunkered in a playhouse that had seats almost identical to the crushed, gilded beauties Emma and I were wading through. A bomb had gone off nearby, peeling the side of the building away and dropping big hunks of the roof into the theater. An entire section of seats, along with some hunkering Jews, were crushed by steel girders. They were some of the first dead bodies Russell and I saw, and their corpses were grisly; one was decapitated, and they were all rotting.

A difference of a few months stood between my last date at a Friday night opening show and the day Russell and I stood in that collapsed, stinking theater in France. We were just two kids who had no business there, nor any idea what we were doing. Just like all young soldiers—fearless, stupid, expendable—we did what we were told, without question. Along with twenty others, we were supposed to protect that crumbling French theater…what a joke. Under constant German fire, we lost ten men the first day. Ten men to protect a half-collapsed building—but that was how it went; that was our war.

Seeing the once-proud theater Russell and I frequented as children crumbling from time's constant assault reminded me how much the world had changed since those Friday nights we once loved. Everything and everyone seemed to be deteriorating around me.

"Wyatt, you okay?" Emma whispered as I stood frozen in the middle of the theater, unable to tear my eyes from a row of crushed seats.

I sniffled before my running nose dripped. "Yeah, kid, fine. Just thinking about my brother. We used to bring girls to this theater when we were in high school, before the war," I said, motioning for her to move toward the gaping hole in the back wall.

"You sure you want to do this today?"

"Yeah, I want to get it over with," I said.

As she was about to step out of the hole in the back wall, I grabbed Emma's shoulder and said, "Let me go out first," wanting to make sure the coast was clear. Clear of what, I didn't know, but being conscious of my surroundings was a big part of my life's work. And who knew what would be happening, street side, in that neighborhood?

She nodded and let me pass.

I stuck my head out of the hole in the back wall of The Prestige. There was a guy dealing drugs on the corner. When I saw him, I had to do a double take; at first glance I'd have sworn he was my sixth grade History teacher, Mr. Cochran. I stared at him for a second, trying to figure out what the hell was going on, then I remembered that Mr. Cochran had been dead since 1960. I shook my head, rubbed my eyes, and glanced around at the rest of the scene. Other than the dealer, there was a guy pushing a shopping cart full of clothes and whatnot across the street. We were pretty well clear.

"Okay, Em."

She followed me through the wall and said, "Don't call me Em, Wyatt. My stepfather called me that."

I nodded, understanding, and added, "When *my* father got drunk—which wasn't often—he always called me 'Wy-tit.' He thought it was funny. I didn't. Sorry, kid. I won't call you that again."

She let out a nervous little laugh and said, "Wy-tit? That's fucking stupid. It's not even funny."

I couldn't help but grin back at her. It was stupid. But as a kid, it seemed like an insult. And an insult from our usually loving father stung. I didn't pick my damn name; he did, so it seemed unfair that he'd make fun of me for it.

I led Emma past the drug dealer on the corner. He spat, "Crank, smack, gak, crack," like a carnival caller trying to draw in customers. But there wasn't anyone around. He just sang it out, loud and clear, beckoning whatever lowlifes might be squatting in the crumbling buildings that lined the streets. We needed to get out of that neighborhood as quickly as possible—a girl like Emma wasn't safe there.

In my line of work, I saw the worst of the human condition. In the later years of my career, in a hellhole in Eastern Europe, I saw sex slaves junked up, raped, abused, and sold for nothing. I couldn't stand the sight of those young women and boys being tortured, but I shot photos anyway. Photos that made me cringe when I developed them. Photos that made me a great deal of money when I sold them… Photos I wished I could take back. Photos that made me wish I'd chosen a different line of work. Photos that made me terrified of what could become of Emma if I didn't keep her safe.

"Come on, kid," I said, offering my hand to Emma as we crossed the street.

"I'm okay, Wyatt," she said, intently watching the dealer on the corner.

The dealer never lifted his head as we walked by; he just kept spitting the same words: "Crank, smack, gak, crack."

We were half a block away when Emma pulled me to a stop and watched as another man—more like a boy with too many hard years under his belt—walked up to the dealer.

"Come on, kid," I repeated to Emma, tapping her on the shoulder, but she didn't move. The dealer handed the man-child a little baggie of clear rocks that looked like the rock candy Russell and I used to buy as kids. The man-child's acne-scarred face came alive at the sight of the tiny crystals.

They made a trade, and the man-child walked away in a kind of jittery shuffle.

Emma kept her eyes on the scene the whole time. I kept my eyes active. I wanted to tell her it was dangerous to stare, but no one was paying any attention to us. No one cared that we just saw a felony.

When the man-child walked away, I patted Emma's arm again. She looked up at me, and I lifted my chin, motioning for us to move on. She finally followed.

We walked down a jagged sidewalk littered with chips of paint and brick falling from another collapsing building. It looked like someone had tossed a bucket of red and white, lead-based confetti everywhere. Across the street, on the porch of an old corner market with rotting white wood siding and a bowing roofline, a couple of guys barbecued over half a fifty-gallon oil drum. The smoke from their grill blew across the street in the gusty wind. They didn't bother to look up as we passed, either. No one looked our way; it was like we were invisible.

A few cars were parked along the potholed street, but it was clear that none of them had been moved in years. It was like the world had aged a decade since I'd been there last. Twenty-four hours or ten years, what's the difference when you've stopped aging?

At the closest bus stop where buses actually stopped, there was half a map taped to the plexiglass wall. Thankfully, it was the half we needed. I looked at the map for a minute and said, "The Redline connects to the Delmar. The Delmar bus will take us to Skinker Avenue. We can walk from there."

Emma nodded at me, but she looked at the world around us, like a child seeing everything for the first time. A crowd of bus riders stood with us, waiting to make their morning commute from that aging part of the city to an office or a business in some thriving part of St. Louis.

We hopped on the Redline a few minutes later. A few transfers and a half-hour after that and we got off at the bus stop on Skinker Avenue. Compared to the dilapidated Marcus Avenue setting, that part of the city was a bustling world of activity. Joggers were braving the cool morning, exercising on the paved track around Forest Park. Dog walkers moseyed with herds of tiny monsters on tangles of knotted leads, hands full of shit bags. It seemed a lot had changed since I'd been home.

We headed for the nearest crosswalk and marched a few blocks down to Arundel Place. The houses Russell and I once owned stood side by side on a street unaltered by time's aggression. 60 Arundel Place, the home I lived in most of my life, was a vine-covered, two-story, brick bungalow with two huge maple trees in the front.

"This was your home?" Emma asked.

"June and I lived here for most of our married life. We raised Wyatt Jr. here. Raised five dogs, four cats, and the slew of rodents that Wyatt Jr. begged us for. I know every dent in every wall. I know every stain caused by leaky pipes and the reason behind every scratch on every cabinet. I know that the gouges our Great Dane, Lucy, put in the hardwood floor, just days after I laid it, are still there. I put years of blood, sweat, and tears into maintaining that house. But I knew I had to sell it when I did. Neither June nor I could stay there after our son died. It was just too much.

Too many memories. When we left, the memories didn't go away, but they weren't right in our faces, either."

I took a deep breath, turned from my home and walked a few more steps down the block. 62 Arundel, Russell's home. He kept the vines off his place—regularly ranting about how bad they were for the mortar—and had replaced the asphalt shingles with terracotta tiles back in the seventies. Otherwise, the two homes were as much alike as Russell and I had been. Like us, our houses had their own individual characteristics, a roofing change here and a window shape there, but, for the most part, we and the homes seemed the same. It wasn't until you looked inside that you saw bigger differences.

* * *

Emma

When we stopped in front of Russell's house, I saw a summer day. A barbeque. Three dogs wrestling in the yard. Two kids playing in a sandbox. Wyatt, beer in hand, looked almost the same as he does now. His twin brother, a nearly identical duplicate of Wyatt, stood at the grill, flipping burger patties. Hilda—in a nearly see-through sundress—came out of the house, carrying a huge glass bowl of macaroni salad to the picnic table. I followed her from the house with a pitcher of sweet tea laced with fresh lemon slices. I could almost taste it. My mother's recipe: sweet, syrupy, lemony tea.

Aside from the jacket, which I didn't feel like I needed anymore, I was wearing the same fucking outfit I had on at the barbecue. I had the same haircut and chipped front tooth. I ran my tongue over its jagged edge, to make sure that the constant reminder of Eddy's swift backhand and his high school graduation ring—not that he graduated high school, I was pretty sure he'd stolen it off someone else—was still there. I carried that reminder my entire life—and now that I remembered it, saw it in that younger version of myself, it was back.

"Mama," a little boy shouted, "Jeffery's got my truck!"

"Share, honey," I'd said, struggling with the frustration of having an only child. I wanted a second, but Wyatt didn't. We had the argument more than once, and he always told me, "I'm gone too often to have another. I'm traveling, working, and you're here alone. I won't do that to you."

"Russell and Hilda are right next door," I'd say, trying to convince him.

"And Russell's gone almost as often as I am," he'd say, even though he knew it wasn't true. Then, "One's enough, honey," would be the end of the conversation. He'd get that look in his eye, and I knew not to push it further.

On the sidewalk in front of Russell's house, I blinked my eyes, tears running down my cheeks, and the barbecue was gone. I was back to reality, or what seemed to be passing for it.

Even in the same clothes I wore all those years ago, with my chipped tooth and 60s, flower-child hair, Wyatt didn't recognize me. Not that I blamed him. Nothing made sense in this strange world in-between. We were neither here in the present nor there in the past; we were drifting between moments like fog on a breezy spring day.

Chapter 15

Wyatt

I wiped a tear from my eye as a million memories about our life in that home resurfaced. Wyatt Jr. crashing his bike into one of the aging maple trees: five stitches in his left knee. Putting up Christmas lights from a rickety wooden ladder: busting my thumb with the hammer as the ladder threatened to fall, and I was too tired or too stubborn to get off and adjust it. Barbecues with Russell, Hilda, neighbors, and friends. My parents…and June.

Always June.

The smile on her face every time I got home from a work trip. The way her eyes lit up when I surprised her with carnations instead of roses because she didn't like roses—"Their thorns," she'd say, "are too much of a reminder that life isn't perfect." Her laugh when one of our dogs would do some new, surprising, doggy thing. June…the love of my life. The woman who never asked if I cheated even though I was gone more often than I was home. The woman who trusted me, nurtured me, loved me… The woman I saved from an abusive stepfather; the woman who saved me more times than I could count. The woman who died of lung cancer but never smoked.

June…my girl.

"It's a beautiful home, Wyatt," Emma said, rattling a few pills from the bottle in her pocket into her mouth.

"Give me a minute?" I mumbled through silent sobs.

"Are you okay?"

"Pain," I said, holding my heart. My chest.

She helped me to the ground, sat down beside me on the grass near the sidewalk, and took my hand in hers. Emma turned my head to her chest, placing my face against her bosom as she rested her head on my shoulder. The pain in my chest tightened and stole my breath away. But after a moment, I felt at ease in her arms.

I let myself cry, burrowing my face in Emma's bosom like Wyatt Jr. did to June every time he crashed his bike or slipped in the freshly sprinkled grass while chasing one of our dogs, or playing with his cousin Jeffrey. I cried thinking about all the time I'd spent away from them, time I could have been with them. I cried until my eyes burned and my nose was full. Until my head ached. Until I didn't have any more cry in me.

I let Emma go, unscrewed the top of Russell's urn, and slowly scattered about half of his remaining ashes onto the grass. I didn't turn it into a ceremony. I couldn't. The words wouldn't have come even if I'd planned something to say. Words were Russell's forte; I was an action guy. When I placed the lid back on the urn, a strong gust took the top layer of my brother's ashes and tossed them to the wind. I closed my eyes and let the memories drift away with Russell's remains.

Still sniffling, I stood, helped Emma up, and wordlessly headed back the way we came.

Three-quarters of my brother had been distributed. The rest of him was supposed to go to the cemetery with his wife. I said it before, but it had never been so clear as it was then: rituals—these odd things we do with the dead—aren't for the dead; they're for the living. They're a reminder of all the good we did together and all the bad we helped one another through. They're a reminder of our lives, our ups and downs, of where we came from and where we're going—everyone but me, that is… I'm stuck here for the long haul. I'll never get out.

With a deep, shuddering sigh, I led Emma down the block, away from my and Russell's houses, our bodies entangled like the vines that covered my home. The further we got, the less it hurt.

"I may be back in this town from time to time, but I don't think I'll ever be able to walk down that street again," I told Emma while we waited at the bus stop on Skinker. She smiled, nodded, and placed her head on my shoulder. At that moment, nobody could have done anything better than that.

* * *

Emma

Making that last turn from our street felt like I was saying goodbye to something important. A last visit to a life I once lived, and a last reminder of the life I could have lived, if I'd made slightly better choices. We all feel regrets, but right then, I was full of regrets for hiding from my past in a bottle of booze and/or pills.

"You grabbed your chest back there," I said to Wyatt as we waited for the bus. "An old man like you could have a heart attack doing something like this," I said, thinking about all the times he'd grabbed his chest or shook out his left hand since I'd been back.

"I guess that's true. I don't know what's going on inside me. I felt a rush of blood to my chest that tightened my heart into a fist and sent pain down my arm. No matter how many times I hoped I'd die or felt like I would, my body just keeps going. I'm old, tired…sad; but on the outside, still young. I'm afraid my body'll go on until the world dies and the planet fries. I'll be here until the end, waiting for my turn. Waiting to finally move on like the rest of my family. Life has become purgatory for me. And I'm stuck—I think it's punishment. I don't know if it's punishment from *God*, but it's punishment for all the bad things I saw and, instead of trying to stop them, I took photos that I'd later sell to corporate giants making a killing off death and destruction. And because I was an accomplice to those horrors, I'm stuck, and I'll never age another day, and I'll never move on. And worst of all, I'll never see my family again."

"Jesus, Wyatt, that's too depressing," I said.

But his statement was like the missing piece of a puzzle I'd nearly completed. "Moving on" *was* the point. If we didn't move on, we'd be stuck here forever, like he said. I'd been swimming in déjà vu and confusion since I awoke under the stage in that old theater, but when Wyatt murmured the phrase "move on" it was like a flashing neon light, reminding me why I was there, why I was back.

"I'm sorry, kid. This life is depressing and today is one of the most depressing days I've been through. I know we don't know one another well, but I feel like I've known you forever. And I'm damn glad you're here today."

I took his hand as the bus pulled up. From an outsider's perspective, we could be a couple in love, suffering the loss of whoever was in the urn Wyatt kept tucked in the cradle of his arm, like a football. If anyone took a second to look at us, they would never guess anything different. But no one ever looked at us. We were just two anonymous souls drifting through a cold, grey world.

Chapter 16

Wyatt

At Bellefontaine Cemetery, just north of Cascade Lake, our family plot stretched seven headstones deep in every direction. Silk flowers from unknown visitors rested at Hilda's stone. Someone had left a reefer pipe on the top of my son's. Leaves were scattered from the huge oak that stood like a guardian over the family's plot.

My father bought the family plot when he retired in 1950. He said, "This'll keep us all together." For the most part, he'd been right. He and Mom were there, side by side, in the middle of it all. Cousins, aunts, uncles: the whole family tree. I was the only remaining leaf left fluttering in an endless fall wind.

"There're extra plots. Why didn't your brother want to be buried here?" Emma asked from behind me.

"I asked Russell why he didn't want to be buried beside his wife and son. He said, 'My heart is scattered across the world, like yours. I'm not happy with the idea of my body rotting in one spot; not after all the places we've been. Send me to the wind so I can keep on traveling.' It was a romantic notion. A bit too romantic for him. The last few months, near the end, he got so delusional he hardly knew his name. In that time, he came up with these odd romantic notions. He was a goofball, not a romantic. He probably saw it on some Goddamn soap opera.

"The next time I tried to convince him to be buried in the family plot he said, 'Just plant part of me in the ground on top of my wife; she always liked for me to be on top,' then he laughed. That was Russell. He always had goofy ideas; some Russell-devised tale that would only play out clearly in his mind. Near the end, his gags became too complex for anyone to follow, including him. He'd keep repeating a punchline, but he'd forget the joke. Other than when his son died, I think life was all a joke to him," I said, holding up the urn.

Emma took it out of my hands, then I used my pocketknife to cut a small branch from the old oak. I sharpened one end and used the branch to peel back the grass in front of Hilda's headstone. I'm sure there was some cemetery policy against what I was doing, but I didn't care, and I was sure Russell would have gotten over my rule breaking. He was more of a rule follower than I was—but that's not hard; I don't even follow the rules of nature.

I dug silently, wishing I'd brought a garden trowel. But I wasn't going back for one now. Once I had the hole deep enough to accommodate the rest of my brother's ashes, I said, "Okay. Hand him over."

Emma handed me what was left of my brother. I poured him in the tiny, unmarked grave and said, "Hell of a ride, brother," before pushing the dirt back into the hole. I laid the bit of sod I'd scraped from the top of the hole on the miniature mound; leaving Russell's final remains exactly where he wanted them: on top of his wife.

I brushed my hands off, stood and walked over to June's grave. It'd been a while since I'd been there, and there were a few small patches of lichen growing on her headstone. I scraped them off with my pocketknife and felt that all-too-familiar stab of pain in my chest.

* * *

Emma

Looking over his shoulder, I asked, "Is that your wife's?" I knew it was me in there, under there, but I'd never seen my gravestone—salmon colored granite with glimmering bits of clear crystals embedded in the stone. At the top, centered, it read:

GAUMOND

On the left side:

EMMA JUNE
WIFE, MOTHER, FRIEND
BORN: JUNE 15, 1925
DIED: MARCH 22, 2002

On the right:

WYATT JEFFREY
BROTHER, PHOTOGRAPHER,
FATHER, HUSBAND
BORN: DECEMBER 27, 1924
DIED: APRIL 3, 2012

I stared open-mouthed at the grave, glancing back and forth between our names and death dates.

I already understood me, and I was pretty sure I understood Wyatt, but seeing his name on that stone and his death date, made his existence clearer. *We* were dead. And *we'd* been dead a long time. I'd crossed over after I'd died, but now I was back because

Wyatt never found the path to step from this plane of existence to the next. To "move on" from this world in-between. Like I'd been when I first came back to this reality, Wyatt was completely lost. Confused. He didn't even realize he'd died. And if I didn't show him what he was, he could be stuck here forever. I still didn't remember anything from the other side, but I knew the purpose for my return was to get him to cross over.

"Yeah, that's my wife, June," Wyatt said, interrupting my revelation. "We were married over sixty years."

"What was she like?" I asked, hoping that the more he thought of her, the more he'd see *me* for who I was. Hoping he'd recognize I was Emma June, his wife of 60 years and not just Emma, a girl he found in a theater. Hoping that realization would help him take the next steps.

"How do I describe someone I was in love with for most of my life? I knew her better than I've known anything or anyone—except Russell. How do I tell you what that's like?"

"Maybe start simple. What color was her hair?"

"When we were young, her hair was auburn. Not red, but a reddish-brown that looked like rust on steel. That doesn't sound right. It doesn't sound pretty, but it was. It was always darker at the top, near the roots, and lighter near the ends. The sun bleached it out in the summer. By summer's end, it would be a little orangy and it would pop against her tan skin. She had freckles, too. Not all over, just a few here and there. A dusting of them on her nose and cheeks. It was cute." He paused and looked over his shoulder at me.

I hoped for a second that he'd see my auburn hair and freckles, that he'd recognize me for who I was. But he was blind to the truth. I had to *make* him see. If I told him who I was, he'd get that look in his eyes and he'd shut down. This wasn't something I could twist his arm to make him realize; he had to come to the realization himself.

"Where did you meet?" I said, sitting down beside the headstone. Beside my grave.

"The bookstore, then I asked her to the movies, of course. We saw *The Wizard of Oz*. It had been out a little while, but she'd never seen it, and if the weekly film wasn't doing well, the theater in our neighborhood would show replays they knew they could sell tickets to. I thought it was a damn shame she'd never seen it, and I insisted she go with me."

"Keep going," I said, urging him to give me more, to remind himself of who we were. Of who *I* was.

"June was tough. I've never met a tougher woman. Again, that doesn't sound ladylike or beautiful or attractive when I say it like that, but it was. After living with her stepfather, she never let a man talk down to her, demean her. I know I wasn't perfect toward her. I wasn't a good husband, and I know there were times she wondered why the hell she was still married to me. But she kept me in line."

I glanced down at the tombstone and said, "Tell me about your best day together."

He glared at me for a second, and I thought I'd overdone it, but then his eyes eased, and he looked back down at the headstone.

"Best day… That's a tough one. We had a lot of good days. Those last ten years, when we ran our theater, were all pretty amazing. Those years made me realize how much I'd missed when I was away at work."

"Okay, maybe not the best day, but a good day," I said. "Any good day. Maybe it'll help you remember."

He glared at me again, then growled, "I remember her. That's not the problem."

"Well, what is, then?" I barked back.

"I don't know. I just…don't think I'll be able to explain her well. She was a complicated woman, and I don't want to paint her in a bad light. She was nothing but good, even though she had her struggles. I don't want my words to make it sound like I had anything but respect and love for her."

"It's okay, Wyatt. Just try," I said, reaching out for his hand.

He looked into my eyes, laid his hand in mine, and I squeezed. He said, "Our honeymoon was a good trip. We didn't take our honeymoon until a few years after me and Russell got back from the war. We did that long trip out west, and it blew a lot of our savings, so I had to get a job and start making money before we could go again. I don't know if I told you, but I worked in the shoe factory during the day while me and Russ were trying to get our journalism careers going. But working all day in a factory and in the evenings writing, developing film, and printing pictures, I got pretty worn out. And I'll admit, I got grumpy."

That's an understatement! I thought.

"June asked me about the honeymoon I'd promised her when we got married—she didn't ask for much. And really, I think she wanted to get me out of my routine more than she needed to get out of hers. She was always looking out for me like that. Anyway, I'd promised her a honeymoon, but we were five years into our marriage and still hadn't gone—so I let her pick…told her we could go anywhere in the country."

But you didn't really let me pick. You let me suggest. And then you picked from my suggestions, I thought.

"She wanted to go to the Atlantic. Like you, she'd gone down to the Gulf once, when she was a girl, but didn't have a good time because of her stepfather. June wanted to see the ocean fresh and clear, to erase the memories of that first trip. We went to Georgia, to a little island off the coast of Savannah. We stayed at a bed-and-breakfast that an old woman named Mable ran. We slept in until Mable rang the breakfast bell, then we'd go downstairs, have breakfast, and borrow the bicycles Mable lent out to guests.

"We rode those bikes on the packed sand right where the water met the beach. When we got tired, we'd lay out our towels and rest in the warm sunlight… I'm sorry, I'm not doing this justice. Russell was the one who'd take my observations and turn them into poetry. I'm just spewing details…"

"It's okay, Wy. I'm getting the picture," I said, and I was. I remembered that day, remembered riding along the surf, dodging starfish and sand dollars in the low tied.

"Wy?" he asked, testing the nickname.

"Is that okay?"

"It's what June used to call me," he said. He looked at the stone, then back to me. "It's okay."

Wyatt went on, telling me the details of that week we spent together on the beach. His details were slightly off, but he had the basics down. It wasn't summer, like he seemed to be remembering; it was fall. There wasn't much sun, but the beaches were nearly empty. All the summer vacationers had gone back to their homes, and many of the brightly colored houses had been shuttered for the hurricane season and the winter. Mable was glad to have anyone that late in the season, and she gave us a discounted rate, cooked the best food you could imagine, and didn't say a word about the noises coming from our bedroom each night.

Wyatt told me all about the days we spent there, but he didn't talk about the nights, and I wasn't ready to press him on it. While the days were good, I don't think riding bikes on the beach was why he'd deemed that vacation one of our best; I think it's because nine months later Wyatt Jr. arrived.

I knew I was pregnant just a few weeks after we'd returned, and when I told him, his eyes glowed in a way I hadn't seen since before the war. I hoped that Jr. would bring Wyatt back to me. I hoped he'd stop running, stop disappearing into a bottle or a project or a new story every time he got the chance. And while he loved his son from the moment he was born, Wyatt never stopped running from whatever had happened to him in that camp.

Chapter 17

Wyatt

I could tell that something was bothering Emma. As I told her stories about June, her eyes kept glancing back at the tombstone, especially my side. I couldn't quite figure out what was wrong with her, but seeing those beautiful green eyes filled with tears as they flickered from me to the tombstone, stung.

She wanted to know more about my wife, and every time I paused, she pushed for more details. When I finally ran out of things to say, she asked, "You met her at a bookstore, huh?"

"Yeah. We met at the bookstore. Russell and I were into books almost as much as we were into movies. We bought one each per month—all we could afford with our other hobbies—and traded off and on, so it was like having two new books in our collection each month. Movies came first in the entertainment department—you couldn't take a girl to a book. But I met a lot of girls in the bookstore.

"June was in the fiction aisle, holding up a copy of a new Agatha Christie," I said. As I relayed details to Emma, I remembered it, like it was yesterday. She had on this blue dress. Blue, like Wyatt Jr's baby blanket…baby blue with white polka dots. The back was open, and there was a kind of bowtie collar around the neck holding up the front. It was a pinup fan's dream. Her shoulders caught my eye from across the store—they were still milky white from the long winter. It was one of the first warm days of the spring, like today, and I had a feeling she was wearing a Christmas present for the first time. Showing it off. Showing herself off. She carried a cardigan that I was sure she'd worn when she left the house and removed as soon as she was out of her parents' line of sight.

That memory stung. But I tried to keep my voice level as I told Emma about that day. About meeting my June for the first time. My words coming out a little shaky, I said, "I was familiar with the Christie book June was holding. I said to her, 'That one's not worth the buck-twenty. But if you want to borrow it from me, you can. One stipulation, though; you come to the movies with me on Friday.' I was bold, brave, and had nothing to lose. If she said no, I could have ten more girls lined up before Friday came. But when I talked to her, nerves I hadn't felt in years roiled in my stomach. I'd mostly gotten over that teenage insecurity by the end of high school—Russell and I dated a lot. We were good-looking and just charming enough to have our pick of the flock... But this girl, she was out of my league. It didn't matter what side of the tracks she came from; she was something special."

Emma gave me a look that said, "Arrogant pig!" I recognized it immediately. I'd seen it on June's face here and there.

I said, "Hey, kid, this was over seventy years ago. Times were different. Men *were* arrogant pigs. Men were forceful; men were always right. Jesus... seventy years ago. Seventy. June and I had a million memories together, and every single one is as vivid as the day we met," I said, taking in a deep, shaky breath, and wiping my eyes again. I couldn't believe I was crying so much in front of that girl, but I didn't feel like she was judging me.

* * *

Emma

He looked at me, tears running down his ashen face as memories of our life rushed him from every direction. My questions kept those memories rolling. His eyes were running back and forth between each side of the tombstone and me as he told me about our life. I knew he didn't see yet, but it seemed he was getting closer. And as he got closer, those age lines around his eyes got deeper.

Being in the cemetery and telling stories about our life as I sat there, beside my tombstone, silently begging him to see what he was choosing not to see, was having an impact on him. He needed time to process. So, after an hour (or two, time seemed to move in strange ways since I'd been back) I stood and left him there to ruminate as I walked around the family's plot, looking at each tombstone, remembering something I loved and something I didn't love about every member of our family.

I loved Russell's sense of humor. Wyatt was right. It was goofy, and sometimes you couldn't really follow the joke, but he always knew how to make me laugh. He saw almost as much horror in WWII as Wyatt…almost. Russell escaped nearly unscathed, though. He maintained his ability to laugh, to feel, to enjoy life. Granted, he was never taken prisoner and tortured, like Wyatt, but he did live through the fighting.

What I loved about Russell was also what I disliked about him. That he went on after the war like nothing had happened; like he hadn't seen their friends' die in the snow, or like he hadn't seen his brother's chest torn to shreds, as if he'd been attacked by a lion. As if he hadn't seen them drag his unconscious body from the prison camp. Russell stayed resiliently happy even after a lifetime of seeing the horrors the world had to offer. But most of what he saw was secondhand, when he developed Wyatt's pictures. He was disconnected from the firsthand violence Wyatt spent his life intertwined with.

I looked at the other side of the dual headstone and saw Hilda's name. My best friend in the world was passionate. I loved her passion for life. When we were kids, she was timid, almost afraid of messing up, but after our winter in the mountains, in that god-awful camper, her timid streak faded. She loved the outdoors and sang church music while she played in her garden. Which I guess was what bothered me about her. How could she be so happy while I was so miserable, terrified, and alone most of the time? While it took years for her to come back to life after Jeffrey died in Vietnam, she did come back to life. I never understood how that was possible. And I guess I was jealous of her ability to move on, while I never could.

I never realized that what bothered me most about everyone else was the same as what bothered me most about myself. I couldn't laugh like Russell. I wasn't passionate about life like Hilda. I couldn't move on with life after my boy died. But I wished I could laugh; wished I felt passion…wished I could move on. I guess looking in the mirror is harder than looking through a magnifying glass.

I started to step away from their headstone, but before I made it a single step; I looked closer at their names side by side, like mine and Wyatt's. Then their list of life achievements, then their death dates. Russell's death date, carved boldly into that stone, was, impossibly, the same as Wyatt's:

DIED: APRIL 3, 2012

I looked back at Wyatt's stone to verify:

DIED: APRIL 3, 2012

What the hell? If they died on the same day, how does Wyatt remember scattering Russell's ashes?

I walked back over to Wyatt, laid my hands on his shoulders and, wanting some answers, asked, "Are all your memories so vivid? Do you remember the wars, your brother, and your childhood in as much detail as the stories you've been telling me?"

"Memories stick to me like cockleburs to a long-haired dog, that's for sure. But they become less intense as time goes by. They change as I change. Did you know that every time you remember something, you're not remembering the time it happened but rather the last time you remembered it? Our minds are unreliable sources of information. As you get older, you'll have a thousand new memories for every old one—which will continue to distort the reality of any memory. I think that's why we can't remember the fine details of our childhood. Sure, we get snippets, but the majority of our earliest memories are lost at sea," he said.

I understood that from his perspective, he'd had a relatively uneventful childhood. But for me, so much of my mind's space had been occupied by childhood traumas. I remembered those days; the sounds of drunken arguments, the meaty thuds of thrown fists connecting with soft skin, the earth shattering sound of broken glass. Maybe I didn't remember everything and maybe what I did remember wasn't quite accurate, but I knew how those early memories impacted the rest of my life.

As if he were repeating a mantra he'd chanted a hundred times before, Wyatt added, "The most important thing I've ever learned is that life isn't all about the past. We shouldn't be focusing on things that happened five, ten, twenty years ago; we can't change those things. It's not about the future, either. What will be, will be. Life's supposed to be about the here and now. Living in the moment… I know this, but right now it's not working for me. I'm here, saying goodbye to my brother, but I'm also off on a fishing charter with Russell and I'm holding June's hand as we stroll through Forest Park, baby crib in tow. Right now, my mind is scattered and my thoughts are everywhere at once."

"I'm sorry about your brother, Wyatt. I'm sorry you've lost everyone you've ever loved," I said. And while I meant it, my eyes, unable to help themselves, darted back and forth between our headstone and Russell and Hilda's.

They died the same day.

"Thanks, Emma," Wyatt said, reaching his hand up to mine. And when I looked down at our hands together, I realized my skin didn't look as fresh as it had that morning. As unblemished by time. It didn't look old, just not young. It was clear my time was waning, and there was some unknown deadline I had to meet. I just didn't know how to meet it—yet.

Chapter 18

Wyatt

I looked over my shoulder and saw a dangerous flash in Emma's eyes as she stared at our overlapping hands. I'd seen that look come over dozens of men in the field. And it was never good.

"Let's get out of this graveyard," I said, glad to have an excuse to go. The thought of sitting there, mourning my brother and everyone who went before him, while I told this girl everything I could about my wife, was making me sick. If I'd learned anything in my life, it was that sitting still and overthinking could drive a person insane.

While I expected the day to be hard…nearly impossible for me, I hadn't considered how hard it would be on her. Spending the day in my old neighborhood, then a graveyard, watching me break down in both; none of it could have been easy. Her own death loomed closer with every passing day, and dragging her along on this tour of sadness was reminding her how little time she had left. Her emotions had to be in chaos. I was an inconsiderate asshole for dragging her along.

I said, "I'm sorry, Emma. I asked too much of you today. I shouldn't have assumed you'd be ready for something like this. I'm grateful for you helping me through it, but it's time to go."

She nodded.

"Come on, let's go get something to eat," I added.

She nodded again, wiping a nonexistent tear from her freckled face.

Did she always have freckles? It seemed like her skin had been smooth, like a porcelain doll's… But the more time I spent with her, the more she looked like June.

Maybe it was just the lighting.

I got on my feet, took one more glance at our tombstone—June's side first—and flicked off another piece of lichen. Then I took a quick glance at my side. My heart fluttered, my eyes went blurry, then, as quickly as it happened, everything righted itself and I was standing on the far edge of our family plot, but didn't know how I got there. It was almost like I'd teleported from where I'd been standing, to fifty yards away, in the blink of an eye.

I glanced over my shoulder a few more times as we walked out of the cemetery toward a restaurant called "LaDonna's Soul House." It was a place Russell, June, Hilda and I frequented after our visits to the family plot.

"The tripe's pretty good here," I said, motioning to an open table as we walked through the front door.

"No tripe for me," Emma said as she sat down. The red vinyl tablecloth squeaked as her elbows pushed it across the table. "That wasn't what it sounded like," she said, smiling. It was an old joke between June and me. Anytime we squeezed into a leather recliner or squeaky vinyl chair that made that fart noise, we'd say, "That's not what it sounded like." It started on our second date after she tried to squeeze into a leather-covered bench in a tight booth at an Italian restaurant. She looked up, red-faced, and said it for the first time. We repeated it hundreds of times throughout our lives.

I looked Emma in the eyes for a second. She smiled, and for the first time I saw her chipped front tooth, just like June's. I stared until she picked up a laminated menu, blocking my view.

"How can you eat tripe?" she asked, glancing at me over the menu.

"How can you not?"

"Puke. You eat Chitlins?"

"Gross. No."

"But tripe is okay? I think I'll just stick with fried chicken," she said, laying her menu down.

"Tripe for me. It's been years since I've had a good mess of tripe, and this place has the best."

The disgust on her face turned into a smile, that chipped tooth peeking out from behind her lips, taunting me, daring me to ask her how she got it. But I knew if I asked, she'd tell me about how June got the chipped tooth; she'd tell the story as if it had happened to her the same way.

* * *

Emma

Inside LaDonna's Soul House, a heavyset girl with long dreadlocks and a filthy red apron walked by. She didn't seem to hear when Wyatt mumbled our order to her, but it didn't matter. We were living in Wyatt's projections—ideas and memories from the life we had. Some of it had happened exactly as Wyatt lived it—like instant replay—other things were creations of his mind—like the hallway of doors and this day, dedicated to Russell's post-death ash-scattering.

I hadn't taken the time to analyze that one yet, but it seemed like he was leading me through the things he would have done if he'd outlived his brother. Or maybe the things he wished he could have done for Russell. It seemed he had more regrets than he knew how to process.

But I knew LaDonna's was real. When we were alive, we'd gone there dozens of times. Wyatt always got tripe. I always got fried chicken and a big glass of lemonade, to which I'd add a shot or three of vodka from my flask. That day, though, unless the waitress was tapped into the spirit world, I doubted she saw us or knew we were there; I doubted the door had opened when we came in; I doubted the menus in our hands were actually in our hands; but I was sure, before long, a pair of dinners and glasses of lemonade would be sitting on our table, because that's how this world he'd created for himself worked. If he thought it was real, it was real. If he thought he was young, he was young. If he thought he'd outlived his brother, he'd outlived his brother. If he thought we were in LaDonna's after another visit to the family plot, we were.

One of the most baffling things in the world between human life and what comes after is the confusion. In life, the mind has the ability to create, the ability to remember, and the ability to forget. In the in-between, those abilities are stretched. Imagine living in a dream for ten years, twenty years. Dreams can be confusing, you wake up after being chased off the side of a cliff by a goat with a dragon's head or diving off a roof into a pile of snow and landing in your old boyfriend's bed or seeing a family member that's been dead for years, and wonder, "What the fuck was that about?"

Dreams and the in-between overlap. They're both run by the mind and powered by the soul. Wyatt's mind had been running nonstop for years. Mine had been gone, crossed over, and was now back on this plane. It was no wonder I woke confused in that theater. No wonder I was attacked by Eddy and ended up in the hospital dying of lung cancer… Those were real experiences in my life, the order, my age, and the fine details were off, but I'd lived them, and they'd scared the hell out of me. Of course, those moments haunted me here, where our fears, hopes, and dreams all become reality.

I was sure now that my purpose in being back on Earth was to help Wyatt. To get him to see the truth. To help him wake up from his decades-long dream so he could cross over. So, I kept on asking questions about *June*, hoping he'd see me. Sitting there in LaDonna's, at our usual table, with our usual order on its way, I said, "You started telling me about how you and June met at the bookstore and how you took her to see *The Wizard of Oz*. Tell me the rest of that story."

"Right, right. Sorry, I get sidetracked sometimes. June agreed to the date as long as she could bring her girlfriend, Hilda, with her. I told her about Russell, and she said, 'I know about you and your brother.' Apparently, Russell and Hilda had been on a date a few years before, but Hilda didn't meet the mark at that point. Russell was too much of a stickler for perfect measurements. I had to do some convincing, but my brother eventually agreed. I don't think he would have if I hadn't made it so clear how much I wanted that date with June. When Friday night came, Russell saw Hilda and gave me a quick wink. Over those few years, Hilda had…developed," he said, mimicking breasts with his hands.

I laughed, "Ahh. Important assets."

"Important for Russell. They never made a difference to me," he said diplomatically, aware of my flat chest. He never complained about my body when we were alive, and whenever I asked him if he liked my miniscule breasts, he'd say, 'You're perfect. I love you just the way you are.' He was such a good politician that sometimes I even believed him. But occasionally I caught him looking in Hilda's direction when she had on a low-cut top or a bikini.

"Russell liked a full-figured girl. I like a girl with personality. And June had personality! When the four of us went out that night, I knew she was different than the other girls. I felt it in the bookstore, but when we sat down in that dark theater and she started cracking jokes about the stupid ads rolling across the screen—you know, dancing Hershey bars and Tootsie Pops—I got the feeling that all the other girls had been practice and this was the real game. She made me laugh, and I got tongue-tied again and again, which never happened to me. That night, after we dropped June and Hilda at Hilda's place, I started talking about her and I didn't let up. I told Russ about her freckles and her perfume. I told him about the long scar on her left palm—the hand I'd been holding. About how cute her chipped tooth was. I talked about the jokes, and the smarts that girl had to have to make 'em. God, she was something. One in a million," he said, shaking his head while I checked out my left palm.

The scar was there, alright, but I was sure it hadn't been until that moment. I'd forgotten about the long-jagged flap of skin that had been ripped from my palm by a rusty piece of sheet metal Eddy once used to patch one of the bedroom doors he'd broken in a drunken rampage. The cut was so deep and the metal so sharp that for a few seconds after it happened; I didn't feel a thing. It didn't even bleed. I just looked at it, like a slice of bologna hanging from my palm. The warm blood running up my arm freaked me out before the pain hit. When I showed it to my mom—she was fall-down drunk at the time—she said, "Goddammit, girl, what'd you go and do that for?" like it was a choice. Like I chose to cut the shit out of myself on Eddy's half-assed attempt at repairing the door he'd broken. Then she said, "Go get some gauze. I'll get the alcohol. You, get the hell off my carpet! We'll tape it up; you'll be fine."

The searing pain from straight rubbing alcohol being poured into a bone-deep cut made me scream, then I passed out. When I woke up, I was cold, shivering, and in shock. Momma said, "Don't you fucking puke, girl, you'll stain my carpet." Then she doused my hand with another round of rubbing alcohol. I kept it together; I didn't puke, but I screamed.

Grandma came busting through the front door a few seconds later. She had a shotgun in her hands, like some old-west hero. She must have kept her ears open for me all the time, waiting for Eddy to start beating on me again, waiting and hoping she'd catch him in the act so she could shove that shotgun down his throat. She was a tough woman, and I don't know if it was euphoria from adrenaline or delusions from the pain, but for a few seconds after she'd appeared, I'd slipped into a daydream. I'd imagined that Eddy'd been there and that, without asking questions, Grandma saw me injured and assumed it'd been his fault—which indirectly it had. I'd imagined Grandma blasting that fucker across the living room. I'd imagined Momma shouting about her cheap pink carpet as Eddy bled out.

Instead, Grandma sat the shotgun beside the front door, helped Momma wrap my hand, and took me to her house for the night. Momma must have had the blood cleaned off the linoleum and out of the sink before Eddy got home. I never heard a word about it. If he'd known, he'd have rubbed my nose in how stupid I was and how careless I was for months.

It took six weeks for my hand to heal, and I never regained complete function. My fingers just didn't have the ability to do fine tasks after that—which made working in the munitions factory during the war hard, but by then I'd mostly adapted to that subtle disability.

Running my fingers across my palm, I looked up at Wyatt. He averted his eyes, but he had to have seen the scar. Maybe he was starting to see the impossibility of all the coincidences that had been piling up since we "met." When he talked about his wife, he *had* to see the similarities in me. The more he talked about her, the more fine details he shared, the more I looked like her. He had to see, he just chose not to believe it, yet.

Before either of us could talk, with perfect timing for Wyatt to be able to deny what he'd just seen, the heavyset girl brought out drinks and two plate dinners. One with fried chicken, mashed potatoes, gravy, and green beans with little pieces of bacon in them and the other, fried tripe with the same sides.

"Thanks," I said to the girl.

She didn't even look at us. It was like we weren't even there; just a couple of ghosts lingering in between where we'd been and where we were supposed to go.

"Okay," Wyatt said, loading his fork full of fried tripe, "I told you a little about my wife. And I'm sure she'll come up in conversation more often than you'll care to hear about her. Now tell me about your missing husband. What kind of asshole disappears when his wife is sick?"

I paused for a second, a spoonful of mashed potatoes inches from my mouth. Stalling, I shoved them in and chewed. They had no taste, no temperature, nothing. It was like chewing a mouthful of thick air. I pretended to swallow, and Wyatt was still staring at me, still waiting for an answer. I said, "He was my knight in shining armor, even though he almost always wore plaid."

Then I told him the whole story of how we met in a bookstore, how we went to the movies, how he saved me from my stepfather after jumping through my window. I told him about how he dumped me in a crummy apartment and disappeared. I told him how lost I felt when he was gone.

Wyatt sat there listening, taking it all in, nodding his head, chewing his fried tripe, without a single moment of recognition on his face. He couldn't see me; all he saw was a cancer-riddled, sewer-rat of a girl—a girl slowly aging and changing right in front of his eyes.

Chapter 19

Wyatt

We left the restaurant, but Emma never even touched her fried chicken. Other than a single bite of mashed potatoes, she didn't bother with any of it. It had to be the cancer, of course. I watched June skip meals here and there when it started to spread. I watched the extra pounds fall from her body, then pounds she couldn't afford to lose slipped away, and then even more. And more. Until there was nothing left but worn-out old skin stretched over frail bones. It was a tough day for me. Burying my brother, visiting my family plot and my old home, watching Emma skip her meal was the arsenic-laced cherry on top.

I had other concerns than just Emma's eating habits, though. When I asked her about her husband, she repeated the story of how I met June—the story I told her just before we went into the restaurant—practically verbatim. I was starting to fear that the cancer had spread to her brain. I feared dementia or some other unknown or undiagnosed mental problems. I analyzed every move she made so I could tell how soon our trip back to the Trois Rivieres hospital would be necessary. She looked good, better than when I found her in her old theater, but not as good as she had when we left the hospital yesterday. She looked tired, and her skin lost some of its luster. It was amazing how fast she was changing.

We hopped a bus back toward The Prestige, the theater on Marcus Avenue, and rode in silence, side by side, intentionally avoiding one another's eyes. The city passed us by, deteriorating more and more the closer we got to our destination. It was like riding a bus through time. The buildings went from elegant, well-maintained structures with brick sidewalks and lush, blooming city parks, to middle-class homes with decently maintained asphalt roads and slightly overgrown yards; then, finally, to run-down buildings and roads paved, neglected, patched but not smoothed, neglected more, patched, and neglected again. The closer we got to Marcus Avenue, the bumpier the roads were and the more deteriorated the buildings became. When the bus let us off ten blocks from the theater, it was like we had traveled to a distant future where the people had forgotten how to trim trees, patch roads, fix leaky roofs, and paint buildings. Nothing was manicured, nothing was clean; everything was falling apart.

Walking the ten blocks from the last bus stop to the theater, I asked Emma the question I wanted to ask three or four times during our bus ride. I didn't know why it bugged me so much, but I had to know. I stopped her on the sidewalk in front of "Marcus Hardware" and asked, "Do you still love him?"

I knew it was a hard question to answer, especially in her confused, possibly demented state. She'd been abandoned by the man she thought loved her, and her life had been in a downward spiral ever since. To admit that she still loved the man who hurt her was to admit that she could still be hurt by him. An open wound, bleeding, and tender, could be cured and forgotten with the right care. But an open wound that kept being prodded would never heal. I didn't think this poor girl had ever been treated right. She'd grown up with a drunk mother and abusive stepfather. She'd been "saved" by some boyfriend who later abandoned her in a crummy apartment, which she apparently lost and became homeless, and now she was dying of cancer, but no one cared enough to help her. Her emotional wounds probably never got a chance to heal. Because of that, her ability to cope with life's constant trials had to be quite limited. The thought that a beautiful, smart young woman like this had just been tossed to the curb made me wish I could do better for her.

She stared into my eyes after I'd asked the question and finally admitted, "Yes. Yes, I still love him. More than anything else, I love him. I'd go to the ends of the earth and beyond if that's what it took to bring him back." The intensity in her jade-green eyes burned her seriousness into me. She loved this man and, for reasons unknown to me, I felt a great sense of relief knowing that.

I grabbed her hand and led her further down the sidewalk, toward the theater. I said, "We can try to find him. You've helped me through one of the hardest days of my life. I'll help you any way that I can. We can use the hallway if you know where to start. And I'll open every Goddamn door in there until we find him, if that's what you want."

"Really?" she asked.

"Yeah. Do you—" I started but stopped myself. We were still a few blocks from the theater, but I could tell, even from that distance, that something was wrong. The skyline wasn't what it should be; something was missing. There were people standing in the street around the old theater. And a dust cloud had risen into the air.

"What is it?" Emma asked when I froze.

"Our exit. I don't think it's going to work."

She looked down the street, focusing her eyes and placing her hand to her brow in a salute-style sun guard. For a second, she didn't recognize what the problem was. Then it dawned on her.

"The building collapsed?"

"It sure as hell looks that way," I said, taking a few more steps toward the theater I visited hundreds if not thousands of times in my life. The closer I got, the surer I became. Bricks, blocks and other theater rubble were spread out into the street like the war-torn streets Russell and I had fought our way through in France. Twisted bits of metal stuck out from the rubble like those makeshift barricades we'd hidden behind when we got into a firefight.

Our screen was gone. Our theater was gone. Our exit was gone.

"It's not a big deal, right? We can just go to some other theater and head home that way, right?" Emma asked.

"No," I said, standing there in mild shock.

"What do you mean, 'No?'"

How did I tell her this? How could I explain that there are only certain theaters that can be used? Screen traveling isn't like hopping on a plane or bus and going anywhere. It's…more random. Impossibly random.

The first time it went wrong, Russell and I nearly died. It was 1982. Russell and I were off the coast of Koh Tao, Thailand, enjoying a little fishing. We rented a longboat for five bucks a day. The boat was shit; it came equipped with a bail-out bucket we had to use to scoop out a few gallons of seawater every half hour. But at five bucks a day, how could we lose?

The water was crystal clear even a few hundred yards off the coast. From above, it had a strong turquoise hue. Perfect in every way. Through the turquoise water, we could see fish swimming fifteen or twenty feet below the surface. We caught Mackerel every other cast, and the Perch and Marlin were biting off and on. We probably drug in fifty pounds of Mackerel over the first few hours. Then we started tossing them back and using them as chum for the bigger fish.

Before the day was over, we each hooked a Marlin but neither of us were able to complete our transaction. Russell pulled in a six-foot sailfish—which we promptly tossed back over the edge of the longboat; the damn thing wouldn't stop flopping around and we both started to worry about its rapier bill running us through. Besides, we didn't have room in the tiny ice chest we'd been filling with Mackerel all day. It was an eight out of ten day for fishing and a ten out of ten day for the Gaumond brothers.

The next day, however, wasn't the same. We took the water taxi from Koh Tao back to the mainland intending to head home to our lovely wives—who would surely curse us for bringing in another cooler full of fish fillets. "There's only so much fish we can eat, Wy," June used to say when I'd bring in another load. Russell told me similar stories about Hilda's reaction to another successful fishing trip. They didn't understand that it was about the trip, not about the fish. Or maybe they did, and their protests were meant to encourage us to switch to catch and release fishing—which we eventually did of our own accord.

Once we got on the mainland, we toted our ice chest, fishing gear, and duffle bags from the water taxi to a real taxi. In the tiny car, packed full of fish and fish stink, we slid across rough dirt roads that were full of livestock, bicycles, and pedestrians. Our driver zig-zagged around all these obstacles better than a dirt bike racer revving his engine through the Mint 400.

It was all business as usual from our perspective. Any non-affiliated country, countries that most people referred to as "third world," had shit like that going on. Russell and I got used to it as we traveled across the globe for both work and pleasure. Fishing around the world was one of our favorite activities, but the older Russell got, the less he liked going to these tiny islands off the coasts of underdeveloped countries, hence our multiple trips to the Florida Keys. But when we were younger, we'd watched some of these countries develop over the course of twenty or thirty years and fell in love with them as we watched. We saw dirt roads become cobblestone. Cobblestone become brick. Brick become asphalt. We saw towns without electricity in the seventies install streetlights, traffic lights, and constant flow electric in the eighties. Everything changes…

Except me…

About a block from the theater we'd used to enter Thailand, the driver hit the brakes, sliding the car to a halt. The rustic theater had been built to seat a hundred people, which by my estimate was roughly a tenth of the population of the village. It never ceased to amaze me how many small towns, towns that hardly had safe drinking water or electricity, found the means to build theaters. This theater was nothing special: a bamboo building with rows of benches made from rough sawn palm trees, a canvas screen about half the size of the smallest screens in the U.S., and a single, third-hand projector that jammed every third or fourth reel. The dirt floor was packed to almost cement smoothness, and the refreshments included coconut water and crispy, dried shrimp.

The first time I found the tiny theater in Thailand, I walked right through the screen in the middle of a showing of Howard Hughes' *Jet Pilot* starring John Wayne. It was a full house despite the fact that the film was being shown in English and no one watching spoke a word of it. The Thai liked movies from the U.S. and didn't seem to care that they couldn't understand the words. I guess it's like us watching operas written in Italian or French and not knowing what's being said but still getting the gist of the story. When I walked in that first time, no one even seemed to notice I was there. I walked around the town and found a beach with water so clear I could see through ten feet of it on a half-moon night. It was perfect.

The second time, I brought Russell, and we thought we timed it so we could enter the theater after hours. But it seemed there were no after-hours in that little theater. At two in the morning, when we came through the screen, a few dozen Thai people were sitting there on the rough-sawn palm benches watching the same movie. Again, no one said a word. It was like they were immune to odd things happening. A couple of white guys loaded with fishing gear, an ice chest, and knapsacks walk through the movie screen, sure, no big deal—movies are magic, right?

When we got back two days later, though, I realized how big of a deal they took our arrival to be. The theater had been burned to the ground. Nothing remained. Not even the projector had been salvaged before the moviegoers started the fire. They must have started it right when we left, too, because the rubble had all but stopped smoldering by the time we returned.

When the taxi driver dropped Russell and me in town, angry villagers threw stones at us and ran us out. We dropped everything but our knapsacks, which had the important stuff—cameras, snacks, water, money, clothes, knives, and passports.

At the docks, we learned that the next closest theater was on Koh Samui, a three-hour boat ride away. We didn't bring enough money for airline tickets, so it was the only possible way home. Russell paid the fees, and we hopped on the boat. Considering the reception we got in town, I felt lucky that the captain, who spoke broken English, allowed us on.

On Koh Samui, the theater was a bit nicer, but still quite rudimentary. Rather than palm benches, they'd used metal fold-up chairs, and the projector spun smoothly, but there was still only one, so they had to pause between reels. We waited until the theater emptied after a showing of *Hell Town*—those Thai must have loved John Wayne—then snuck through.

At that point, I still hadn't done much research on the hallway of doors' organization. I figured that if a door seventy doors to the left of my St. Louis door led to Chumphon, Thailand, then the next closest theater would be in the same area of the hallway. But it wasn't so. I don't know why I made that assumption considering that my door to Lhasa, Tibet was right across from my door to Cairns, Australia.

Of course, there was the other possibility… Russell's notion that the doors and the hallway itself were in my head—a metaphysical passage created by me that operated under my own accord; a mentally created gateway that could do anything I imagined… That would explain why, on summer days when the heat was nearly hot enough to burst thermometers—like those in cartoons where Mickey or Donald were really sick—I'd always find a new door to someplace cool. And on blustery winter days, I'd find tropical beaches. Anything *seemed* possible.

That day, though, we walked through the screen on Koh Samui, into a section in the hallway of doors I'd never seen before. The lighting was different; the paint was chipping from the walls, and the carpet squished under our feet like it had been flooded.

"Where are we?" Russell asked me frantically when he saw that none of the doors were labeled. "I don't know," I replied. "We came to Thailand from the left hallway. Logic says we should go right, right?" I asked him. He shrugged, and we both turned to look to our left. Down that hallway, the lights were burnt out, the flooding had molded the walls, and there was a sharp curve just down the way. We looked at one another, then looked both ways down the hallway, and without a spoken word we turned right and walked.

We walked for an hour before we started to get concerned. We walked for another hour before we decided to have a snack and clean out the unnecessary items from our packs. We sludged through wet carpet and mildewed halls for another hour before we decided to start trying doors randomly, hoping just to get back to the U.S. where we could catch a train or bus to a town we knew.

The first door we tried led us through a screen, or part of a screen that was in shambles. They hadn't been using the screen to show movies for a long time. I think they'd been using it as a backdrop for another kind of show. There was animal crap on the stage and the fliers scattered across the floor said, "Puta y Burro."

I'd done a story about the kind of brutality women in those shows faced a few months before and I knew we weren't where we wanted to be.

The next door we entered was across the hall. Nothing sinister was going on in that theater, but it was cold in there. Colder weather than I'd been in in years. We peaked out the exit door at the back of the theater and found a frozen wasteland that stretched out eternally in every direction. There were just a few military barracks style buildings and a snow-covered runway. That was it, nothing else but frozen, permafrost-covered ground and wind.

"Where the hell are we?" Russell'd asked.

"No idea," I responded. I'd only come across one other theater as isolated. I'd been assigned an interview at Pituffik Space Base in Greenland. The base had a few bunkers, some barracks, and a crummy little movie theater that only had two films. After the interview, I understood that deployment to Pituffik meant you'd screwed the pooch on a previous assignment. The first lieutenant I was interviewing had admittedly messed up by leaking Secret information to a journalist he was sleeping with. She published; he got a one-way trip to Greenland after being busted from Major. My interview was for *Soldier of Fortune Magazine*. It was supposed to be about the dangers of "pillow talk" and military procedures. It never even got published, but I got paid anyway.

Russell and I left the frozen wasteland behind and, in the hallway of doors, tried to find our way back home. We were in and out of a dozen other doors before we wound up in an elaborate, gilded theater with half the building missing. With a series of violent, shell-shock flashbacks, I froze. It wasn't long, but it was long enough for Russell to follow me through the door and close it behind him. Bombs were crashing around us, and gunshots ricocheted off the walls. I turned back to the screen, reaching for the silken silver fabric. I placed my hand on the screen, hoping to energize it for a quick exit. Before I could, though, frantic shouting drew my attention. It wasn't the "Get off my lawn" or "Move your car, I'm trying to park" kind of shouting. This shouting was so intense that it begged, no, forced me to find where the noise was coming from.

From the language and the color of the shouters, I guessed we were in Lebanon—there was quite a conflict going on over there at the time and, by some twist of fate, Russell and I stepped right into the middle of it. My Leica was in my hands, though I didn't remember getting it out of my bag. I took a few shots, maybe just to feel normal in an abnormal situation.

The shouting started again. A man in the same riddled building as Russell and I was waving his arms frantically. It was clear that I was supposed to be looking up at something. Most of the buildings were in shambles, but across the street, in a tower that somehow still stood, a rebel with an RPG aimed directly at the theater spotted us. I moved forward, stole a photo of that rebel, then froze again.

The Lebanese hadn't been yelling at us to hide so we didn't get shot. They were yelling at us to hide so that RPG toting, Hezbollah Jihadists didn't see us and target their cover. But once we were spotted, he did target us. I dragged Russell off the stage, and the two of us ran as fast as we could. When the RPG hit, rubble and concussion splashed down on our backs like a Northern Pacific wave crashing on a rocky beach.

Much of the debris was small and inconsequential, but a few full-sized cinder blocks landed on us, breaking Russell's ribs and my left fibula. Shrapnel had embedded itself in my chest. In agony, I looked back over my shoulder to see the damage. What had remained of the theater was gone, pulverized to dust. Again, we were stranded with no idea where another theater was, but instead of a tropical paradise; we were in the middle of hell.

I kept shooting photos, trying to make the most of the nightmare in which we'd awoken. I'd been in Lebanon before and made good money shooting the riots that preceded the war. Maybe a follow-up would pay off.

Still on the ground, covered in rubble, white with dust and sand, Russell's breathing was ragged and labored; I feared a punctured lung. I shot a photo of him, blood trickling from his mouth, a single tear cutting a path through the dirt on his cheek. That photo later found a home on the cover of *Life*—despite his and Hilda's objections. I *had* to sell it, though; it was some of my best work.

My leg was broken, and I had bits of steel sticking out of my upper chest, but I could walk. Russell's weight, which rested on my shoulder as we stumbled through fragmented roads and piles of brick, made the broken bone in my calf feel like a knife digging itself deeper with every step. Whenever I got into situations like that, I refused to let myself think of the worst-case scenario—that we might not get out. I kept trudging along, Russell breathing raggedly in my ear, which pushed me to move faster, despite my own pain.

A million thoughts were running through my head as we stumbled through the remains of shopping centers, homes, libraries, hospitals, and who knew what else. It was the first time since The Big One that I was injured in battle. It wasn't life-threatening, but we were totally alone. Americans claimed no part in that war, and even if I could find friendlies, I doubted they'd help us.

I worried about my June—I always worried about my June—but I worried what life would be like for her if we didn't come home. And I worried about Hilda. With Jeffrey already a casualty of war, she'd be all alone if Russell died. And I worried about Wyatt Jr.; what would he do without a father?

With all that nonsense running around my head like a marathoner on a tiny track, I froze up again. We were in the middle of some desolate and destroyed street in Lebanon; I was sure of it now, and, like so many boys I saw in Vietnam, I was locked up in panic. Russell clung to my shoulder, breathing raggedly, mumbling, "We gotta go, Wy. We gotta get outta here before the Germans catch up." In his state of pain and confusion, he'd apparently flashed back to one of our narrow escapes from the Nazis. It was like we were reliving the same battles, just from different wars.

The moment that Russell and I were both mentally breaking, a tall Jewish man walked out of the rubble in front of us. A look of confidence was accompanied by a small grin on his bearded face.

It was Hersh—Hershel Solomon—the man I saved in a death camp in Germany thirty-some years before. The man who occasionally got me special "journalistic" assignments from the U.S. government was also the man who got me into Lebanon the first time. He was the one who got me an interview with Arafat when he based his operations in Tunisia. Hersh always sent me front-page stuff, big-paying stuff. Of course, I had to do some things for him in return. Things above and beyond the normal duties of a photojournalist. Most importantly, though, Hersh was one of the three men in the world I trusted, Russell and myself being the other two—and sometimes I didn't trust myself.

"Welcome to ze party, boys," he said, with his heavy German accent.

"A Goddamn Kraut!" Russell shouted, wheezing through his blood-filled lung, his hand looking for a non-existent sidearm.

"Relax. It's Hersh," I told my brother.

"The only friend you two are going to find on zis street. You Protestant pricks just going to stand zere, waiting to be blown up? Come on," Hersh said. At that point, Russell and Hersh had only met once before, the day I was dragged out of the Stalag. They talked on the phone often, though. When I was in the field, they'd relay messages for me, set up meetings, get me stories. When I was looking for an assignment, Hersh had a habit of showing up randomly. Usually with some tit for tat bullshit. But sometimes he'd show up just to have coffee.

We followed Hersh back the way he came, through a maze of shelled-out buildings, crumbling streets, and the stink of war. They never talk about that in movies. No one brings up the smell. From rotting food to rotting corpses, from sulfur traces of gunfire to groups of men, stale and stinking from weeks without a bath or shower, it all reeked.

On D-Day, the smell of shit, piss, blood, open, festering bowels, and days old corpses was enough to make half the soldiers puke before we ever stepped from the Higgins boats onto the beach. If they weren't puking from the smell, they were puking from the waves. If they weren't puking from the waves, it was the nerves. If none of that had them tossing their breakfasts, it was the sight of other men, hard men, men they'd been to battle with, puking their Goddamn guts out, that made them lose it. I didn't think I'd ever get the smell of puke and blood out of my nose. The smell of battle is something that no words can describe, so no one tries to describe it. Like a bad migraine, *headache* doesn't even come close.

Hersh led us into a storm sewer and sat us down on the cool, wet brick. Dark shadows covered his eyes, but his strong, bearded chin stood out in a ray of sunlight that snuck through the cracks in the sewer grate. I snapped a picture as he said, "Gents, you've come in on the wrong day."

"You have no idea. How do we get out of here? How do we get him to a hospital?"

"We're not technically part of zis war. So, you won't have much governmental help here. But we've got friends. You know me, Wyatt, always a favor available for a friend, especially one I owe my life to. By ze way, check your chest," he said, nodding his head toward me. "You may need a hospital, too."

I looked down and saw the two-inch by four-inch piece of shrapnel sticking out of my pec. I pulled the metal out with a grunt and said, as calmly as possible, "Help us get out of here and we're even." A constant drip from the ceiling was running down my back; water cooling my roasting skin.

"We're in Saadnayel, and the closest safe spot for Americans is probably Beirut. I'll get a car and meet you topside in ten minutes."

"Wait," Russell said quietly, "if the Americans aren't here, what are *you* doing here?"

"I said we're not *technically* part of zis war. You zink anyzing happens wizout Red, White, and Blue hands being in ze mix?"

"Go," I said.

When he left, Russell was quick to say, "He's a Kraut, and you still trust him?"

"He's a *Jew* from Germany turned U.S. spy before the war even broke out. I trust him with my life."

"Good enough," Russell grumbled, but I could tell he wasn't happy with it.

After an hour and a half-long car ride through rubble-filled streets with potholes big enough to swallow a car, we arrived at another movie palace. A helicopter sat in front of it, and a dozen soldiers on every side of the theater stood guard. The outside of the building was immaculate despite it being surrounded by wreckage. From the look of the theater, I guessed it had been built way before the moving picture had been invented and was later remodeled when the big boom of movies started to take hold of the world.

Hersh walked us through the door of the Beirut theater. The screen and chairs had been removed, and there were tables and cubicles set up everywhere. It wasn't a movie theater anymore; it was a war room. I recognized some of the Americans in the room, but there was top brass from all over the world working diligently over maps and documents.

"What the hell is this?" I asked.

Hersh pointed to the back corner of the theater, where an emergency medical bay had been set up. "Go get cleaned up. We'll get you home."

"Can we just go to another theater?" Emma said, shaking my shoulder as she dumped a handful of pills into her palm.

I shook my head and tried to refocus.

St. Louis…right. Beirut was a long time ago. We're in St. Louis, I reminded myself.

I looked back at the pile of rubble that had once been The Prestige theater. I knew we were stuck, and that I'd have to be a lot choosier when we got back into the hallway of doors. I couldn't take this sickly girl through some Godforsaken war zone.

* * *

Emma

The old me, the living version who was terrified her entire life, would have been fucking distraught. She wouldn't have said anything directly, but Wyatt would have known how upset she was. Inside, her heart would have been racing, and her brain would have been going a million miles a minute. And while that version of me had vanished long ago, even as a ghost— or whatever I was—I recognized what an impossibly frustrating situation we were in. Wyatt's delusions had incorporated very real memories from our life into his ceremony of self-pity. And if he couldn't control his delusions, we'd never get back to our theater in Ely. We could end up chasing figments of his imagination all day while he tried to figure out what was happening in his twisted mind.

As we stood there, staring at the old theater that'd just collapsed, I knew why he was confused. Shortly before we moved from St. Louis to Ely, on a sunny fall afternoon, Wyatt suggested, "Let's go for a drive, see the old neighborhood one last time before we get out of this hellhole for good." Though we lived in St. Louis most of our lives, we didn't venture from our neighborhood—especially not as far as Marcus Avenue—often. We'd heard stories and knew it wasn't like it was when we were young. But Wyatt was never timid when it came to getting into the action and, despite the horrors we'd heard about our old neighborhood, he wanted to see it.

With the top down on our old Corvette, Wyatt drove to Marcus Avenue, past the places he'd taken me on dates during our brief, pre-wedding courtship. The corner store—that building where the two men were barbecuing in a 50-gallon oil drum— used to sell those little wax soda bottles filled with colored sugar water, candy cigarettes, candy buttons, bubblegum cigars and chocolate. We'd buy candy there and sneak it into the theater. I felt like a real rebel.

Gawking at the broken-down pile of rubble that used to be The Prestige theater, I realized it was the same as it had been the day we'd taken that last drive. The day we took that last tour of Wyatt's old neighborhood, I saw a change in him. I think it broke Wyatt's heart to see that the house he grew up in lay in ruin.

We didn't bother driving through my old neighborhood, Mill Creek Valley. It was gone long before we'd moved from St. Louis to Ely. The city had torn the entire neighborhood down in the late 50s to make way for a fucking highway and some massive "urban renewal" projects. I think they leveled it just because nearly all my neighbors were black and as the Civil Rights Era was starting to gain steam, there didn't seem to be a better way of putting black families in their place than tearing down their neighborhoods, churches, schools, and community centers to build highways so rich white people could commute from the suburbs to the heart of the city.

My family was long gone before they razed The Valley. Eddy died from a heart attack in the late 40s, and my mom had sold her house and moved into a small apartment in East St. Louis. After Eddy died and Mom moved away, I never once went back to The Valley. I'd erased it from my life just as city planners erased it from the map.

Wyatt was standing there beside me, just gawking at the collapsed theater, mouth open, frozen in one of his stress memories. I knew I wasn't supposed to; I knew that the doctors warned against it, but I wasn't the timid girl I'd once been. I wasn't the cancerous old woman I'd once been. I had nothing left to fear, so I shook him and asked, "Can't we just go to some other theater?" It was logical to me, especially since I was fully aware of the fact that we were ghosts and no longer needed to worry about the laws of physics. He, on the other hand, was still confused about our state of being. He still thought he was some kind of un-aging superhuman, and I was some random person he'd saved.

"I've done that once, travel blindly in reverse. It's not a good idea," he said. "We'll have to figure something else out." I didn't know what he meant by "I've done that once," but I was sure he'd created something interesting in his mind.

What other traps has his subconscious set up for us?

Without waiting on him any longer, I took to the street. I had no idea where I was going, but I knew we had to move. When we were alive, I saw him get lost in his stress memories for extended periods of time. He'd freeze in some awkward position, with a confused look on his face, and stare off into nothingness. Shaking him awake was a mistake I only made once in life. But I didn't have any fear of Wyatt anymore—I didn't have any fear of anything. What does a ghost have to fear? The only thing that bothered me were the age spots that'd spread up my hand, to my wrist, and were slowly making their way up my arm, like some kind of timer flashing the last few minutes before the game was over.

I needed to get his mind rolling toward the truth, not stagnant in one of his delusions. "Come on, Wyatt," I said, heading down the street. He followed as I marched, our feet clanking against the rubbly sidewalk. Just like the last time we drove down those crumbling streets, I could tell it hurt Wyatt to see what he'd once loved reduced to waste and rubble. It wasn't crime, drugs, or a broken-down theater that bothered him. It was aging. Seeing a building he used to go to every Friday night collapse had been a clear reminder of our mortality, the only thing that scared him.

As we marched down Marcus Avenue in our ethereal bodies, I imagined the sound of our footsteps on the pavement. A rhythmic sound. A clickity clack of heavy boots on dry concrete. I focused on that sound, and I could hear it, like we were really there, marching through that sunny spring weather.

I closed my eyes, and I was home. Not Ely home, but *home* home—Arundel Place home—because, more than anywhere else in the world, that's where I wanted to be. I wanted to go back, to see myself interacting with a younger Wyatt, Russell, Hilda, and the kids. But as we marched down Marcus Avenue, I saw myself inside our old house, alone, drinking a large glass of red wine, listening to *Bonanza* reruns as Ben Cartwright said stuff like, "We can't ignore the rest of the world. We're the only stabilizing influence in the country." Horse hooves clickety-clacked on the show, and our feet mimicked that sound as we walked, and as we walked, I thought back to our past, and as I thought, I was there. I was somehow both on the street, walking with Wyatt, and on our sofa—a brown leather monstrosity that felt cold all the time—

drinking a glass of cheap merlot. A sink full of dishes soaked in hot, bubbly water, waiting to be scrubbed, rinsed, dried, and put away. But when Wyatt wasn't there, I'd finish my wine before I'd finish the dishes.

Somewhere inside, sometimes deep inside, that younger version of me knew I still loved him, but his extended absences were not making my heart grow fonder. Some days, as I drank alone, I wondered why I didn't just leave. I could disappear, find a job, take care of myself for once in my fucking life. But then I'd drink more, and I'd lose my nerve, and I'd wash the dishes and pass out on the couch.

That night, I slugged down the rest of my gas station merlot and poured another glass before deciding I'd do something other than stare at the TV. Drunk and high on pills, I grabbed one of Wyatt's spare cameras, a roll of film, and started taking pictures. It was a whim. I had no reason to think I'd be any good, but I didn't care. I just wanted to *do* something…anything. With Wyatt Jr. being off to college, I was bored out of my mind, drinking too much, starting to really enjoy the pills, and I felt myself growing angrier, lonelier. For the next few months, when Wyatt was gone, I took rolls and rolls of photos. I piled the spent rolls, undeveloped, in my underwear drawer. When I finally worked up the courage to have Russell show me how to process them, I was surprised by my results. Not amazing, like some of Wyatt's work, but not half bad.

Russell said, "You've really got the magic eye. I was wondering where all the film was going."

"You won't tell Wyatt I've been shooting?"

"No, honey, this is good for you," he'd said.

A few years after I started working in the darkroom with Russell, practicing, I finally got the nerve to frame one of my photos and hang it in the house. It was a candid of a small child looking out the window of a city bus; the awe-inspiring skyline,

Gateway Arch and all, reflected in the bus's window. I used to stare at that photo and drink. I'd wonder who she was and drink. I'd think of my own childhood and drink. I'd think of the daughter I always wanted but never got, and I'd drink.

Wyatt asked where I got the photo a few weeks after I hung it. "I bought it at a craft fair," I'd said. I don't know why I lied. But it seemed like something he'd be against, like I was working, which was something men did, and women shouldn't have to do. "It's…really good," he replied, and then we never talked about it again. I never hung another photo of mine. The walls were lined with his pictures, and mine stayed either in a box in the basement or, if I was really fond of one, I'd put a print of it in the photo album in my underwear drawer. All but that one photo lived in the dark. That one stayed on our walls for the rest of our lives.

Like I was watching a movie, I watched myself sitting on the couch the night I decided to pick up a camera. I saw the sadness in my eyes. The loneliness. And I heard the clickety-clacking of horse feet on the TV. And I remembered our footsteps on the sidewalk; remembered we were supposed to be walking in St. Louis. And suddenly, I was back on Marcus Avenue. Slowly marching with our ghostly footsteps making an inaudible ruckus in my head.

Wyatt shook my shoulder and said, "Emma…are you okay? I said your name three times, and you didn't respond."

"Fine, Wy. Just thinking…" I said.

Interesting…I thought. I'd never escaped into my memories like Wyatt had. And apparently, I'd done just that as I'd been walking down the sidewalk. It made me wonder what else I could do that I'd never done before.

What else can a ghost imagine into reality?

Chapter 20

Wyatt

After I pulled her out of her dazed dream, Emma's pace quickened with every step. There's something instinctual in our nature that tells us that when we're uncomfortable, we need to move faster. Even if we don't know where we're going, or why we're uncomfortable, we need to move. I'd felt that many times throughout my career. And no matter how many times I'd wanted to run, I found that it was usually better to stay still; assess the situation before moving. Emma was a victim of that human fallacy as her hiking boots clashed against the rubble-covered sidewalk. Her feet were moving twice as fast as they had been at any point in the last few hours. And while I could have kept up with her, I slowed down, forcing her to slow down; hoping that a slower pace would take her out of fight-or-flight mode. I didn't trust her cancerous lungs to keep up with her rapid pace and wasn't ready for another loss just yet.

She looked over her shoulder at me from about ten paces ahead. Her glance was one of urgency, like a woman with a full bladder trying to make her way through the horde huddled in front of a bar's only working toilet.

A few agonizing blocks later, we were back at the bus stop we'd come from. A dirty-grey city bus covered with ads for cologne and a local news channel stopped in front of us, billowing black smoke like a tire fire. We walked past the driver and sat down on the first seat closest to the accordion section. Emma still seemed nervous, but her breathing slowed when the bus started moving. I didn't want to tell her that I didn't know the next steps of our journey home. I didn't want to tell her it was possible our evening would get worse before it got better. So, I didn't say anything.

I started to put my arm around her, hoping that it would soothe her. It was an intimate gesture, I know; I just hoped she knew I wasn't trying to be flirtatious. She was just a kid, and I didn't want to come off as an old pervert. She must have known my intentions were respectable, though, because she snuggled deep into me, her body relaxing.

As the bus stopped, started, stopped, started its way through the city, Emma said, "You said that you traveled in reverse before and that you didn't want to do it again. Why not?"

"Last time we traveled in reverse, me and Russell ended up lost in Lebanon during their civil war. See this scar?" I said, pulling my shirt down just low enough to show the upper part of my pec. It was a jagged thing that zigged back and forth like a lightning bolt. Amongst the multitude of scars on my chest, it stood out as the only one with an irregular shape. The rest were straight lines and the nearly perfect circles of cigarette burns.

"I had a two-inch by four-inch piece of bent steel buried in my chest and a broken leg. Compared to Russell, my injury was nothing, but it still hurt like hell. It's just too dangerous to go in reverse. Like you said, the hallway of doors is basically infinite. And there's no order to it; a screen in a theater just a few blocks from here could land us right where we want to be, or it could land us miles away, in some unknown part of the hallway. Last time I tried that, the floors were wet and the whole area smelled like mold. Who knows how long that hallway is. We could march for days and not find a door that leads us home."

I went on telling Emma about Lebanon. As the bus continued to start and stop its way through the city, I told her about everything that happened on that trip. About the time I ended the story, the bus stopped again, and a man I thought I knew, a man I'd just been telling Emma about, stepped on.

* * *

Emma

When the bus stopped, a man with 1960's, hippy hair and a full beard climbed aboard. Imagine the typical white Jesus you'd see in an off off off Broadway rendition of *Jesus Christ Superstar.* For a split second, I thought it was Russell; he'd dressed like that back in the 60s and 70s. He thought he was the 5th member of the Beatles—he even played a few of their songs on the guitar. Wyatt Jr. was trying to teach him, but Russ didn't have the musical talent Jr. had. But that didn't stop Russell from singing along with *Sgt. Peppers,* and *The White Album* while he printed photos and edited articles.

At first glance, the man who'd boarded the bus could have been mistaken for Russell, but, in a way, he could also have been mistaken for Hersh, Wyatt's lifelong friend. Hersh was a tall blond man that could have passed for one of Hitler's Aryans, but he outed himself as a Jew by wearing his Peyot long and proud. In reality, though, the man on the bus was neither Russell nor Hersh, just a man who shared a slight resemblance to both.

But Wyatt's face had fallen, and he was staring at the man who'd just boarded. Staring, and I could tell his mind was racing.

When the man sat down across from Wyatt, he sat a backpack, a patch-covered remnant of the counterculture movement, onto the floor, beside his wide bellbottoms. He opened it and pulled out a copy of *The New York Times.* The front page said: "Nixon Discharges Cox For Defiance; Abolishes Watergate Task Force; Richardson And Ruckelshaus Out."

What the fuck? That paper, like the man's outfit and hair, had to be 40 years out of date, and the man was reading it like it was new…

But when I looked around the bus, I realized it wasn't just the man, but the bus was also outdated. It wasn't the bus we'd boarded. It was half the size, the accordion section had disappeared, the seats were padded and covered in thick, heavy, brown vinyl. The windows were open, and the spring breeze was filtering out the faint smell of exhaust that seemed to be leaking through the floor.

As Wyatt stared at the man reading the New York Times across from us, I looked out the window and saw that the cars had gotten older, too. They matched the bus.

"Where are we going, Wyatt?" I asked. But he didn't answer; he just stared at the Russell look-alike and the newspaper; lost in another stress memory. Lost in his past. Lost in this world between what was and what will be.

But I saw the truth.

This wasn't a bus to another part of the city, not in any conventional way. This was a bus rolling through our memories. Literally rolling through our memories like a reel change in the theater—except when the changeover took place, the projectionist put on the wrong reel. We'd flipped further into the past and as we rode the bus through St. Louis, we rode through parts of the life we'd lived. We passed the school Wyatt Jr. went to from kindergarten to fifth grade.

We passed our first apartment.

We passed the shoe factory Wyatt worked in after the war.

We passed the factory I'd worked in during the war.

We passed restaurants and shopping centers that had long since closed and been replaced by skyscrapers, parking garages, hotels.

The bus stopped and started, and men and women got on and off, but the Russell look-alike sat across from Wyatt, reading his newspaper without ever changing the page. He was like a statue, frozen in time while Wyatt tried to figure out if he really was his brother.

While Wyatt watched that man, I watched the rest of the passengers and saw that as black folks boarded, they started sitting nearer to the back of the bus. And then, a few blocks later, there was a sign hanging from the ceiling that said: "Colored Section".

All the while, Wyatt sat there, staring at the man with the newspaper. The man's hair had grown shorter, more tightly cropped to his head. His beard had disappeared, and his bell bottoms had been replaced by brown trousers. His backpack was now a leather briefcase.

The front page of his *New York Times* had changed from that bit about Nixon to a headline that read, "Germans Attack Poles on 4 Fronts".

I'd been wondering how Wyatt got to this point, how he'd become so confused that he didn't recognize me even as I told him details of our life, showed him my chipped tooth and scarred palm, but at that moment it became quite clear that after I'd died Wyatt must have slipped down that same horrible road his father and brother followed on their way out.

As Wyatt sat there staring at this man, as his appearance and newspaper changed, I understood that Wyatt was confused because his mind had fragmented into a thousand tiny pieces rather than one network of information. Fragments that didn't fit together anymore, like puzzle pieces with their tabs broken away. Everything he'd told me and everything we'd experienced was a memory or a regret or a moment he'd wished played out differently. None of this was how we'd lived it, but rather how he'd remembered it or how he'd wished it'd happened. On a subconscious level, I think he was aware of this. He was the one who told me that every time we remember something, we're remembering the last time we thought of that thing, not when it actually happened.

I wondered, *When a man with Alzheimer's dies, is his soul as confused as his body had been?* And as I asked myself that question, I understood that had to be the case. Wyatt applied meaning where he could because that's what he'd been doing the last years of his life, just like his father and brother before him. If he saw the man across from him on the bus and thought he was Russell, he believed the man to be Russell. If he wished he'd scattered his brother's ashes, he believed he'd scattered his brother's ashes. If he thought he could walk through movie screens and travel to the places he'd been, he could walk through movie screens and travel to the places he'd been. This wasn't reality; we were stuck in the inner workings of a confused man's mind.

We'd boarded a bus, and in Wyatt's mind, we were on every bus he'd ridden through our city, through our lives, simultaneously. We were in the 1930s, the 40s, 50s, 60s, 70s, 80s, and 90s all at once. If I blinked, that man's newspaper might read "Men Walk On Moon" or "Hitler's Last Failure".

There was no telling how long we'd sit on that bus, sifting through Wyatt's memories as he tried to make sense of his world again. And other than the age spots starting to pepper my shoulders and neck, I was in no rush. In fact, I was interested to see what it was like inside that head of his.

I leaned back in my chair and watched time pass forward and backward, through this part of our life and that part of our life. I watched the man across from Wyatt change a dozen times, and I watched headlines from his newspaper change as black folks sat in the front, with the white folks, and then in the back, in the segregated section. I put my arm around Wyatt and let him ruminate as we rolled down block after block, year after year, headline after headline.

Chapter 21

Wyatt

At first glance, when he got on the bus, I thought it was my brother. He'd gone through this odd, hippy stage when Jeffrey was away at war. That ended after his son came back in an aluminum box. But I realized pretty quickly it wasn't my brother, but Hersh who'd boarded the bus. He'd just let his sidelocks grow longer than usual.

Since The Big One, it wasn't unlike Hersh to show up randomly under odd circumstances. When we first met, in prison camp, Hersh was stick thin, barely mobile, his skin was laced with infected burns and cuts. Nazis had been using him as a waiter, busboy, and ashtray for weeks. They did that. They'd take a Jewish American POW, seclude him from the rest of us, make him work until he dropped. Then, once he was down, they'd beat him to death or simply toss him into a mass grave, where he'd freeze or die of starvation.

Hersh had been a German citizen, up until the time Hitler got elected. When he saw the direction his country was going, he moved to the U.S., joined the Army, and fought against his countrymen. He was the worst kind of scum, according to the Nazis: traitorous, Jewish scum.

When I was detained in the Stalag, Hersh was no one to me, just another imprisoned soldier. Another victim of a brutal war.

But after watching what the Nazis did to him, it was clear that he was the target of bullies.

I hate bullies.

When Hersh's body finally gave up and he collapsed to the ground, I taunted the Nazis. I shouted the few German curses I'd learned at them until they took their attention away from Hersh and focused on me. And they focused on me… Focused so hard it nearly killed me. But despite the torture and mental anguish that accompanied the choice, I never regretted standing up for him. It's one of the few things I've never regretted. No matter the cost, how can you feel bad about saving a man's life?

The last time I saw my old friend was during the first few months of George H. W. Bush's Gulf War. My wife was too ill to be left alone for long—it was her first round of cancer—so I didn't take the months-long assignments I had in Korea, Vietnam, Afghanistan (during the Soviet occupation), and the multitude of skirmishes in the middle east. Instead, I took short assignments from secondary newspapers like the *Miami Herald* and *The Indianapolis Star*. My heyday of publishing was over. I was well into my seventies by that time, and my name and notoriety had run their course. I still loved to get out there and shoot the action, though. So, I took whatever assignments I could get—Hersh set up most of them.

I was on my second day of a five-day assignment, shooting and interviewing soldiers who'd seen their friends fall in the line of duty—a cheesy repeated story told and retold in every war I'd been through. *"How did it feel to watch your friend fall? How do you feel about America's stance on insert issue here? Do you think your friend's sacrifice is worth it?"* And so on… I did that assignment a dozen times before and at least half of those times for more reputable news outlets, but the world had lost interest in foreign wars.

On my last assignment, Hersh set up my interviews in an old building, just outside the safe zone in Iraq. I was interviewing a young man about losing his best friend in a firefight with Hussein's Republican Guard, and Hersh was there, doing whatever it was that he did for the U.S. government, when a shitstorm rained down on us. No planes buzzed overhead; no warning shots told us we were under attack. There was just a kid, a toddler really, walking in the street with a knapsack almost as big as he was; then the world shook and the front of the building we were in collapsed. Another poor, starving child blown to pieces in the middle of a rich man's war and all I could think was, *Why the hell didn't I get a picture of that kid before his parents or whoever hit the button?*

I crawled deeper into the building as a rain of bullets poured down on us. Time passed. People on both sides died, including the young man I'd been interviewing. Hunkered down in the back of that adobe building, I swore to myself that if I got home to my June, I'd never leave her again. I pictured her in the hospital, hooked up to IVs, her hair falling out, her skin turning yellow and pale. I shouldn't have left her, and I knew it, but I needed…I never knew what to call it…escape, an adrenaline rush…something that I was ashamed to need. I loved my June, but whenever I stayed home for too long, I got that itch. The itch a man full of regret gets when his mind has too much time to consider all the things he's done wrong.

About the time I found myself swearing to some God I wasn't sure I believed in that I'd stay home by my wife's side if I got out of there, Hersh poked me in the back with a long metal rod. I let out a gruff, grunting scream, thinking I'd been shot. When I turned, realizing I hadn't, I saw Hersh, under a metal grate in the floor. He was waist deep in a storm sewer that ran under the building and had a big stupid grin on his face. "I zought zat one got you," he said, still smiling.

"You bastard!" I whisper-shouted.

He lifted the grate, helped me crawl down, and walked me through the sewers again, extracting me from what could have been my end. When we were topside, fifteen blocks away, he gave me one last assignment. It was an easy one. "Go home and sit wiz your sick wife." I did, and other than visiting Russell in St. Louis, I never left her side again. And I never saw my friend again. I didn't even know he was still alive until he showed up on that bus.

The driver stopped the bus; new passengers got on, old passengers got off, and the bus started rolling again, turning a corner. I started to wonder how long Hersh had been following me. It had always been his style to just show up, but why now? I thought about my brother's obituary, printed in the *St. Louis Post Dispatch*, like the nursing home did for every other man who died there. I assumed Hersh must have seen it, known I'd be in the city, and tracked me down. He was a spy, after all. Spies did those kinds of things.

But oddly, my lifelong friend never said a word. He just sat there reading his newspaper, ignoring us. As a spy, he'd always been subtle about things, and I started looking around at the other passengers, wondering if one of them might have been the reason Hersh was staying silent. If one of them was following us for some unknown reason.

I tried to stay calm, tried to keep my head on my shoulder. If I was being followed by some ancient foe's hitman, getting paranoid wasn't going to help. Hersh was there, and until he told me why he'd shown up, I needed to keep myself and Emma calm—not that that was an issue. She sat beside me on the bus, her hands in her lap, silently watching the city pass us by.

Other than the first time Hersh randomly reappeared in my life, it never shocked me when he showed up. The first time I saw him after we were liberated from the Stalag, I'll admit I didn't recognize him. He just walked up to me and said, "Wyatt, how about a cup of coffee?"

I was intimidated not just by his German accent, but by the fact that he outweighed me by forty pounds—all muscle—and had a coldness in his eyes that emanated strength and confidence. I guess after living through what he did, nothing in the world could really bother him. Every war-torn region he worked, every job he'd been assigned was just another day, another dollar, another regime to overthrow, another dictator to unseat.

Even as she lay dying, I never told June about the professional relationship I had with Hersh—never told her what kind of work he got me. I definitely never told her that most of my work over the last decade of my career came directly from my old friend. And I never told her about the connection between my chest scars and Hersh. To her, he was just a friend from the war. Nothing more, nothing less. I should have told her all of it, but she was stressed enough without worrying that I was doing more in the field than photojournalism.

When I started working with Hersh, I was still in vogue enough to get big jobs from *Life*, *Time*, *Newsweek*, and *The New York Times*. I had a reputation, and every piece of shit I wrote or shot, Russell sold. By then he was more of an agent than a partner. I'd send him work, and he'd touch it up and sell the piece to three or four different news outlets around the world. He was excellent at his job. Without him, I'd have been a flop. I called as often as possible from wherever in the world I was, and he'd give details about requests from different editors.

In 1972, Russell told me to meet a potential client in Lak Sao, Laos. I didn't quaver. But when I sat down in the café where I was supposed to meet my client, and a huge white man with long sidelocks and an all-white suit asked if I wanted a cup of coffee, I nearly shit myself—I thought he'd died in that POW camp. Hell, he was more than half dead when I finally gathered the courage to object to the way those Nazi assholes were treating him. The liberators that saved me showed up soon after I stuck my neck out for Hersh. I don't know for sure how long it was, I'd passed out when my Nazi captors started peeling the skin off my left pec, right above the nipple, and I was still unconscious, laying in a pile of mostly dead soldiers, when the Americans busted through the fences. Along with me, they saved four dozen Americans—including Hersh.

After we met in Laos, and he gave me that first assignment, I fed Hersh info, and he fed me the occasional job. I gave him rumors from my contacts in East and West Germany, all over the Middle East, Asia, and so on. As an operating journalist, I heard a lot of rumors that couldn't be sold, but that Hersh was happy to get. When he needed me for something specific, he'd find me, hand me a brown envelope with directions here or there, for an interview or a photo shoot with this monster or that one, or to place a bug in so and so's house during our interview. I never killed for him, and I never pretended to be anything but a photojournalist. My reputation was real, and my cover was real. I just worked a bit deeper on some stories than the typical journalist would. In truth, though, a lot of us did those kinds of things back then.

I was a small fish on the scale of things, but I loved feeling like I mattered—like I was still relevant. I wasn't really a spy, not like Hersh, but I was a sort of operative, and I was proud of that. I did my part to help the Red, White, and Blue maintain the balance of power.

The bus stopped again, and Hersh stood, glanced at me, then got off the bus. He never said a word. I'd known him for over 60 years, and he never said a word. Maybe it was because I wasn't alone.

* * *

Emma

When the Russell look-alike got off the bus, Wyatt stared at him, watched him step off and walk away as the bus drove on. He didn't say a word about the setting of this nightmare changing over and over as we rode the bus through a dozen different eras of our lives. I didn't say anything about it either. I honestly doubted he even recognized that anything was different. Instead, I asked, "Where are we going, Wyatt?"

"What?"

"How are we getting back to your theater?" I asked. This was his world, his mental game. My role in this whole afterlife mission was to get Wyatt to move on to the next plane. To lead him through his confusion, so he could see that his life was over, and that it was time to go on to…whatever was across that final border. But in order to do that, I had to show him something he couldn't deny.

Since The Prestige theater had collapsed and we had no money, no car, no train tickets to get to Ely, I hoped the situation itself would leave Wyatt in a mental paradox so huge even he couldn't deny something odd was going on.

I hoped he'd see that traveling through movie screens is impossible.

And while I looked for the right questions to ask, the buttons to push, I noticed that the city bus we'd been riding through our past had taken another turn, one I didn't expect, couldn't explain.

The driver announced, "End of the line," as the bus came to a final stop in the neighborhood I'd grown up in: Mill Creek Valley.

"Let's go," Wyatt said.

"Where?"

"It's the end of the line, so we have to get off. I recognize the neighborhood; there's another bus stop a few blocks from here."

Of course he recognized the neighborhood, he'd brought me home after dates. He'd snuck into my bedroom when Eddy was away on a hunting trip. He'd beat the hell out of my stepfather and saved me from my own childhood prison.

I glared at him for a second, then I stood and got in the queue to get off the bus.

"You sure about this?" I asked.

"Let's go, kid. It'll be fine," he said.

"But where are we going to go? How are we going to get back to Ely?"

"I have an idea about another theater near here. It's worth a shot," he said.

"I thought you didn't like traveling in reverse?" I asked as I took the last step toward the bus's stairs.

"But if I know where the theater goes, it's okay. And I think I know where this one will go. I think you will too, once you see it. Come on, it'll be fine. Trust me," he said, holding his hand out to me, urging me off the bus the same way he'd urged me into that theater in Canada. The same way he'd urged me to go on that last tour of our old neighborhood before we'd moved to Ely.

I took his hand but said, "I know this neighborhood. I'll lead the way."

He squeezed my hand and walked beside me, down a street that had been demolished in the 1950s. If a paradox was what his mind needed to see the truth, a paradox was what I'd give him.

The last time I was "home," I was just a scared child. It was the night Wyatt beat the hell out of my stepfather while Eddy was strangling me on my bed. Momma stood behind him, hardly saying anything while Eddy choked the life out of me. It was a night that haunted me the rest of my life.

When I'd returned to this plane, I'd relived that moment—in a way. I'd blended memories from my life in with the tragedy of my childhood, creating this skewed, but very real reenactment of horror. I don't know why I had to relive that first, before I had any memory, any understanding of what was happening to me, but I think it had something to do with establishing trust in Wyatt. He'd saved me when I was young, and he saved me again when I'd returned from the other side. The only major difference was the setting. Eddy never strangled me in the theater, but I had to appear to Wyatt in a theater, or else he never would have found me because everything in his mind was connected, loosely, to the theaters he'd visited in his life. So, I suppose it made an odd kind of sense.

It also gave me a taste of the confusion Wyatt had to be feeling. He wasn't waking up to reality as I had; he'd been confused for too long in the last stages of his life. His slow, dementia-riddled death stole away his ability to understand that his life was over. And as a result, he never moved on. He just thought he was still living his life, going on about his business. I imagine he's relived Russell's death over and over again. I imagine that he's been repeating this self-flagellating trip through all the theaters—all the memories—on some kind of repeat, like a dusty record playing the same part of the same song repeatedly.

Sometimes the things we deal with on a daily basis become normalized in our minds. As a kid, I tried to tell myself that it was normal to be afraid at home. Wyatt had spent a lifetime convincing himself that the things he saw in war, the photos he took, were normal. It's how we cope. Even when it seems like something no one would ever get used to, we eventually accept the horrors of our lives and move on. Being terrified shaped a lot of my youth, and after Wyatt and I were married, every time Wyatt went on assignment, I felt that lonely, vulnerable terror again. It wasn't until I got prescribed benzos and found out how much stronger they became with alcohol that I was able to relax, raise my son in peace, pick up a hobby, enjoy life a little bit. I lived most of my youth in terror and most of my adulthood in a stupor, but that stupor got me through. And now, in the afterlife, as we walked directly toward the origin of my fear, more than anything else, I was awash with the helplessness I felt as a child in that house.

I think helplessness must be the worst feeling in the world. When your child is dying of AIDS and you're helplessly watching him slip away, or when you've been diagnosed with terminal cancer for the second time, and you know your choices are suffer through painful treatments or accept that you're about to die, the helplessness becomes overwhelming. The sick feeling in your gut as you accept you can do nothing to change any of this makes you want to puke.

"Doing okay?" Wyatt asked, real concern in his voice. He wasn't cut out for the kind of emotional journey we were on—he was a physical being. But he was trying.

"No," I said, feeling more and more out of touch with reality the closer we got to my childhood home. I remembered what it was like to walk home from school down those crumbling streets. I remembered being afraid, but not of the poor neighborhood, of the monster in my own home. I remembered that as a child, the world seemed very small.

The closer we got to my old home, the darker the sky became, and the thicker the air turned. It was like some divine warning shouting: STAY AWAY! DANGER! STAY AWAY! I pushed those warnings aside and marched down Aurora Street. The once-paved street that circled the homes had turned back to gravel. Every few feet, potholes of murky grey water were being filled by the mist that fogged the air. The grey mid-afternoon sky turned my old home into a 1940s horror film, black and white, with an air of violence tipping an unbalanced scale toward something disastrous.

Walking through *The Valley* was like walking through a nightmare. Long grass and other junk, like rusting pedal tractors and old bicycles, had been stockpiled, turning each yard into a landfill. Green mold grew all over the sides of the homes and abandoned cars. At least every other driveway had a car that had been dead so long small trees were growing through them. Porches were falling off the sides of the homes. Bags of garbage had been left out long enough for dogs to sift through and abandon. Some of the asphalt-sided homes had blue or green tarps tied across the rooflines, like band-aids being thrown on wounds that needed stitches. It was a wasteland—way worse than I remembered. But of course, if Wyatt could create the hallway of doors in his purgatory, I supposed I could create this scene to mimic how I felt about my old home. Even the graying sky could have been a reflection of my mood.

I took in a great big breath, let it out into the rainy, humid air, turned a sharp right into the driveway of an inconspicuous wood-sided bungalow numbered 34. "Home," I grumbled to Wyatt as I stepped onto the collapsing porch. It was the home I grew up in, only more rundown, poorer. I walked by it a dozen times when Wyatt was at war. The munitions factory I worked in was just a few blocks away, and after a day of work, after I felt a bit proud, a bit bold, I'd walk by and hope I had the guts to confront my mother. I even stopped once or twice with the intention of going in, so I could tell Momma off. But I never had the guts to knock. I was always afraid Eddy might be there, drinking a beer and listening to old records in his stained and holey underwear.

Now, though, without any hesitation, I lifted my hand and knocked on the storm door. When my fingers wrapped around the thin metal, a loose, bone-chilling rattle filled the grey silence.

"Hold on!" a gruff, cigarette-damaged voice hollered from inside.

From the voice, I expected the woman on the other side of the door to be ancient. She wasn't. I didn't remember Momma being beautiful. Maybe it was because I wanted so badly to hate her. But every part of her appearance, as she filled the doorway, was undeniably beautiful. Curled blond hair hung loosely at her shoulders—bouncy, thick, like Veronica Lake in *I Wanted Wings*. Green eyes, my eyes, stood out against her smooth alabaster skin. She looked to be in her mid-twenties; not old enough for the cigarettes to do any damage. In ten years, she'd look thirty years older, but right now her body was winning.

I got the sense that, in the world in-between, we subconsciously chose how we wanted to look. Wyatt was young, handsome, tan, always with a clean-shaven face, and until I saw the darkness behind his eyes, he'd been free of the scars that peppered his chest. I was younger, had perky—even if small— boobs and a flat belly—no baby stretch marks yet. My skin was clear of zits but hadn't started to wrinkle. The only thing I didn't like about my look was those pesky liver spots that started on my hands and were now all over my chest and arms.

Momma must have been proudest of her look in her mid-twenties—just before she met Eddy—and I could see why. She was beautiful—the exact opposite of the neighborhood she was living in.

"Hi, Momma," I said, feeling more regret for completely cutting her off than I expected. I didn't even know if I was here or if I was imagining all of this, but I had a clear pang of guilt seeing her there.

"Emma June," Momma said, looking me up and down. "I heard you skipped town."

"Not town, just the neighborhood. I came back to see you."

"You came to see me?" Momma asked, then took a heavy drag from her cigarette. She turned her head and blew the smoke away from me, then picked a piece of loose tobacco off her tongue.

"Yeah. We need to talk," I said, moving closer to the door.

"And you brought him?" Momma said, pointing at Wyatt.

"He's a friend, Momma."

"More than a friend," she said, taking another heavy drag on her cigarette.

"I just came to talk," I said harshly. "If you don't want to talk to me, I don't fucking care. I'm happy to leave."

"Well, ain't you turned tough?" Momma said, stepping back and opening the door wider. She looked me up and down as I entered my childhood home. It hadn't changed since I'd been there last. The old home came equipped with dark wood paneling, low ceilings, thin louvered windows, turquoise curtains and matching appliances. A washing machine rattled loudly from the covered back porch. Momma completed the picture of white trash horror with a staticky radio blaring a bad recording of Stuart Hamblen's "Big Rock Candy Mountain" at an ear-piercing volume.

"Have a seat. I'll get some sweet tea," she said, turning down the radio and heading into the kitchen.

I sat down on the blanket-covered couch. Wyatt wiped a few cookie crumbs off the spot next to mine, where Momma must have been having her lunch, and sat down, too.

"You grew up here?" he asked, as the paradox he'd just been smacked with started taking hold. How could that woman be my mother, be living in this house, if I wasn't his wife?

"Yeah. You're going to love Momma's tea. It's like liquid sugar," I whispered.

"Tea?"

"Yeah, Wy. Tea. You know, the drink," I said, but he looked confused. *Good!*

I was enjoying the confused look on Wyatt's face; it was the first time he lacked confidence since I'd been back. But I was also excited about Momma's tea, hoping I'd be able to taste it. It was the only thing we had plenty of when I was a kid, and it was usually the only sweet thing in the house. She made it by the gallon, and

Eddy and I drank it so fast she could hardly keep up. Funny, that drink was one of the best memories of my young life.

It was just a drink, but I could still smell the faint bitterness of the tea bags steeping and then the sweetness as she poured the hot water over way too much sugar.

When Momma came back into the living room, she had three mismatched cups of tea so dark it looked like coffee. She handed me a pink aluminum cup. She handed Wyatt a faux crystal champagne flute and took a coffee mug with her to an armchair—also covered in blankets—on the other side of the room. She kicked one calloused foot onto the coffee table and asked, "You here to ask for some money? You know I ain't got none, so don't even bother." She seemed almost proud to be able to shut me out so quickly, remorselessly.

"We're not here for money. I just had some questions about...Eddy," I said, pointing at a picture that hung from the wall beside her.

She looked over her shoulder at the photo, hesitated, then turned her steely gaze on me. "Yep, that's your stepfather, Eddy," she said, being a smart ass like she always was. "What about him?"

"What do you have to say about him?" I asked. I could feel Wyatt tense up beside me as he set his tea on the coffee table and leaned toward the picture on the wall.

"You know the basics. I can repeat 'em fer him," she said, pointing at Wyatt. I nodded. "We met, got married. After a few years, he got fat, drunk, and angry—well, he was always angry, but when he got fat and couldn't get it up anymore, he got angrier. Every year he got fatter, drunker, and angrier. When you took off with that boy," she said, pointing at Wyatt, who looked shocked by her gesture, "he got even drunker and angrier until one day he got so drunk and angry that his heart blew up in his chest. His death was the first good day of my life."

"That's horseshit," Wyatt burst out. He stood and moved half a step closer to Momma—which was significant in that tiny house—pointed at the photo on the wall, and shouted, "You can't lie about this. I know that man. I beat the hell out of that man when he tried to strangle my wife to death! You can't tell me that the man in that picture is this girl's stepfather!" he shouted, pointing at me.

Momma glared at Wyatt for a second; a slight change came over her. I want to say it was remorse, but I'm pretty sure it was shame. "That's him. That's my shitty, abusive, dead husband. This girl's my daughter. And you're the man who saved her from us. I'd know you anywhere. I memorized your face and pictured it when I got the notion to pray. You did fer her what I never could'a."

Wyatt sat back down, his face flushed, his eyes blinking rapidly like he was going to have a seizure. He grabbed his chest, and his breathing changed.

"You okay, Wyatt?" I asked calmly, grabbing his hand and wondering if this was it; if this was the thing that would push him over the edge of delusion and into reality.

But instead of continuing his heart-pounding reaction to what Momma was saying, he simply nodded and squeezed my hand.

I held Wyatt's hand and glared at my mother. "Go on, keep talking."

"Well, when I met Eddy, he was some kind'a bum. Homeless, moving from town to town, working a bit here and a bit there. We didn't fall in love; I never loved that fucker. No one did. But after your daddy died, I was struggling to keep a roof over your head. Eddy got himself a job at the service station, fixin' cars, pulling in decent enough wages, and…he moved in. You and me had been on our own since your daddy died in the train yard, you remember that story, right?"

"I remember. He got crushed between two boxcars."

"That's right. Poor bastard. Eddy was nothing like your father. Your daddy was a good man, and Eddy was a Goddamn pig. I knew it. But it was the Depression; people was poor. People was starving. I hated it, but I needed a man; fer you as much as fer me. I needed someone to pay the bills, no matter what it costed me. You was just a little kid, and we was about to be homeless. He came 'round just about the time I'd'a done anything fer some security."

"This is my wife's story, Emma. Not yours! I don't know what you two are playing at here, but I don't like it," Wyatt said angrily, squeezing my hand. That look, that terrified, confused look filled his eyes. This moment, this revelation, was shoving a mirror in front of his face and forcing him to look. And he was scared.

Good!

"I'm not playing at anything, Wyatt. Didn't you hear what Momma called me when I walked in? Did that ring any bells? How about this house? Seem familiar in any way? How about that first bedroom down the hall?"

Wyatt stared at me, his mouth slightly open, eyes narrow, questioning, angry. One hand was on his chest, the other still gripping my hand tightly.

Momma kept talking like she hadn't heard anything. Like she was talking to herself as much as she was to the two of us. "He may'a done some horrible things to you and the same things to me, but he also kept us from starvin'. And back then that was about the best a woman like me could hope fer."

I closed my eyes and remembered the beatings she took when I was young. Before he started beating me, he'd focused all his aggression on her. And when she finally broke, he needed to break someone else so he could feel strong. I was that someone else.

Tears rolled down my cheeks, and I understood, perhaps for the first time in my existence, that Momma was a victim, too. Yes, she should have done more to protect me, but she was scared; she'd suffered. Maybe she'd suffered worse than me.

I understood fear. I understood suffering, and part of me wanted to forgive Momma for her weakness—that was something I never thought I'd feel.

Chapter 22

Wyatt

With "Momma" working her guilt game on Emma, and Emma working whatever game on me, I couldn't sit still. I couldn't take anymore Goddamn bullshit. I got up and paced around the twelve-foot-wide room. Most pictures on the walls were of a sloven looking man that I hated—June's stepfather, Eddy. There were pictures of my June on the wall, too.

What the hell is happening, I thought as I looked from picture to picture, then around the room, then back to the pictures. The photo closest to Emma's mom was a perfect black and white rendition of June's stepfather before I scarred up his face. Right beside it, one of June in a light-colored dress with lighter colored polka dots. The dress I'd seen her in the first time I met her.

Impossible!

But now that I looked at it, the house did look a hell of a lot like June's momma's house. Emma's momma herself looked a hell of a lot like June's momma, only younger, prettier.

My June died. I knew that. I'll remember that pain for the rest of my life. June's momma died. Eddy died. I knew that, but...

They kept talking while I stared at the few pictures of my wife's family that sat, collecting dust, in cheap frames. In every one of the photos, Eddy's shirt was either off, halfway off, or stained, filthy. He almost always had a beer in his hands and never smiled. He never seemed to shave clean, but never grew a beard, either. In every picture, June and her mom looked miserable.

And it made me mad! The thought of him hitting June with his sloppy hands or choking her until her breathing stopped made me mad!

I kept looking around the house while Emma and her momma talked *at* one another in hushed, angry tones. As I paced, Momma kept glaring over her shoulder at me as if I was going to steal something. The house itself wasn't dirty, but it wasn't clean either. Momma was a half-assed housekeeper. She swept and did the dishes. Hell, she probably even wiped off the table and knife-gouged countertops every few days, but there was a thick layer of dust on all the sit-arounds. The tops of the fridge and stove looked like they hadn't been touched in years—a greasy film covered them.

She didn't have a TV, just an old record player on a small side table with beer bottle condensation rings marring the top. I could picture Eddy setting a cold beer on the table, rubbing his fat belly, a sloppy sandwich dropping condiments onto his already stained shirt as he looked through the shelf of records above the player. There weren't many, and most of them were country and western style, like Jimmy Rodgers or McKinney's Cotton Pickers.

I walked down the hallway, looked at the first bedroom on the left; the pain in my chest grew stronger. I had a sudden flash of a younger me pummeling an older, sloppy, drunk man. My fists turned to hamburger as the man's face turned from flesh and bone to offal discards from the butcher's shop. It was like a bad dream.

None of it's real. She isn't my wife. Her stepfather was the man from the theater, not the man that tormented my June. She isn't June! My mind screamed, but every impulse in my mind was misfiring.

Everything I thought I understood was wrong. What I felt when I looked into that room, the first room on the left— anger, hate, violence—couldn't be mistaken. I knew where I was, but it didn't make one Goddamn bit of sense.

I marched back into the living room and blurted, "Why did you let that man hurt your daughter?"

"That ain't your business. You did your part, and I'm thankful. Just keep your nose out'a the rest?"

"I'm here for Emma, here to get her questions answered, here to help her get past this shit; something you can't say for yourself," I said as I looked at Emma to see if my outburst was upsetting her. Her face was neither mad nor sad, but somehow content. Somehow more June than Emma.

"Momma, why *did* you let him hurt me? Money isn't a good enough reason," Emma said calmly. Once she asked it, it seemed everyone in the room knew that was the question we went there to get answered. Never mind my confusion about the man in the picture, the man in the theater, my wife, or Momma. All that was irrelevant. Nothing mattered other than Emma getting an answer to that question. She'd waited long enough.

"Why?" Emma repeated. "I was a little girl. I didn't know how to behave in a way that wouldn't earn a beating. And… I was waiting for you to save me. I was waiting for YOU!"

"How could I help? He beat me half to death. Sometimes before his pecker gave out, he'd beat me half unconscious and then he'd rape me. That man all but destroyed me. When he started hitting you…"

"What? He stopped beating, raping, and destroying you?"

"No. No honey, he never stopped…except the raping, and he only stopped that 'cause his dick stopped working. But then the beating got worse. He never stopped. And he never would'a stopped. Eventually, he'd'a kilt me, so I kilt him before he could do me in," Momma said.

Emma's mouth dropped, but Momma went on: "That and because of what he did to you. I just wish I did it sooner. I kept telling myself I had time. That if I waited a little longer, I'd find the strength and the right moment; the right way to get us outta there. I should'a kilt him the first time he hit you. I should'a kilt him the second, and the third. And I definitely should'a done it the first time I heard you struggling to get away from his nasty, explorin' hands. But I was terrified. I wanted him dead. I wanted you safe, but I didn't know what to do."

"I was your daughter, and you let that man," Emma pointed at the picture, but Momma looked away; Emma added, "Look at the fucking picture!" Momma did. "You let that man do to me the same things he was doing to you. The things that nearly 'destroyed' you. How could you? Even being terrified of him, how could you let it happen?"

"I thought he'd kill us both," Momma said.

"Bullshit! Even a weak woman will rise up to protect her child," I shouted. But neither of the women looked at me. It was like I wasn't there.

"I'm sorry, Emma June. I'm so sorry. I hate myself fer it. I hate myself fer what I let happen. I was a bad mother, and I hate myself fer it," Momma said, blubbering.

"I'm sorry you didn't save me. I'm sorry you picked a monster to take care of your child. I'm sorry that you didn't kill him before he beat and groped the innocence right out of me. I spent my life high on pills and booze, hiding from the memory of that monster. Wyatt saved me once. He left me often, but I loved him my whole life because he saved me just once. If you only tried, Momma. If you only tried, I…I'd have loved you forever, too."

"Oh God, Emma June…please…please…pl…"

I watched Emma take a deep breath in. She held it. She held it for so long I thought she'd pass out. Her face should have turned blue or red or purple, something, but she never let it out. She never shed a tear; she never sniffled. She just held her breath while she watched her mom beg her for forgiveness.

When she finally let out that breath, her face changed. She aged ten years in the space of one breath. I rubbed my eyes, trying to unsee what I'd just seen. I looked at Momma and was shocked to see that she'd aged, too.

"It's not real," I told myself. "I'm just tired. It's been a stressful week."

But when I looked at them again, it was obvious that a decade had disappeared in the blink of an eye. Both of the women were older and more tired. The cigarettes had done their work on Emma's mom…casting wrinkles around her mouth and bags around her eyes.

"It's not real!" I growled, "It's not real!"

Out of nowhere, the corpse of a fat man in a stained wife-beater—the shirt's nickname finally making sense—appeared on the floor. Momma was on the floor now, too. She was much older, crying and cussing over the body of that dead, fat man. An empty syringe lay on the floor beside Eddy.

Emma leaned forward, placed her hand on her mom's shoulder, and asked, "What was in the syringe?"

Momma looked up at me, then at Emma, then back to me. Like me, she was confused, lost. Didn't know how the hell she'd gotten to the floor. Didn't know how the hell Eddy's corpse showed up in that room. She asked, "What?"

"The syringe, Momma? On the floor? What did you do?"

"It was air. Just air. That's all. That bastard got drunk, passed out… I was cleaning up a hospital room after a girl died, and I heard docs talking 'bout her having an illegal abortion. The doc said, 'The air got into her.' He said it 'Went to her heart.' I figured if it worked for her… I stole the biggest shot I could. Stole one out'a the trash so if the air didn't work maybe he'd get some disease. I dumped a heavy dose of Seconal into his beer. When he passed out, I pumped a shot of air into his veins. Then another. And about halfway through that second shot, he flopped 'round a bit, then stopped moving. His eyes and his mouth lay open, and his chest lay still. I waited 'til the next mornin' to call the cops. The coroner took one look at Eddy and said, 'heart attack.'"

"You really killed him?" I asked.

"It was too late…my Emma June was gone. Gone forever with you. I knew she walked by the house some days, wanting to see me, but never got the courage. I saw her out there, pacing in front of the house, in her blue jumpsuit. I hoped that once Eddy died, she'd come back to me. But you never did," she said, turning her eyes to Emma.

I looked at Emma, too, who was crying and wiping tears on a handkerchief I'd gotten my wife in Japan during the Korean War.

"I didn't know," Emma said between sobs, "I didn't know you did that."

"I didn't want you to. You went through enough. When you sent him to Eddy's funeral," Momma said, pointing at me, "I knew I waited too long. I knew it before, but I really knew it when you didn't show up. I thought you'd at least want to spit on his grave."

"Momma," Emma said, reaching her arms out to her mother. They stood and wrapped their arms around one another and, almost as soon as they embraced, Momma and the corpse on the floor faded away. In seconds, they were gone. Just gone.

Poof, like a Goddamn Houdini act.

Everything came into sharp, Kodachrome, focus.

Emma wasn't just "Emma," some girl I found in a theater; she was Emma June. My Emma June. She hated that name; she called it "hillbilly," so I called her June because her stepfather called her "Em," and I didn't want to remind her of that man.

How could I have been so Goddamn blind?

Did she know who I was?

Why didn't she tell me?

At that moment, though, none of it worried me. The impossible scene that had just taken place didn't worry me. What worried me was that my mind had failed to make some basic connection. My mind had failed like my brother's and father's minds. My mind had failed and couldn't be trusted any longer.

* * *

Emma June

"Momma," I mumbled, tears rolling down my face. But she was gone. "Moved on" was the phrase that kept running through my head, and I knew that phrase fit what happened to her. She just needed to tell me what she'd done. She'd been waiting since she died for me to set her free. A moment of my time and her sentence to this purgatory, this in-between, was over.

And suddenly, I couldn't think of anything except my grandma at Piggly Wiggly when I'd first returned to this plane. Was that subtle statement, that she'd "always done right by me," all she'd needed to move on?

Who else was lingering, waiting for me to save them?

Wyatt stood behind me, watching me sob, but not daring to touch me. Even as uncontrollable sobs rolled from my mouth, I wondered how close he was to seeing the truth. It was almost time. He was almost there. We were getting close. I could feel it. I could feel his change.

"Wyatt?" I asked, turning to him.

"Yeah," he said, nervous, confused.

"Did you see what just happened to my mother?"

"Yeah."

"What do you make of it?" I asked. It was an old phrase of ours, a phrase Wyatt and I found ourselves asking one another often in the first few years of Wyatt Jr's life. Like: "Did you see what just came out of that kid?" "Yeah, what do you make of it?" Neither of us ever had an answer because the things that go through young parents' minds are too terrifying to say out loud.

"I don't have a clue what to make of it," he said tentatively while kneeling beside me and putting his arms around me. "Is this okay?"

I looked up at him, grinned, then dropped my head onto his shoulder, and squeezed him. Being wrapped in his arms, in his protective grip made me feel at home, at peace. I let out a sigh I didn't know I'd been holding in and felt the warmth of him— warmth that I knew shouldn't have been there.

"How long have you known?" he asked.

"That I'm your wife? For a while now. I've been trying to get you to realize it without telling you. I doubted you'd believe me if I told you. I kept bugging you to tell me about your wife because I thought telling me all those stories would help you realize. I thought you'd see."

"You're right, I probably wouldn't have believed you. The coincidences have been adding up… I thought…the cancer… At the end, June was confused. I thought cancer had you confused, too," he said, pushing me away and holding me at arm's length rather than right next to him.

He looked directly into my eyes and called me what he'd called me when we were alive. "June, tell me what's happening?"

"I don't think I can tell you that either. I think you have to figure it out for yourself—just like you had to learn about me for yourself."

"Learn what? What the hell is going on? Your mom just disappeared! But only after you both aged ten years right in front of my eyes, and the corpse of your stepfather appeared and then disappeared. There's no way to explain this other than…it's…it's…a dream. Right? I'm dreaming? I imagined it all."

I put my hands on his hands. They were coarse, rough; like they had been in our old age. I didn't want to be in that house anymore; I was tired of the reminders of my past. Maybe I understood my mom a little more. And I'd helped her move on, but that didn't mean I wanted any more reminders of the first seventeen years of my life.

I was ready to be home. It had been a long day. Long, painful, but productive.

I imagined us back in Ely—but it was more than imagination. I saw us there. I saw myself cooking dinner over our stove and Wyatt just coming back in from his afternoon walk. I saw us as we were in our old age, when we were happiest.

I told Wyatt, "Close your eyes, old man."

He did, and I closed mine, and in my mind, I saw us in our home—or, rather, the theater Wyatt had created that looked like our homes.

And when we opened our eyes, we were there.

Chapter 23

Wyatt

I woke the next morning unsure if I dreamed it all or if Emma, the girl I found in the theater, really was my June. Hearing my wife's familiar little snores, while she slept beside me in our king-sized bed, I had no doubt. How she was there was another question; one I didn't dare try to answer.

Instead of ruminating on that unanswerable question, I tossed on some threadbare sweats and headed for the trail. It was a crisp morning, but it was later in the day than I usually ran. I crossed the paths of a dozen people walking and jogging the trail before I was halfway through; before I started to feel…off. It started as my mind raced back to the things I saw the night before. June, her mother, her stepfather, the aging, the disappearing. Impossible things.

How did we even get home? What did we do after we got home? We were there, at June's old house, then I woke up this morning…

A few miles into the run, that "off" feeling turned on me, becoming a mixture of fear, panic, and anger all at once.

What the hell is happening?

I saw June's face, as she aged. I saw her eyes turn cloudy and the wrinkles creep in around them. And her mother… And Eddy's body.

I wondered if my father's disease had caught up to me. Dementia. My father had it, my brother had it, and with the confusion I was feeling maybe I had it, too.

But hallucinations aren't part of dementia, are they?

As I jogged, feet slipping in the muddy earth, my heart raced. Not the normal accelerated heartbeat of a jogger, but the racing I usually only felt from exceedingly high doses of caffeine. I kept running but my heart got more and more uneven with every step. My left arm tingled, and I had to squeeze and shake it to try and bring the life back. My heart was off, my mind was off, and my soul felt thin.

Worn.

It all started with June. When I found her in that theater… Until then everything had been fine, normal. All this had something to do with my wife's…ghost.

I cut my run short and, in a rush to get home, headed through the woods, making my own trail from the lake back to the theater. Focusing all my energy on my feet and almost none on keeping my upper body safe from the whip slap of maple saplings and low branches, I was bombarded by punishing lashes. They hurt just enough to take my mind off the pain in my chest. When I hit the sidewalk on the edge of town I pushed my heart to its limit. Feeling like it would explode, I grabbed my chest and pushed myself a little further.

My pace had slowed to that of a snail, and I almost dropped to my knees—the pain in my chest…

Inexplicably, I thought of Paradise Garden, of Russell's room there. Of the cold tile floor. And of Nurse Hope.

When I ran through the open front door, into the theater, my breath was ragged and hot, my head was pounding, I was nauseous and had a rush of cold sweats.

"June?" I shouted, trying to catch my breath.

"Wyatt?"

"My chest," I said, falling to the ground just outside the kitchen.

* * *

Emma June

I moved Wyatt to the bed, covered him with a quilt I made back in the 60s—a quilt our Great Dane, Lucy, destroyed in the 80s—then thought about our situation. We were just a few steps away from getting out of this world in between, and we needed to hurry. The timer was ticking away; the age spots had spread to my chest, my face… My hair was greying, crows' feet had turned into deep creases around my eyes, and my tits were sagging.

I sat in one of the recliners—mid theater, where Wyatt and I always sat when we watched a movie—and I thought. And as I thought, I realized I wasn't playing with a full deck. Wyatt outlived me by a decade. If I wanted him to move on, I needed to know what happened after I'd died. And because I wanted it, needed it, and because in this world in between anything you want can be manifested, I instantly knew. I knew it all.

In 2002, Wyatt had his first heart attack. He was 78 years old. It was the day I died. When his heart was stable again, and his body healthy, he started running again, started doing what he called his "Jack LaLanne fitness regimen." He and Russell started that stupid routine when they were younger, trying to stay fit as their bodies aged. Those slow, shuffle-footed runs around Ely and modified push-ups might have bought him a few more months. But just a few.

By the time we took off for our final vacation, the Alzheimer's had already dug its fucking teeth into Wyatt. I was just too sick and too preoccupied to do anything about it. Before we went on our little road trip, the one I never returned from, the disease had crept in slowly: he'd misplace his keys, miss a reel change on the projector, forget where he parked the car, forget how to get to our house in Ely… I played it all off as "age" and nothing more. But deep down, I knew what it was.

I remembered the first time we went to visit Wyatt's father in Paradise Garden. And the last time. No one in my family lived long enough to be moved into a home like that, so until Wyatt's dad got placed there, I'd only heard stories about nursing homes. I really didn't understand what age and that disease did to people. But by the end of Wyatt's father's life, I did. I saw it, and I saw how it crushed everyone around him. Rather than engage with his family like he always had—even when he didn't know who he was engaging with—at the end, he sat in his room, lights out, staring at nothing.

I could hardly think of a worse punishment than forgetting everyone you loved. Well, I could…seventeen years with Eddy was enough to make me wish I could forget parts of my life. But Wyatt's father forgot all of it. His wife, his kids, his grandkids. He forgot everything he'd ever done or felt, or thought. As he sat there, his eyes open, glancing between his visitors, I thought I understood the hell he must have been in. He was powerless, just a shell of the man he'd once been. And seeing that once hardheaded and caring man broken down to a husk sitting in a dark room crushed me, too.

I was eternally grateful I didn't live long enough to see Wyatt going through that. But knowing that's how he went, that's how he spent the last few years of his life, stung. But it could have been worse; at least he had Russell…

After I died, and Wyatt sold the house in Ely, he boxed up all our things, stacked them in the corner of the "living room" in the theater and started sleeping there. I think he just didn't want to let the old building go. I think he felt more comfortable there than in our empty home. But when he forgot to pay the bills and the power went out and the water was shut off and he'd wake up nights, freezing and scared, then he'd go for a run to warm up. Then he'd get lost, mixing memories of St. Louis and Ely and every other small town and big city he'd visited. The Ely police eventually got tired of taking him back to the theater. They told him he either had to live with family or move into a home.

The next week, he checked himself into Paradise Garden and shared a room with his brother.

While he and Russell's minds were deteriorating in the nursing home, he'd still get up in the middle of the night, and dive into his exercise routine. He'd do his pushups and sit-ups, then he'd jog right out the front door. Somewhere between the nursing home and our house on Arundel, he'd get lost. Most of the time, the St. Louis city cops would pick him up and bring him back. Sometimes the Paradise Garden staff would catch him and walk him back home. Twice he made it all the way to our old home and, thinking he'd "locked himself out," he'd go in through a basement window, climb up the stairs and start shouting at the new owners.

The new homeowners were very understanding, but that's not to say that when an old man shouts, "Get out of my Goddamn house!" in the middle of the night, it didn't scare the hell out of them. Eventually, after a slew of complaints, Paradise Garden put a monitor on Wyatt so that if he got near the doors, they would alert the staff, and they could stop him from running out into the night.

Wyatt and Russell shared their second-floor suite in Paradise Garden for the last few years of their lives. No visitors, no excursions out of the home. And without mental stimulation, the disease stole what was left of their minds.

Russell finally succumbed to age on a sunny spring morning. Wyatt's heart took him just a few hours later. They came into the world together and went out together. Russell was Wyatt's one true love on this planet—the only person he couldn't live without. They were everything to one another.

The nurses loved the Gaumond brothers because when their minds were lucid, they'd tell stories of their adventures together. They'd talk about traveling, they'd talk about assignments that led them down rivers through ancient jungles, and they'd talk about important people they met. They'd talk about the good things, but never about the wars. Their fragile minds finally let their most painful memories slide, and all they had left was each other and a bulletin board full of pictures.

When Wyatt died, they said it was shock, from seeing his brother pass. Like fools, the nursing home staff took him to the hospital to be with Russell when they pulled the plug. They thought Wyatt had the wherewithal to understand because he was so good at faking awareness, lucidity, clear-headedness. By the time he got back to the nursing home, his heart was already pushing its threshold. By the time they got him back to his room, his age-weakened blood vessels simply burst. He collapsed to the ground and died before the nurse—a pretty young woman named Hope—could make it across the room. She gathered him up in her arms and actually shed a tear as his soul escaped his body.

Memories are powerful things. They kept Wyatt and Russell connected through one of the most mentally debilitating diseases the world has ever known. And now that I knew all the parts of his life that I'd missed, I understood that I simply needed the right pieces of evidence, the pieces that would spark the right memories, to remind him what had happened. I needed to prove he couldn't walk through movie screens and that he never distributed his brother's ashes; that everything he thought was real was an illusion.

But how the fuck do you convince a man he's been dead for a decade? Even after he accepts that he's seeing ghosts…

I dug through the boxes in the corner of the living room. The boxes that gave me chills when I'd first seen them. The boxes that Wyatt intentionally steered clear of. They were like a card catalog of Wyatt's life, our lives. All I needed was the right book, the right picture, the right film, and he'd see what I saw.

The first box in the corner was an old leather suitcase that had a gold monogrammed RG—Russell Gaumond. It was full of photos and a few other knick-knacks from our lives. There were black and whites from our trips out west, our winter in the mountains, Hilda's growing stomach. There were tiny glass bottles of sand and stones from beaches around the world, each labeled with a phrase like, "Atlantic, Florida," or "Indian, Madagascar." They were Russell's treasures, packed away, waiting to be rediscovered.

In the suitcase, I pulled out stacks of photos of the four of us, before our kids were born; then the six of us, as the boys grew; then the four of us after the boys had passed on. Even in my ghostly form, I could feel every memory, every joy, every heartache.

Maybe those were all I needed to break Wyatt down. Maybe seeing pictures of himself as an old man would be enough for him to realize that if I was his dead wife, and he was with me, he had to be dead, too.

Chapter 24

Wyatt

I rolled over in bed, my breath and heart rate back to normal. Through blurry eyes, I could see June digging through the stack of old boxes in the corner of the theater. My... *our* family's things. Some of which had been packed and stacked in that corner for years. I almost objected to her digging through all those boxes, all those memories, but then remembered they were as much hers as they were mine. She had every right to them. As long as she didn't bother that box with the red stripe in the projector room, everything would be fine.

She'd started with Russell's leather suitcase. The photo collage that hung from his bulletin board in the nursing home had been packed away in a plastic bag. June was pulling photos out of that bag and examining them one by one. Sitting cross-legged, her eyes concentrating, she reminded me of a young Wyatt Jr. looking at bugs under a magnifying glass.

Without looking back, she asked, "How are you feeling?"

"I feel fine, surprisingly. I thought Father Time was about to catch up with me. Felt like Death was wrapping his bony hand around my heart and squeezing the hell out of it. How'd you get me into the bed?"

"You weren't that heavy," she said without looking up. Seemed odd, since most of our lives I'd weighed about twice as much as she did...but now...in her state...

I asked, "Didn't think of calling 911?"

"No… You seemed fine when I checked on you," she said nonchalantly as if life and death were inconsequential. I suppose they are…if you're…if you've already…

"If you think I'm going to die ever, don't bother with 911. I'm ready to go when my time comes. Okay?"

"Same goes for me," she said, still not looking up from the pile of photos on her lap. But I could see the sarcastic grin spread across her face behind the curtain of her hair—now thickly laced with strands of grey.

"Do you remember this?" she asked, waving a photo of the six of us in Montana, at Glacier Park, canvas tent and backpacking supplies laid out in front of us like we were taking inventory. I just wished we'd done that before we left the parking lot. It wasn't until we hiked all day and started setting up our backwoods camp for the night that we realized no one had packed the Goddamn tent poles. The adults had all slept through worse than a cool night without a tent, but the kids hadn't. After a day of hiking—carrying kids and equipment most of the way—it felt like an impossible mission to gather enough quality sticks and branches to prop the vast stretch of canvas into shape.

It didn't matter how the trip started, though; that week in the mountains passed in the blink of an eye. Funny how things we enjoy, like a camping trip with our favorite people, go so quickly. Like life, I supposed; in hindsight, it's all a quick trip. My mom knew that. She was in her fifties when she died. The youngest of all my family to go. When Russell said she was getting bad, I took a return flight from the Congo to sit with her. I held her hand and watched the light fade from her eyes. Dad sat on the other side of the room, reading a newspaper, almost as if he couldn't be bothered to watch; I like to think he was so upset he couldn't handle the situation, so he avoided it. Russell sat on one side of Mom's hospital bed, holding one hand. I sat on the other, rubbing her shoulder. Our wives had taken the kids out of the room while it happened, but Mom was sharp right to the end. She knew who we were, where everyone was, and while she looked at ease, at peace, she took her last breath to warn us just how short time was. The last thing she said to us was, "Don't take your time for granted, boys. There's not nearly as much of it as you think. It goes so quickly…"

And it had until June died. The time since she passed crept by. But now, she was back, digging through our family's boxes of post-mortem flotsam and jetsam. A chill ran up my spine, and for the first time, her presence scared me.

Why did she come back?

"I'm going to jump in the shower, June. If you find any good ones, keep them out for me," I said, reaching down to touch her shoulder. I hesitated, letting my hand hover there, unsure what would happen if I tried to touch her. Now that I knew what she was, would my hand go right through her? Would it be like the kind of cartoon Jr. used to watch? That coyote would run right off the cliff and hover there until he realized he'd run off the cliff. Would it be like that with her now? Now that I knew she was…would my hand go right through her?

But I risked it and when I laid my hand on her shoulder, she was firm, real, not just some mist hovering around. And somehow that eased my mind. Like there was some semblance of permanence in her being there because she was as physically real as I was.

* * *

Emma June

While Wyatt showered, I abandoned the boxes in the corner and cooked for him. Cast iron on an open flame. Imaginary bacon, eggs, and potatoes. Because I wanted to smell that intoxicating aroma of salty sustenance, I did. I was making the rules. It was my world now, my in-between, and no laws of the other side or Earth applied to me.

As I cooked for Wyatt that morning, I thought of how much I used to love preparing a meal for my husband and son. It was so incredibly domestic of me but seeing the look in their eyes when they took a bite of something I created, made me feel whole. I think it all went back to my grandma, whose snickerdoodles made everyone lucky enough to eat them smile. There's something heartwarming about feeding people. When the smell of hot oil in a cast-iron skillet filled the kitchen, fears, regrets, and anger eased…temporarily.

The more time Wyatt spent on assignment, the less I cooked. Especially after Jr. moved off to college. I cooked less and less and drank more and more. In the late sixties, when Wyatt was in Vietnam for months at a time, and Jr. was away at college, I fell into a deep depression. News from the war was awful. There were reports of soldiers, American soldiers, doing atrocious things and having atrocious things done to them. While Wyatt wasn't a soldier anymore, he spent months there taking pictures, interviewing, digging up the grimiest stories he could find, to sell to the highest bidders. He was like a smut peddler, selling gore instead of sex.

Wyatt's willingness to follow soldiers into the thick of the battle gave him endless exclusives. He sent so much material home that Russell enlisted Hilda's help for editing stories—which left me even more alone. But I understood why they worked so hard to get the horrors of that war published. They wanted the war to end so Jeffrey could come home.

The long days when Hilda and Russell were working and the long nights when they were sleeping were the worst. At least in the evening, they'd distract me over dinner and drinks. But even that didn't keep the depression at bay.

Depression hits hard and keeps hitting until we find a way to overcome whatever it is that makes us depressed. But how could I overcome this? Wyatt had been away in Korea and on other international assignments, but during Vietnam, there were times we went months without contacting one another. There was an entire year I only saw him once, on a two-day layover in Chicago on his way between this assignment and that one. I didn't have a clue where he was most of the time. Russell would get packages of stories and undeveloped rolls of film every few days. Phone calls came once a month if we were lucky. He kept shooting, Russell kept selling, and while the money rolled in, depression flattened me like a steamroller.

If there was a stretch of time between packages, I found myself wondering if Wyatt was still alive or if some Vietcong had dragged him off into a jungle, killed him, and left him to rot. Those fears only got worse when Jeffery was sent home from Vietnam in an aluminum box. When Hilda fell apart, the depression really started to wear on me, to eat at me. My waistline shrank, my paranoia grew, and soon I ended up with a prescription to *Miltown,* and later to *Diazepam.*

After I got the pills, and after the shock of losing Jeffery settled, I started to get used to Wyatt's absences. Almost enjoying the silent nights when Hilda and Russell skipped dinner. I had my pills and a bottle of booze to occupy me. I can't say I stopped worrying about him being in dangerous places because I always worried about that, but the drugs numbed me. For years I was numb. Completely, utterly numb. I didn't remember helping

Wyatt Jr. move out for college. I didn't remember Hilda coming over to my house and weeping on my shoulder. I didn't remember when Russell tried to kill himself.

But I do now.

Standing there, over a hot stove, cooking imaginary food for my dead husband, some part of me didn't want it to end. I didn't remember what was on the other side. I don't think we're allowed to know what comes after life on Earth, but lingering in that theater, smelling fried potatoes, bacon, and eggs, I felt like I could stay there forever. And I started to understand Wyatt a little more.

I got the coffee going as the eggs turned from liquid to solid. I fixed a plate for Wyatt before heading back to the living room to sift through Russell's old leather suitcase a bit more. Like cooking, watching my son grow, and shooting secret photos when Wyatt was away, looking at Russell's pictures made me feel good. One photo in particular got my heart racing. Wyatt and I standing in front of our recently purchased house, baby Wyatt Jr. in my arms, and a pair of open-mouth grins.

Where did those kids go?

Where did the time go?

Holding that picture to my chest, and holding back tears, I could hear Wyatt in the bathroom, probably covering the drain of the makeshift shower he'd installed in those months after I'd died, before he'd moved into Paradise Garden. Soon he'd head into the kitchen, grab his plate of food in one hand, coffee in the other. Then he'd sit behind me, on our old sofa, and look over my shoulder at the pictures from Russell's suitcase.

Maybe with just a little luck, or by massaging the right memories, Wyatt would see what was real.

Chapter 25

Wyatt

June had already fixed me a plate. I grabbed it off the hot stove and walked to where she sat, going through our family's old things. I plopped down on the sofa, ate a bite of eggs and potatoes and drank syrup-thick, black coffee. Though June was about done going through Russell's suitcase by the time I sat down to eat, she had a stack of pictures set aside, images of special days for me to look through. Just like they had when I put them in the suitcase a few days before, each image ripped my heart out. I could hardly eat, but the food was so good, food I'd been missing for so long, that I couldn't waste it.

"I like this one," June said, handing me a picture of the three of us—June, Wyatt Jr., and I—standing in front of our house in St. Louis. I sat my plate down and took the snapshot from her.

"Look how happy we were," I said, fingering the glossy, black and white. "That was the day you came back from the hospital, after Jr. was born. You were beyond thrilled. You always wanted kids," I said, thinking how funny it was that we spent years planning for the big life events—baby, house, retirement—and how, when those events came and went, they didn't seem as big as they had in our minds. At the same time, those big life events we never got to experience seemed huge. I never got to see my son get married. I never got to hold a grandchild in my arms, to see its cooing smile…

"You remember the day I told you I was pregnant?" June said, grabbing my arm and leaning onto my shoulder as she held out a photo of the six of us standing in front of our houses, shortly after Russell and Hilda moved next door. Jeffery was a little older than Wyatt but small for his age. He was making a goofy, cross-eyed, tongue-out face, and Wyatt Jr. was laughing. God, I loved to hear that kid laugh.

"I remember. You were so excited, then, right after you told me, the cops knocked on the door. They were harassing everyone in the building because the downstairs neighbor just got busted for selling drugs and they wanted to see if anyone else worked for him or bought from him. We had to get the hell out of there. We shouldn't have stayed that long," I said, setting the pictures down and kissing her on the forehead.

"We had no choice; we didn't have the money. I always thought that was why you started taking the other assignments…the dangerous ones."

I nodded somberly and said, "At first it was a means to an end. I'd been working shitty little assignments, making peanuts—you remember. An editor asked me to submit something from Korea, something firsthand. I took the risk. Withdrew most of our savings from the bank, quit my day job at the shoe factory, put down half our savings as a down payment on the house, and used the rest for a ticket to Korea and supplies I'd need. I told you the magazine covered the cost of that trip…I lied. I bought a one-way ticket and prayed that it would pan out. I got lucky; we got lucky; within a month I tripled the salary I made at the factory and deposited the first few house payments in advance.

"When Russell came to Korea, we doubled our business. I could take the photos and write while he figured out what to do with them. In the first few weeks, we saw where the real money was. Very few photographers were willing to walk into a battle zone for a good shot. The market wasn't flooded, and I had a good enough eye, and I've always had a keen sense of observation.

"But honestly, honey, money wasn't the whole reason I worked overseas so much. On that first trip, I saw the ugly truth hiding inside me: life in the U.S., domestic life, wasn't going to be enough for me. I needed…something else to feel alive."

"And you couldn't get that from reporting traffic accidents and political scandals in St. Louis. Or from glueing and stitching shoes," she said, monotone and hurt.

"No. I want you to know it wasn't you. I missed you when I was away. But…after the war, nothing short of life-threatening situations made me feel alive; made those knee-jerk reactions to every loud noise, every scary thought fade into the background."

"But you loved us. I know you did," she said, holding out a few more pictures from the day we moved into our home. I took them from her, remembering the sun warming our shoulders. There was a faint but very definite smell of fresh bread from the bakery half a block behind our house, and the spring air was laced with the smell of dirt and fertilizer. It was a good day to be home. One of my best days.

She showed me a dozen more selections from Russell's suitcase: vacations, trips to the zoo, snowball fights in the front yard, barbecues, and camping trips. Each picture hurt a little less than the previous, and I started to think we could actually get through the boxes together, sorting out the things we wanted to keep.

After dozens of pictures and hundreds of memories, the tension in my heart was building. The odd tingling pain shot down my left arm when I reached out for another photo. But I needed to see these pictures, postcards, trinkets of a life well-lived; to face the past, to move beyond that past and the pains it brought me. I needed to do it while June was there, and who knew how long she'd be with me.

She could disappear like her momma at any minute.

After Russell's suitcase, June pulled down her own box—which hadn't been touched since she died. In her box, I kept every family picture June had collected throughout her life. She kept every photo, from those my parents had taken before the Depression to those I took just before June's cancer got too bad for her to leave the hospital.

There were images from all over the world. Envelopes and photo albums were overstuffed with pictures of family and friends that I hadn't thought of for years. There were also dozens of print sheets from photos June had taken and never shown me. I didn't see her shots until after she died. I didn't even know she was interested in photography until I found those beautiful candids she'd taken of kids in every part of our city. Kids on buses, kids on playgrounds, kids digging through trash for scraps of food. I should have taken her overseas with me; she had more natural photographic instinct than I did. Maybe because she could connect emotionally to her subjects—because she was taking pictures of something she wanted so badly. Maybe because she saw beauty where no one else did.

I just wish I'd known. I'd have loved to see her shoot.

There were also a few hundred postcards I sent to June from around the world. Often, they were the only form of communication I had with my wife. For years, I thought she'd thrown them out. It wasn't until after she died, and I was going through her dresser, that I found them tucked away with her underwear and bras. The same place she hid her print sheets and negatives.

June reached back and handed me a stack of pictures from my childhood. It seemed like they'd been taken an eternity ago. One picture was of a dirty pair of twins in overalls, cane fishing poles over their shoulders, real Huck Finn types—which made sense; it was Missouri. I didn't remember where we'd been fishing, but Russell and I'd obviously spent more time swimming than fishing. Our dripping, mud-covered clothes matched our toothy grins. I didn't remember ever being as happy as the kid in that photo looked. But it had been taken in a different age; an age when things were simpler. An age when everything was right and none of the wrongness that plagued me since the war was even a glimmer in my future. I didn't know I'd lose myself in that war. The thought never even crossed my mind—why would it?

For a while, as we sat looking at pictures, neither June nor I said a word. We just handed pictures back and forth…living in the memories. It wasn't until we got to a family photo of Russell, Hilda, June, and me in Washington, on our mountain, four or five decades after our first trip there, that something changed.

"Who's this?" She asked, pointing at the man standing behind the aged version of her in the photo.

I took the photo from her, looking at the four people, my wife, brother, and sister-in-law and… It was a dim photo, and I don't know exactly how to explain it but the me in the photo was as old as the rest of my family. I never aged. I knew that. It was a fact. As I sat in our theater, holding that photo, I still looked thirty; it was one of my life's greatest torments. I stayed young while Russell and the rest withered away in front of me. But there I was in the picture, an old man, cane in hand, leaning awkwardly out of balance on the mountainside.

I didn't like the way it made me feel, so I handed it back to her.

"Who is it?" she asked, pointing at the elderly version of me standing behind the elderly version of her.

"That's…that's got to be Russell," I said, setting aside any other possibilities.

"Then…who's this?" She said, pointing at the elderly man standing behind Hilda.

I scratched my head. That *was* Russell; I'd recognize that silly grin anywhere. The other man…he had to be Russell, too— Russell was the one who walked with a cane. He had since a bad fall down his basement stairs in 1992.

"Must have been something I was messing around with in the darkroom. I probably burned him in after I processed the first negative. I mean, I couldn't be in that photo; I was the one who took it. Right?"

June didn't say anything for a bit. She just sat there holding that picture in her hand, staring at it. I looked over her shoulder, unable to shake an odd sense that I was very wrong about something.

All I could think was: *God, they aged.* All of them carried canes. They had more wrinkles than an English bulldog. Hilda was hunched over from degenerative spinal disease. June's body was half the weight it had been only a few pictures before—she was fighting the cancer for the first time, and at that point she was losing the fight. When June started going downhill, she asked for "one more trip to the mountain." She practically begged for it. And with both of us thinking she was at her end; I had to appease. Hell, I'd have carried her up the side of the mountain if that satisfied her last request.

"God," June started, unease filling her voice, "we really did wither away right in front of you. You watched us grow old and die. How did you…how does one deal with that much loss?"

"It's the hardest thing anyone ever has to deal with. After you know and love a person that long…their death takes part of you with them."

June hugged me, setting a pile of pictures down. "But I'm back now, Wyatt."

"Yeah…you're back," I said, wanting to ask her how that happened, but afraid of the answer. "I hope we'll have each other for a very long time."

June nodded and said, "I'm not going anywhere, Wyatt." She wiped a tear and went back to the pictures.

* * *

Emma June

I hoped the picture of the four of us in Washington would have more of an impact on him. I hoped he'd see himself as an old man, see his brother there, and…just accept it, just accept that he's as dead as I am. But, of course, I was talking to a man who, on a bet, once burned the negative image of a gorilla onto a snow-covered mountain and sold it to the *National Enquirer* as proof of the Yeti—you may have seen it, it's quite famous. It made the front page of the *Enquirer* and even showed up in a few other papers. With that kind of skill, why wouldn't he believe it was some kind of prank he'd pulled and simply forgotten about?

The pile of pictures that we sifted through kept growing and despite my best efforts, Wyatt was no closer to remembering his death than he was to acknowledging that he couldn't walk through movie screens, that there was no hallway of doors, that he aged just like the rest of us. I was almost ready to give up on the photos when I ran across one Wyatt's father took just before he and Russell went to the war. It was an old black and white of the four of us at Hilda and Russell's wedding. The Mississippi River was high in the background, and the sky was almost white—it was the type of cloudy/sunny day where fair-skinned people get a sunburn but never need a hat. The corners of the photo were worn and folded as if it had been carried in someone's pocket or wallet, or heavy, canvas Army coat for years—a coat that had been hanging on the back of our dining room chair since I'd returned to our theater.

"Recognize this one?" I asked, knowing it was the only photo he took with him to the war. Russell told me years later that for the first few months Wyatt would sit up at night with his Zippo lit, just staring at it. He also said that after he'd been saved from the POW camp, Wyatt never looked at the picture again. Russell said he'd catch Wyatt feeling for it in his pocket, without ever taking it out to look at it—like a type of silent mourning for what he'd lost.

He took the photo out of my hand and stared at it for a minute. Silently. A small change came over his face, then he grabbed his chest as he gasped for air.

Chapter 26

Wyatt

I didn't know where she got it, but I hadn't seen that Goddamn photo since The Big One. I'd purposefully pushed it out of my mind. Too many memories, too many heartaches. It was the last photo taken of us before we left… I didn't want to, but compulsively; I grabbed the photo out of June's hand.

That squeezing in my chest started again. I felt like I couldn't breathe, like an elephant was standing on me and I was going to be squeezed to death.

"I recognize it," I said, gasping for a deep breath and holding my chest.

"Russell and Hilda's wedding. Do you remember that terrible cake your mom made?"

I tried to breathe slowly. "It was like…she used corn flour…and lard. It was gritty…and dense, nasty. But Dad…wouldn't turn loose of any money for the cake…he wouldn't even give her the few dimes it would have…cost to get good ingredients. I think…she made the worst cake she could, just to piss him off."

"Knowing your mother's silent vengeances, that's probably true. Do you remember that old man—I don't remember who he was—but he shouted at your mother, 'This is the worst Goddamn cake I ever ate.' And then she smiled, as if to say, 'Mission accomplished.'"

"Uncle Raymond. He was…Grandpa's brother. Always was…a bastard, and he took my grandfather's dislike of my mom as a mission to make her life miserable," I said, the pain in my chest easing.

"I remember," June said, then she grinned at me like she had some kind of top-secret secret that she was finally going to let me in on. With playfulness in her voice, she said, "Wyatt, do you want to go back there?"

I set the photo aside, took a deep, easy breath and asked, "Where, St. Louis? We were just there. You saw what it's like now. You really want to go back there?"

"Not just to St. Louis," she said. Then, pointing at the photo I'd just set aside, she said, "*Then.*"

"How do you mean?"

"Do you trust me?"

I hesitated, then nodded. I'd trusted her my entire life.

"Then let's go," she said, standing up and reaching her hand out to me.

As soon as our hands met, the pain in my chest disappeared, and I felt lighter, younger.

"Come on, Wyatt. This'll be fun," she said, pulling me to my feet.

* * *

Emma June

I held Wyatt's hands, and I led him through the theater, and as we walked, I imagined us moving through the morning mist, the sun eking over the horizon as it warmed our little part of the world. I imagined a clean brick street with cars defined by glimmering chrome and tailfins and two-tone paint driving by. I said, "Close your eyes, Wyatt," and while I led him through the theater, toward the all-glass front doors, I imagined the two of us traveling to our past. I thought of all the pictures I'd just sifted through and all the memories that came with them. I thought of our past, and I thought of that bus ride from the day before, and I knew I could show him what he was missing.

I closed my eyes and led Wyatt through the front doors of our theater.

In less than a second, without the showmanship of a hallway of doors or bright lights or upturned pools of water, we were seven hundred miles and sixty years away from where we'd started the day. We stood on Marcus Avenue; the air was warm and sunny, but not hot. It was spring; flowers in terracotta pots were blooming, the morning mist was quickly fading, and the world was as perfect as I could imagine it.

Everything was fresh, clean, clear, and the sidewalks were bustling with busy shoppers. Down both sides of the main drag, the buildings had been restored to their former glory. The Prestige theater on Marcus Avenue, the one we'd frequented as a young couple, the one we'd seen collapse in our older life, was back up and in prime condition. The marquee read, *Mr. Lucky*. The old corner store, where the two men had been barbecuing in an oil drum the last time we'd been there, was freshly painted, and all the windows were clean glass, rather than plywood. An *OPEN* sign glowed in bright neon red.

"Open your eyes, Wyatt," I said, squeezing his hands.

He looked around. His mouth opened. He paused. Then, shocked, he asked, "Where are we? What the *hell* is going on?" His voice trembled. It was a side of him I never saw. He was always the strong one, the one who'd walk into a battle zone to get a picture, the one who'd fearlessly travel to underdeveloped, dangerous countries without speaking a single word of the local language. I never saw him scared in my life. Angry, yes; stuck in a stress memory, yes; but never scared.

"I think you have to figure it all out for yourself, Wyatt. I can guide you, but you have to figure it out."

I was just starting to get the hang of this world in between. Wyatt had years to develop his "hallway of doors." To convince himself that it'd been real in his life. That was the furthest his skeptical mind could stretch. My mind, however, was always a bit more flexible. In the in-between, I knew I could have anything I imagined. Anything but control of Wyatt's free will.

Even in death, free will was uncontrollable.

"You want to see where you grew up? You want to see your grandfather's home? You want to see our first apartment? You want to see us as kids? We can. I know how," I said. Our roles had changed completely. I was no longer the one that needed to be led around like a stray dog; I was on the other side of the leash.

"How's it possible?"

"It's just like your hallway of doors. Only I can go anyplace because these places are here," I said, pointing at my temple. "And here," I said, pointing at his chest.

"What do you want to see today? What was your best day in this city?"

Wyatt held his trembling hand out to me. I took it and smiled silently.

"I want to see what *you* loved about this place," he said.

We walked the day away like we did when we were young and too poor for a car. We walked through sixty years of streets, houses, apartments, restaurants, stolen kisses in dark alleys, and movie palaces that played black and white masterpieces on silver screens. We walked through our life in St. Louis together, one last time. A last look at the wonders we were lucky enough to live through.

And as we walked, I saw Wyatt age, and I felt myself aging, too.

262

Chapter 27

Wyatt

After a day in our past, June and I slumped on the worn-out sofa with our feet up on one of the boxes that she'd been sifting through that morning. I wanted to ask her more about our long walk through St. Louis; about how she recreated the streets, houses, apartments, and theaters to fit the time periods in which they were most important to us. Like the theater on Marcus Avenue, with flashing lights running up and down the marquee, *Mr. Lucky* spelled out in black letters against the lighted white background. It wasn't just reminiscing. She put us back in those places and times—we relived them. She showed me the early days of our relationship and marriage; the days just after Wyatt Jr. had been born; the middle days when I was gone more than I was there; the days after Little Wyatt moved away, after he died, and finally, after we decided we couldn't stay in that city anymore. She showed me our lives in slow motion instant replay.

We'd walked for what felt like hours, but to experience everything we'd experienced in those hours would have taken a lifetime. Was this her "life review?" That moment they say where your life flashes before your eyes just before you pass over? Had she somehow shared that with me?

When I was a young man, which suddenly seemed a lot longer ago, I spent a lot of time thinking about my grandfather. My dad used to tell us that on Black Tuesday, my grandpa was one of the men who jumped out of a window, plummeting to his death, in the wake of the great crash. I was only four years old when the crash happened, and since I never saw my grandpa, I had to take my dad's word for it. His vivid retellings of grandpa's descent made me first terrified of heights and second curious about death. What exactly did it mean to die?

Russell and I spent countless hours under the night sky debating the Christian notion of the soul like they talked about in church. Mom once said that Grandpa was "in Heaven, watching over us all," but there wasn't any certainty in her voice. She was usually so certain about everything, but when she said that, her voice quavered, like she couldn't stand to lie to us, but had no choice in the matter. Dad, on the other hand, always said that if there was a hell, Grandpa was there, roasting hot dogs with the devil. As kids, neither Russell nor I knew what that meant, but we both chuckled about the image it conjured up in our imaginative young minds. The chuckling earned us one of Dad's razor-sharp glares.

It wasn't until our fifteenth year that Russell and I met Grandpa, who hadn't actually jumped to his death on Black Tuesday—in fact, nobody in New York did—but had disinherited our dad because he married our mom; a woman that was, according to our grandpa, "below him in every way." Dad claimed he hated Grandpa. In all truth, Dad never expected to see him again, and as such, tried his best to make Grandpa seem pitiful and weak, to rationalize his anger. Once we met Grandpa, though, we realized he was just the opposite of Dad's descriptions. The Great Depression never besmudged his white-gloved hands. He lived big when others, including us, lived small—I think that's why Dad was so angry. For a fraction of his wealth, Grandpa could have solved all Dad's financial troubles. My parents could have kept their first home. They could have fed Russell and me something other than fried bologna and potatoes. But Grandpa was a stubborn man, just like Dad. Both were too proud to admit they did anything wrong, both too proud to ask for forgiveness.

After Russell and I met him, Grandpa was our inspiration to "Get spiffy and pick up some dolls." That's how he said it, anyway. He wanted us to be powerful, wealthy men with a hundred girls hanging from our shoulders, like he was. We took his advice and ran with it—and we chased girls, and we dated, and we spent every penny we had taking girls to the shows. It didn't make Dad proud, but after finding out that he lied to us about our grandpa, Russell and I weren't interested in making Dad proud anymore. Teenagers can be ruthless when they realize their parents aren't infallible beings, but just humans trying to figure out the world as they go.

A few months after we met him, Grandpa picked Russell and me up in his 1939 Fleetwood. He took us to a show and then out for dinner. At dinner, just as some juicy steaks were placed carefully on the white linen tablecloth, Grandpa grabbed his chest. His face turned blue. He spilled twenty-year-old scotch down his white suit, tumbled out of his seat, and died. He was 66 years old, too young for the Alzheimer's that would later destroy our dad and my brother to touch him.

That night was the only time I ever saw my dad cry. He didn't cry when Mom died, or when Russell and I went off to war. He didn't shed a tear for his in-laws' passing. But when Grandpa, a man who'd written him off, a man he claimed to hate, died, he wept like a kid with a skinned knee. In my entire life, that never made sense to me. Until I saw June forgive her mother, that is. It became clearer still when, just as they were about to embrace, they were separated again. I think my dad expected to forgive and be forgiven, to embrace Grandpa like he had as a child, to feel the warmth and comfort that only comes from a loving parent. But just when they got back on speaking terms, Grandpa was taken from him—this time with finality.

Slumped down on that couch, feet brushing up against my dead wife's feet, the conversations Russell and I had about the soul carved a river through my head. June had settled deep into the cushions and was resting her eyes—that's what she always used to call it when she was about to fall asleep but didn't want to admit it.

She looked at peace. More so than she had since I found her in that theater, under attack from her stepfather. The torment my wife must have felt both living and in death had to be incredible. She lived stuck in between the hell of her past and the uncertainty of her future. As I always did, more than anything else, I wanted to protect her. To keep her from harm. In this case, that meant helping her move on to whatever came next. If she moved on, she'd vanish from my world, like her mother had, but I could accept that if it meant she'd finally be at peace.

As she snuggled deeper into my shoulder and I placed a longing arm around her, I wondered if my dad and grandpa forgave one another in the afterlife. I wondered if my son forgave my many misgivings or if he was waiting in some horrible in-between state for me to find him and beg for forgiveness. I wondered about Jeffrey, Hilda, and Russell.

How many of my friends and family are lingering? How many are waiting for me?

"June," I whispered, shaking her just a little. She took a deep breath and sat up, on full alert.

"What, Wyatt? What's going on?"

"Nothing," I said, taking her hands. "I just wondered what you think happened to your mother…when she disappeared," I said, hoping to prompt her. She didn't deserve to be stuck there with me. She deserved to move on to whatever was next, as her mother had. I couldn't let her wait for me anymore. She spent too much of her life waiting for me.

* * *

Emma June

"Momma? She disappeared, Wyatt," I said, not wanting to go into details. He was so close to the truth now. His question was opening lines of thought that only had one outcome. He would see. He would realize. And he'd glance in the mirror and see the wrinkles on his face or look down and see the scars on his chest, and he'd remember. I knew he would.

Like Momma and Grandma, Wyatt needed a push to move on. I hadn't spoken to Momma in fifty-some years. A few minutes together in a place where we could sit down and finally hear one another changed everything. When she felt at peace, my mother moved on—the same was true of Grandma in the Piggly Wiggly; as soon as she felt at peace with her life, she moved on.

Wyatt needed to feel at peace with his regrets, with the things he'd left undone. He needed to forgive himself for not being able to scatter his brother's ashes, for not being there for our son when he was growing up, for not being there for me. Wyatt needed to forgive *himself* before he could go.

"I know she disappeared. I saw her disappear, June. But where did she go?"

"Where do you think she went? What do you think *I* am? You saw my grave. You remember my death. What does that tell you about me?"

"I'm sitting here talking with the ghost of my wife. I don't understand it, but I've accepted it. Today, my wife's ghost led me through the experiences we'd once had. A lifetime of experiences in one day. I know what you are, and I know that because you're…what you are, you were able to show me what we lived through, all the good I'd forgotten. But what I'm asking is, where do you think your mother went and where will you go when…when you're not here anymore?"

"Momma moved on, Wyatt. Eventually, I'll do the same."

He paused, thinking about that for a minute. The furrow of his brow got deeper, wrinkles spreading across his forehead, as he considered the phrase. "Why haven't you 'moved on?' Is it because of me? Because I'm still here?"

"Yes," I said, smiling.

"So, you've been here the whole time? Stuck in that theater? Reliving that horrible moment?"

"No," I said, shaking my head. I grabbed his hands and turned to face him more directly. "I wasn't there the whole time."

"So, what's on the other side? What happens when someone 'moves on?'"

I couldn't answer that question. Every time I tried, I got the same feeling, like a word stuck on the tip of the tongue that just refused to fall. I said, "I can't tell you, Wyatt. You don't get to know that until you move on, and if you come back, you don't get to remember it." I hoped it would give him some incentive once he realized what he was—he always liked a good adventure, a new destination, a new journey. I can think of no greater adventure than stepping from in-between to the other side—the ultimate unknown.

"Being…what you are, do you have any special knowledge about anything?"

"Can I see the future? No. Can I see the past? Yes. And so can you. What do you think that walk through St. Louis was? That wasn't just my mind at work there. That was us, working together to remember our lives together. *Our* lives, Wyatt."

"Our lives…I never forgot us."

"I know you didn't. But you've got some of the details jumbled," I said. His eyes flickered around the room like he was trying to figure out which details were off. When his breathing changed, I said, "I think it's enough for tonight. I think you need to let your mind rest. It's been a big day for both of us. How about a movie? We can sit in your favorite spot and turn the movie up loud like we used to when we first moved in and there were just two leather recliners in this theater."

"Okay, Doll," he said in his best—but still terrible—Bogart impersonation.

Chapter 28

Wyatt

Of all the movies we had, June chose *The Shining*, which was fine because it was the only movie we owned that I hadn't watched enough times for the films to wear thin. I didn't usually go for horror movies; I'd seen enough horror in real life. I lived with nightmares about the people I killed in the war, about rotting corpses in crumbling towns, and rice paddies. I didn't need to see nightmares like that corpse in the bathroom of the *Overlook*. But I was sure I wouldn't be watching much of the show; my mind had other things to keep it busy.

I thought about offering popcorn, soda, and candy, but I wasn't sure she could eat it. I tried to think back about her eating habits over the previous few days, but everything was foggy. I didn't remember if she'd actually eaten anything. I thought she might have eaten something that morning—eggs? toast?—but again, it was foggy.

"You want anything to eat?" I asked, not wanting to be too presumptuous.

"I'm not hungry, but if you want something, go ahead," she replied. That was my wife. She spent much of our life together giving me that line. Even when she was alive, I hardly remembered her eating anything. She was rail-thin in her seventies. Before she died, after the cancer had its way with her, she'd turned into something unrecognizable: a horror movie prop with my wife's

270

features. Though I'd never tell her, in the end, she resembled something out of those death camps in The Big One. It didn't make me love her less; it just made me sad.

"Okay. Make yourself comfortable and I'll go up and start the first reel," I said, laying my hand on her shoulder. Under her thinning skin, I could feel her bones, like cypress knees bulging through wet soil on the edge of a pond. No matter how many times Russell and I talked about the soul and the metaphysical, we never would have guessed at the physical characteristics of a ghost. Everything I knew about ghosts I picked up in movies or books. And with my hand resting on her shoulder, I realized I didn't know shit. My wife was solid, and under my hand I swore I could feel her pulse. She felt alive. And as much as I wanted her to move on, I dreaded it.

I was tired of being alone.

I gave her shoulder one more squeeze and headed off to start the movie. To get to the projection room, I had to hike up a narrow staircase hidden behind a secret door in the main lobby. A panel behind the popcorn and soda machines was spring loaded and opened when pushed—Russell's design. I pushed on the panel, and when it popped open, I headed up the stairs. For the first sober time in my life, I lost my footing. I'd been in a lot of tight spots in the wars, but with each step up that two-foot-wide, dark, hidden staircase I got more and more confused, claustrophobic, and scared that the walls were closing in on me.

My vision went blurry, and I had to sit down, catching myself on the handrail. I could neither focus on the steps nor the walls. That ache in my chest was the worst it had been since it started a few days before.

About the time I melted to a seated position, June shined a dim flashlight up the staircase and asked, "Wyatt?"

"I'm okay, just having a bit of vertigo and a little chest pain."

"No, you're not okay. Come on, I'll help you up the steps."

I blinked, tried to rub the dizziness out of my eyes. While trying to refocus them, June put her arms around me, tossed my arm over her shoulder, and helped me stand.

"One step at a time, Wyatt," she said standing beside me and holding a great deal of my weight.

"Uh huh," was all I could seem to get out. I didn't understand it, I'd gone up there just the night before and didn't even get my heart rate up. But now, in addition to my heart pounding and the vertigo, my knees hurt, and my hand longed for a cane.

At the top, I breathed heavy as I jiggled the handle, trying to push open the metal door that kept my family's most valuable possessions safe, but it was locked. The pain in my chest was overwhelming. I dug the keys out of my pocket and tried to find the right one, but I couldn't remember which one went to the lock. I couldn't seem to remember anything. I hardly knew my name. I hardly knew the woman standing beside me.

I dropped the keys on the ground.

She grabbed them.

She slid the right key into the deadbolt on the first try. And with the clanking sound of the bolt being snugged inside the mechanism, she twisted the handle, and the door opened, and an obnoxiously bright light filled the staircase.

"Ah, what the hell?" I asked, squinting as June pulled me into the projector room.

"What?"

"Why's it so bright in here?"

"Relax, Wyatt," she said, guiding me to the stool I sat on when we ran the theater, and I had to wait for reel changes.

"Where's the movie?" she asked, looking at the shelves and shelves of metal film canisters.

"The reels for *The Shining* are on the far left, under *Portrait of Hell.* Have you ever worked one of these before?"

"You forget who you're talking to. We used to run this theater together, remember?"

I looked at her and, through blurry eyes, saw her for who she was: I saw every age line, every grey hair, every scar she'd acquired in our time together. I saw her as she was the moment before she died, and I saw her the night I stopped her stepfather from choking her to death. I saw every grimy thing that ever happened to her, but I also saw her skin in the perfection of its youth, her eyes without cataracts, her smile with unstained teeth. I saw her naked and nervous the night of our wedding. I saw her holding Wyatt Jr. by an open window, her perfect hair blowing in the breeze on the first cool, fall evening after we moved into our house in St. Louis.

I saw her completely like I never saw her before. And seeing her like that made the pain in my chest and the dizziness I felt even more intense. For a second, I thought I'd fall off the stool and die right there. But my clear distress didn't seem to bother her.

"Furthest to the left?" she asked, but as she did, her eyes shifted to the box in the corner of the projection room, under the *Portrait of Hell* canisters. The box with the red stripe down the center. She gawked at it long enough for me to see that she saw it. A chill ran up my spine and the pain in my chest and confusion rushing over me redoubled again.

I fell to the ground, clutching my chest, and grumbled, "That box. Don't touch it!"

* * *

Emma June

I knew what it was. It was *his* box. Like those downstairs: one for me, one for Wyatt Jr., a suitcase for Russell, a small box for Hilda and an even smaller box for Jeffery. The bit of cardboard with the red stripe emblazoned across it was *his* box.

I knew, because I wanted to know, that a few months after Wyatt died, a distant cousin brought Wyatt's things to our theater for storage. Everything we'd owned went to a cousin Wyatt hadn't seen since the girl was five years old. She was a third cousin with a huge extended family. She got a phone call on a sunny spring day from our attorney, who said, "With no other living relatives and no will, you're the next of kin. You'll get everything." Cousin Charlie didn't want any of it, but she signed the paperwork and accepted it anyway. She'd paid the taxes on the theater and sent servicemen over twice every year to fix anything wrong with the building. She left all Wyatt's things there, thinking that one day she'd have an auction, sell the original prints of Wyatt's most famous photos… or maybe she'd put them together for a museum. But Wyatt's cousin never made plans to do any such thing. She hated that theater and the feeling she got inside of it.

Wyatt's personal items, the things he'd kept in the nursing home, had been tossed unceremoniously into the box in the corner by a young CNA at Paradise Garden. That box and Russell's suitcase sat at the nursing home for months waiting for Wyatt's cousin to pick them up. If not for Hope, they'd have been thrown out.

When my husband moved from our theater into Paradise Garden, he took a single overnight bag, and a small suitcase full of clothes. In the overnight bag, Wyatt packed the lifetime of postcards he'd sent to me. Postcards from all over the world. Some had little stories on the back; some only said, "I love you and miss you," in his quick, sloppy longhand. I saved them all and squirreled them away to look at when I was lonely.

In his confused, post-life mind, Wyatt buried the box with the red stripe out of sight, so he didn't have to think about it. Things like that could happen in the in-between. The memory of it was still there, but he could deny what that memory meant. Like Momma looking twenty-five and Wyatt looking thirty, we can be and do and think anything we want in the in-between. The only problem is, we forget the truth because living the lie is much easier. Just like how Wyatt could walk through movie screens, and I could bring us from the Ely of the present to the St. Louis of our past, anything was possible here, if we believed it hard enough. And Wyatt wanted to believe that box had been in the theater since before we moved in. So, in his mind, it had been.

As we lingered in the projection room, haunted by Wyatt's box, it dawned on me how little material possessions matter. We couldn't take anything beyond the grave, and even if we could, we wouldn't have a use for it. Besides, if a material object was important, like my favorite outfit from the 60s, I'd have it; just like the rest of my memories. I knew this only because that's what I'd accomplished in the world between. I'd gone from a completely blank slate when I arrived, to a version of myself that held more memories and more experiences than I thought any living human could recollect. I saw the life I'd lived, from birth to death, in a single, crystal clear, panoramic image.

The rest of Wyatt's memories—the ones he'd let slip away after he'd died—were in that red-striped box in the corner of the room. His last months at Paradise Garden were in that box. His soul's connection to the physical world was in that box, waiting to be released. He just had to reach out and open it, and he'd understand everything.

"What's in that box, Wyatt?" I asked, pointing.

At some point, Wyatt had fallen to the floor and was clutching his chest, but I wasn't worried; maybe he needed to feel like he was dying to realize he already had. He muttered, "That box was…here when we…moved in."

"I don't remember that box being here when we moved in, honey. I remember the stack of gymnastics equipment and a leaking ceiling. An old mattress and a ratty old blanket under the stage—clearly someone had been squatting. I remember a backed-up toilet and a grease-coated popcorn machine. I remember hand-painting the marquee and you haggling over the price of fluorescent lights. I remember buying the recliners. But I'm sure that, aside from a few reels of dirty movies, and that crazy Japanese horror film, and three half-working projectors, this room was empty."

"I don't think so…kid. I think…it was here," he grunted.

I shrugged. "So, you've never opened it? You think it's been here as long as we've owned the theater and it's never been opened?"

"*We* never opened it and…I don't know, I just don't like to think about the damn thing. Never wanted…to open it. Thought about throwing it…out a hundred times…never could though. As much as I…don't like to think about that box…I can't fathom tossing it."

"I don't see what all the mystery's about. Shouldn't we just open it?" I asked.

Sounding a little stronger now, Wyatt barked, "I'm not opening it. I don't think you should either. You going to get the reels loaded?"

He was so close now. He felt his death lingering in the back of his mind as he relived the symptoms of the heart attack that killed him. He'd been experiencing it in little bursts since I'd been back, and while he didn't realize what that pain in his chest was, I knew… And I knew he just needed another little push.

I grabbed a canister and moved toward Projector One. But as I walked across the tiny room I asked, "What if I open the box and you go downstairs?"

"Please don't, June," he begged as he pushed himself onto all fours. His voice was a little smoother and his face was a little less pale, but he still looked like he was at death's door.

"Okay, Wyatt, I won't touch it," I said as I spun the reel into Projector One and loaded the film. "I'll leave it for another day."

I threaded the film through the projector, and as I did, I imagined something very different than *The Shining*. I imagined the memories in that box; memories that terrified Wyatt. I imagined his last moments. And because I imagined it, because I wanted it, it became real.

Chapter 29

Wyatt

My chest still hurt, and I still struggled to focus my eyes, but now the pain was a mild inconvenience, rather than the debilitating ache it had been. While June got the projector set up, I climbed to my feet and picked up one of Wyatt Jr's guitars—not the expensive one, but the first one I gave him. That old guitar had seen dozens of sets of strings and thousands of hours of play; it had gouges and chips where his unsteady hands let it fall to the floor, and where his attempt to revolutionize the pick industry ended abruptly after his homemade metal pick cut right through the worn out first string and gouged the varnish. That old guitar wasn't a pretty thing, but it was the instrument he taught himself to play on. Giving him that guitar was one of the best things I ever did for him.

"We're ready, Wyatt," June said behind me as she closed the cover on the projector.

"Do you remember this?" I asked, holding up the guitar. I knew she would; how could she not? I heard his best playing at multiple stages of his development; she heard the years he spent practicing in his bedroom. She took him to his teacher's place for lessons and encouraged him when he got down. More things I wasn't there for.

"Of course. He played that thing constantly. Do you remember the day you gave it to him?"

"His tenth birthday."

"You were just back from Jerusalem, or someplace. We didn't even know you were in the country. You just walked in, guitar in hand, and everyone started laughing."

"You bought him books and clothes."

She grinned at me; it was the grin I spent hundreds of hours thinking about, missing. I grinned back and said, "Should we go down?"

"Go ahead. I'll get it rolling when you're in your spot."

I nodded; she always used to do that for me, get the movie going while I sat in my favorite seat, perfectly centered in the middle of the theater. She always got the movie rolling because she knew that, even as an old man who'd seen a million films, I still got excited about the opening credits. Though they changed the format from the long list that used to be played at the beginning to just a few names rolling across the screen, I still loved to see them. It was like the anticipation of the thing was sometimes better than the thing itself. Like the big events in life, the lead-up excitement was sometimes better than the reality.

I got situated where I could rest comfortably without straining my eyes or neck. I hoped I'd be asleep before Jack's descent into madness made him turn on his family.

The screen went black, and the staticky sound of crinkled and filthy film rolled through the projector. June sat down beside me and grabbed my hand just as the film smoothed out and the music started. Though I hadn't seen *The Shining* in years, I knew immediately that the movie she put on wasn't *The Shining*. Instead of starting with a camera flying over that lake in the mountains, there was a still frame image of Russell's room at Paradise Garden.

"What's this?"

"Just watch," she said, squeezing my hand.

"Something new?" I asked. I wanted to sound cool, calm, but even I could hear the nervousness in my voice as another round of dizzying pain ran down my left arm and up the back of my head.

"Did you know Russell told me about that theater you two found in Thailand back in the 80s? The one with the palm tree benches. He said that the first night you were there, they were playing some old Howard Hughes movie in English, and nobody there other than you two, spoke English. He said that instead of popcorn, they were serving some dried, salted shrimp. And he said that you got so excited that they were playing a movie you'd seen together as kids, that you were practically bouncing."

"He told you about that?"

"You guys were the biggest movie junkies I ever knew. I asked him once where the strangest theater was. That's the one he told me about. He told me about a lot. Sometimes I think I only kept up with your life through him. Most of the time I felt I knew him better than I knew you. I spent way more of my life with Russell than I ever spent with you, until we moved to Ely, that is," she said, then she squeezed my hand again and rested her head on my shoulder.

In a smooth panning motion, the film showed Russell's room at Paradise Garden. But there were odd little differences. Like Russell's bulletin board being full of postcards instead of the pictures I'd taken down just a few days before. The cards were from the collection I sent to June every time I visited a new country—over a hundred in my life. I couldn't even name them all without looking at a globe or atlas. Some of those countries changed names two or three times over the years. Uprisings and overthrows were easy news to sell.

Sometimes postcards were the only contact I'd have with my wife for months—another thing I wasn't proud of. I could have written more or found a phone, but I was selfish with my time, my freedom. On those postcards, I'd send little stories of what I was doing in those countries and confessions of love; sometimes a combo of each. I remember sitting on the coast of Malta, looking at the blue-green water, writing something like:

> My love, today I'm in Malta. I'll be here for the next two weeks. They're opening a new War Museum, and I'm supposed to get stories from survivors of The Big One and discuss how the war changed their lives. The impossibly green water around the archipelago makes me dream of your eyes. I miss and love you with all my heart.
>
> Yours,
>
> Wyatt

Of course, I wouldn't remember the details of any of those cards if June hadn't kept them all and if I hadn't studied them after her death. I wept over them—each one a moment I could have had with her. Each a lost day…

After a few seconds, the camera panned from the bulletin board to the left, showing an old man in a worn-out blue bathrobe, sitting in a rocking chair in the corner of the room. He hadn't shaved in a long time, but it had to be my brother. Though I never remembered him having a blue bathrobe, and he hadn't had a beard since the 60s, one doesn't mistake one's own brother often.

"What is this? Where did you get this?"

"Just watch, Wyatt," she said, still squeezing my hand.

My brother stood up, stretched his arms, and yawned. He flinched as he did so and brought his right hand to his chest. He looked pretty much as he did just a few days ago, but…thicker. He must have weighed thirty pounds more than he had the last time I saw him. Which meant this film must have been taken shortly after he moved in rather than right before he died. Even the way he moved was that of a much younger man.

The camera stayed on my brother as a voice from off-screen said, "You're not supposed to be out of bed." The camera panned to a nurse standing in the doorway. She was a pretty thing. She'd been there the last time I'd been there, the day I gathered Russell's things. Her name was Hope.

"Do you remember me?"

"I… Jane? Joan? June?" the man on the screen mumbled. Russell got bad at the end. His speaking changed from clear sentences to scattered noises and phrases. Sometimes he'd talk about what was going on around him. Mostly he'd ramble about things from the past.

"Do you remember what happened this morning?" Hope asked.

"Where's Russell?" The man on the screen said. A chill ran up my spine. This was familiar. Like a scene I'd watched in a movie many years before.

"Hop back into your bed, and we'll talk about that," Hope said.

When he did—not so much hop as sit carefully—the nurse pulled the blue bathrobe apart and placed a stethoscope on his chest. When she did…I saw the scars all over his chest…my scars.

"You're not supposed to be out of bed because your heart's been acting up since this morning."

"Just need, just need, just need to go on my…my run. I need my run," he said, trying to get up again. "A run," the man said, glaring at the nurse.

I turned to June and asked, "Where the hell did you get this footage?"

"What's wrong with it? It's just a movie, Wyatt."

Hope's voice filled the theater's speakers as she answered the man's question. "No running or walking until we get your heart calmed down, Mr. Gaumond," Hope said.

"Wyatt…my, I'm…uh, my name."

"I know, Wyatt. I know who you are. Do you know what happened this morning?" Hope asked the man on screen.

"What the hell?" I barked at June.

"SHHH!" she said as she pointed at the screen.

"Wyatt," Hope said, "do you remember where we went this morning? We took a van to the hospital. Do you know where your brother is?"

The man on screen moved more quickly than I'd expected anyone that age could move, hopped out of bed, and walked over to a bulletin board full of photographs, the photographs that I'd untacked from Russell's board just a few days before. He pointed, mouthing something but unable to get the words out.

Hope nodded and said, "We're going to miss him. Your brother had personality. It wasn't always the best personality, but he was full of it. Some of the people who come through here are…their minds have gone, but their bodies keep moving around. Russell wasn't always sharp, didn't always know who we were, but he was always funny. He was a flirt, but he never got handsy. He was a good man. We miss good men when they're gone. I'm so sorry for your loss, Wyatt."

The man on screen turned back to Hope and said, "Miss him? My…loss?"

"That's right, Wyatt."

The man on screen glared at her, anger filling his eyes, then he shouted, "They pulled the…they pulled the Goddamn plug! My brother's dead!"

Hope's face sank.

The camera panned to the man on screen and switched from a wide angle to a closeup of the man grabbing his chest. Off-screen, Hope's clog-covered feet clunked across the room. She entered the scene, eased him to the floor, and pulled him into her lap.

She whispered, "It's okay, Wyatt, you can let go."

"WHAT THE HELL?" I shouted again. It was too real and too familiar. The man in the movie looked like my brother but had my scars. The room looked like my brother's but had my things. How could anyone fake that?

This was…that old man was…

We watched a little longer as Hope rocked the man in her lap and repeated that it was okay to let go. The man's face went from lively to blank in a matter of seconds. In some kind of fast forward special-effect I'd never seen before, the movie changed angles to a hovering view that was looking down on the scene but slowly ascending toward the ceiling. Everything went silent.

Later, a doctor walked in, followed by two men in black suits. One with a white collar: Father Curt. The other, Ken, the funeral director my family had used since the 1960s. Ken was much older than he had been just a few days before, when I'd collected Russell's ashes. Hunched over and leaning on one of those metal canes with four feet, he looked like he belonged in that nursing home rather than wheeling people out of it.

The three of them spoke, but there was no noise. Just heads and mouths moving as the camera floated above the scene, recording from that uncomfortable angle. Two more men in black suits came in, wheeling a gurney. They loaded the man into a black bag, onto the gurney, then wheeled him back out. Ken shook hands with the doctor, then with Father Curt, and followed his team out of the room.

Then the scene jumped to the nurse, Hope, alone in that room, weeping as she pulled postcards down from the bulletin board and laid them carefully into a box with a red stripe—the very same box that sat in the projector room.

And I understood.

"June?"

"It's okay, Wyatt. You have to understand what you are before you can move on."

"What I am?"

"What we are," she said.

"What we are," I said, standing and pacing the aisle of our old theater. When I got to the living space, I realized the floor didn't match our old theater. The floor matched our house in St. Louis.

I paused and looked over my shoulder at June. At the movie screen as Hope sifted through my things and tossed them into that box with the red stripe.

"You see it now, don't you?" June asked.

"I understand…I've…I'm…like you."

June nodded as she walked toward me. She wrapped her arms around me and squeezed. "Close your eyes, Wyatt. Close your eyes and think of where you'd like to be, who you'd like to see."

"June?"

"Close your eyes, Wyatt. What was your best day?"

I closed my eyes and rushed through the thousands, millions of memories I'd had. Before I consciously settled on a memory, before I knew it was going to happen, the theater melted from around us and the summer sun shined in my eyes.

* * *

Emma June

We stood on the beach in Florida, where we'd had our last big family vacation. Wyatt's mom and dad had flown down; Russell, Hilda, Jeffery, Wyatt Jr., Wyatt, and I had driven down together. We rented a van and took a few days to camp in the Smoky Mountains in Tennessee. None of us knew it would be the last time we'd vacation together, but it wouldn't have mattered. Everyone important to the family was there, right on the beach in the prime of spring, before the heavy summer crowd and hot summer weather. Cool ocean air blew through the cottage we'd rented, keeping it comfortable at night. The smell of salt and the constant cooking were like candy for the nose.

The kids were young enough that they didn't mind sharing the fold-out sofa. Russell and Hilda were okay with the smaller of the two bedrooms. Wyatt's folks took the bedroom with the bathroom attached, and Wyatt and I slept on the sun porch. With all the windows open, we buried ourselves in thick blankets as that cool ocean air filled our room.

Every morning Russell and Wyatt fixed a full breakfast: bacon, eggs, coffee, pancakes, waffles, hash browns, ham steak, you name it; it was there. During the day, the men would stay at the beach and fish while the women went shopping or cooked or played in the sand with the kids. A few times, Wyatt's mom, though she looked exhausted, watched the boys while Hilda and I went to town to play.

One afternoon, David caught a small shark and pretended it was attacking him when the kids came over to see it. Aside from David's slightly deteriorating mental state (he kept calling Jeffery Wyatt and Wyatt Jr. Russell), it was the perfect vacation—no sunburns, no bee stings, no fights. It was almost as if we all knew it would be our last outing together.

A week after we got back to St. Louis, Wyatt's mom announced she had terminal cancer, only a few months to live. Just a few short years after she passed, David's Alzheimer's got the better of him and he had to move in with Russell and Hilda; then, when he became too much to handle, into Paradise Garden.

Wyatt chose the place, but once I saw all our family there, I knew this was the moment I'd been working toward. Wyatt started to understand who he was, what he was, first at my mother's, then a bit more on our excursion through the past. He was almost there, and when I showed him the "movie" of his death, the memories that'd been packed away in that box with the red stripe pushed him to the brink. All of it led up to this moment. Florida, the last time we were all together; a complete, happy family. It was this place and all these people he needed to see.

Wyatt saw himself on the movie screen, saw how he'd died, and finally remembered it; now it was time for him to move on. And we dare not dawdle in this world in-between. There's too much our minds are able to manipulate to make a situation seem real. If we didn't get him to cross over now, it was likely he'd wake up tomorrow and believe the whole thing had been a dream. And if he didn't go, if he didn't cross over, I knew I'd stay with him, and we'd roam the world…just two spirits reliving parts of our lives under a foggy veil of truth. It wouldn't take long before I'd forget where I was supposed to be, where we should have been. And if we didn't cross over now, I didn't know if there'd ever be another shot to move on. This was the moment. This was why I'd returned, and we had to go…soon.

We stood hand in hand on the beach. Wyatt's mouth hung open as he stared at our family, all smiling, all accounted for.

David stepped toward us first and wrapped his son in a hug. Wyatt let go of my hand and put his arms around his father in a way I'd never seen while we were alive.

"Son, we've been waiting for you," David said, relief flooding his voice.

"Dad?" Wyatt asked. His voice young again, pre-war, none of the gravel he'd spoken with throughout his life. His hair was dark again. His back straight.

"It's me," David said, laughing. "Good to see you, son."

"Junior," Wyatt said as he looked over his father's shoulder at our son.

"Hey, Pop. Been waiting for you. Missed you, you know. I know you're a stubborn man, always were, but I didn't expect it to take this long for you to come around. We all got tired of waiting and decided we'd have to send Mom back to get you. Like that time you guys came to New York to see me play at Carnegie. You remember? You kept bothering Itzhak Perlman, telling him how good I was and how he needed to make me a permanent part of his 'act.' It was so embarrassing. Uncle Russ had to send Mom in to get you. She distracted you while Itzhak made his getaway. Like *that* day, we figured she would be the only one who could get you here. Get you ready."

"Ready?"

"To move on," Jr. said.

"And you're all here for me…" Wyatt said as his mom stepped up from behind Jr. and waved her little single-wrist-flick wave.

"Mom!"

"Wyatt, give us a hug," she said.

"Mom, how long have I—" Wyatt started but his mom interrupted him.

"Nearly eleven years, son. You got lost in your own world. You got confused. It happened to me, too. But I came around quicker than you did. It's nothing to be ashamed of. It happens when people can't accept the truth. Or when they're not happy with how it all ended up. Your father was lost for a while before he realized he was reliving the same few moments over and over again. Your brother came right away, though. Nothing curious in that boy's mind. Never was," she said, turning over her shoulder and winking at Russell. "But as your dad said, you always were the adventurous one. Always looking for the next great thing. And here you are, finally ready to cross over to that next great adventure."

"Here I am," he started, then he turned to me. "June, you came back for me?"

"I suppose I did. I didn't remember anything at first. You found me locked in some kind of *nightmare*, but you saved me…again. Once you took me to Canada, I started to remember everything. Just before we went home, to Ely, it all came back to me."

"What if you'd been stuck, too? Or what if—"

"We're not worried about 'What if's' Wyatt. In fact, there's not a whole lot to worry about here. Why don't we have a seat at the table, have some of your mother's fried chicken, and we'll talk about it," David said.

"Mom, I can't handle this," Wyatt said, turning his tear-filled eyes to her. I knew how he felt; it was overwhelming. Though I'd only been gone for a short time, it felt like I hadn't seen any of them in years. I thought I knew what to expect, but being back on the human plane, even as a spirit, even just for a short time, fucked up my mind. Every family member he'd been mourning since his mother died was there. And they were happy and well. And they were all expecting us to follow them to the other side, but not before we sat down to one final meal.

Chapter 30

Wyatt

My family sat around the plaid-covered picnic table; the ocean breeze was perfectly balanced—not too hot, not too cold, not too windy. They started loading their plates with mashed potatoes, fried chicken, gravy, green beans with little chunks of bacon in them. All of them had a mug of sweating beer. They watched me, smiling, urging me to eat up, take a sip of my beer, to take in the moment.

And June—who never gave up on me, who never stopped loving me, even when I didn't recognize who she was—grabbed ahold of my hand again, giving it a knowing squeeze. The love of my life had risked everything for me. I'd saved her once when we were living, and she'd risked her soul to save me from an eternity stuck in between life and whatever comes after.

I wanted to hug them all. I wanted to put my arms around my mother and cry like I had when I was just a child. But at the same time, I didn't need to. I felt their love like a warm blanket as I loaded up a plateful of Mom's cooking.

"How have you been, Hilda?" June asked as Hilda sat down on the other side of her, filling her fist with a chicken leg.

"Don't worry June, everything's been fine. I watered your plants while you were away," Hilda said. June laughed. It was an old joke between the two of them—I never got it but anytime Russell and I would tell them we were planning a trip, one of them would say, "I'll water the plants," and they'd both giggle like schoolgirls.

We sat around the table and ate and talked and ate, never getting full. Every time we'd go for another drink, the mugs refilled themselves. Same for our plates. The food never got cold, and the beer never got hot. We told stories and laughed. I'd forgotten what it felt like to laugh like that. I'd forgotten a person could feel so complete.

Eventually, as the plates cleared themselves of dinner and cheesecake came and went, people started to get up from the table and move toward the beach. June stood, took my hand again, and helped me up.

And I was an old man again, needing a cane but too stubborn to use one. When we stood, I felt a change come over the group, like they'd released me from that constant hug.

"June?" I asked as I held onto her, tears running down my cheeks. Her eyes were watery, too.

"It's time, honey," she said.

"Time?"

"To move on…to the other side. You've been here long enough."

"What's *on* the other side?"

My brother put his hand on my shoulder and said, "She doesn't remember, you stubborn bastard. She gave that up for you. But here, in this place of transition, a place we set up just for you, I remember everything, and I can assure you, it's just another stage of life. You've done what you came here to do. You told the untold stories, and you showed the world that beauty can be seen in tragedy. You can't do any more. It's time to let go. Time to move on."

"And you'll all be with me?"

"We've always been with you, son," Dad said as Russell let go of my shoulder and June let go of my hand. My father stood in front of me as I looked back over my shoulder at the cabin, at the dunes, at the town, at the life I was leaving. I wasn't ready to move on, to leave everything I knew behind. My dad saw me staring over my shoulder, at the past, and grabbed me, held me tight, and I was a child again, wrapped up in his arms after a long day of play. As he held me, I knew that my dad had been waiting for this moment for so long. He'd been waiting to lead me on.

He let go of me and looked me in the eye, then nodded and stepped back, letting June take over.

And when she put her hand back in mine, I was a teenager again, and so was June. And our bodies and our minds were fresh, and it felt as if we had a lifetime ahead of us. "I'll be with you," she said, squeezing my hand. There was a slight rosiness in her cheeks and flirtatiousness in her eyes.

My father looked at June, then at me and smiled. I could feel the warmth he'd always kept from us when we were alive. A lifetime of love spilled from him in that one smile, and I understood that he'd wanted to be caring, wanted to show love, but men in his generation didn't do that. Couldn't do that. And then I understood him.

And though I didn't want to move on from the perfection of that moment, I knew then that it *was* time.

Out of the corner of my eye, I saw Jeffery move gracefully through the wet sand, into the green-blue ocean. A low wave washed over his ankles, and he dove, like a kid, into the break. My mother and Hilda followed, holding hands as a low cresting wave took them away. My father and Wyatt Jr. went after them, racing like kids, into the water. Russell and June grabbed my hands and led me to the edge of the ocean. They let go of me and walked forward into ankle-deep water, waiting.

"I don't think I can do this; can't you just pull me in?"

"This has to be something you do for yourself. Free will, brother. Just be brave one more time."

I took a step forward on my own, my feet almost touching the cool water. I took another step and felt the water's embrace. I laid a hand on Russell's shoulder and planted a kiss on June's cheek. "Thank you both for this."

"Thank your wife; she's the one who saved you from yourself, you pigheaded old fool. Thinking you could walk through movie theaters…didn't you ever tire of reliving the same few memories? The same few days?" Russell said, laughing but not waiting for a response as he turned and ran into the void.

"Together?" June asked.

"Together. Always," I said.

Holding hands, we walked into the ocean. I couldn't help thinking about my movie screens, that feeling of stepping into the unknown. I took a deep breath, sure it was unnecessary—the dead don't need to breathe after all—closed my eyes, and dove into the water.

For a second, everything was black. For a second, I thought I'd made a mistake, been tricked.

Then I felt the sun beating down on me and overwhelming gratitude for everything I'd been given. I felt every part of my life; every scratched knee; every mournful moment; every love and hate-filled second. I felt the small things that once annoyed me but now seemed so trivial. I felt everything I'd forgotten: the pain, the pleasure, the taste of life… And it became part of me again, and I knew I was moving on, to whatever came next, having lived a full life.

My life wasn't perfect, not even close.

But the journey had been long and good and surprising and, most importantly, mine.

About the Author

Jeremiah Bass's enduring love of literature started at a Scholastic book fair in a tiny elementary school in Southern Illinois; his love of the written word has followed him ever since. He holds an MAT in Curriculum and Instruction and an MA in Creative Writing. He's an English Composition and Creative Writing instructor at the University of Wisconsin-Stout. Bass's short stories and essays have been released in a variety of print and online publications, and he's thrilled to have his debut novel, *The Silver Screen,* released in both print and digital formats.